hard

hard

**EROTIC FICTION
BY R.J. MARCH**

alyson books
los angeles | new york

MANUFACTURED IN THE UNITED STATES OF AMERICA.

THIS TRADE PAPERBACK ORIGINAL IS PUBLISHED BY ALYSON PUBLICATIONS,
P.O. BOX 4371, LOS ANGELES, CALIFORNIA 90078-4371.
DISTRIBUTION IN THE UNITED KINGDOM BY TURNAROUND PUBLISHER SERVICES LTD.,
UNIT 3, OLYMPIA TRADING ESTATE, COBURG ROAD, WOOD GREEN,
LONDON N22 6TZ ENGLAND.

FIRST EDITION: DECEMBER 2002

04 05 06 a 10 9 8 7 6 5 4 3

ISBN 1-55583-736-0

LIBRARY OF CONGRESS CATALOGING-IN-PUBLICATION DATA
MARCH, R.J.
    HARD : EROTIC FICTION / BY R.J. MARCH.—1ST ED.
    ISBN 1-55583-736-0
        1. GAY MEN—FICTION. 2. EROTIC STORIES, AMERICAN. I. TITLE.
PS3563.A6342 H37 2002
813'.54—DC21   2002027708

COVER PHOTOGRAPHY BY STEVE CADRO.

Contents

As I recall, I did not care for the way he smelled, slightly sour under his cologne, something fruity, faggy, what all the boys were wearing. What was it—Armani? The smell was something like overripe melon. He told me to put my arms around his neck; he wanted to lift me. He was a big man, as big a man as I'd ever seen. I felt small, childish. I reached up and around his bull neck, lacing my fingers together. He was smiling, and I felt him as he leaned over me, getting his arms under me, the hardness of him in his pants. His breath hit my face in a short little puff, and it was a nice smell and had nothing to do with his sourness, which came, I was thinking, from under his arms. He picked me up easily, like a little wifey, his new little bride. I felt I didn't know him well—at least not well enough for this—but it happened anyway, and I wasn't stopping it.

We were outside. I could smell other things. I could smell the sun on the apples and the dusty perfume that blew off the tall grasses he carried me through. Across the field I could see a stand of trees and beyond them, sparkling water—a dark little brook. He put his chin against my head and licked my temple, and I heard him humming, the tune halting with each step. I wondered if I was getting heavy. I asked him and he laughed.

I am not a boy—not anymore. I wasn't then either, not when he picked me up and carried me across the field. I was a man with mannish features, a broad back and scarred knuckles, an eyebrow split in two in a barroom fight by another man foolish enough to think me inconsequential, a man with more than a split eyebrow.

This man, this carrying man, Dan, was not a fighting man. He was big enough to never have to defend himself with his fists or with thrown chairs and busted bottles. All he had to do was stand and give you a look. He was a man wise men walked away from.

"What's that over there?" I asked him, pointing at a heap over to our left, a rusty skeleton of something, and I felt him shrug and was lifted by it. He cheek was rough against my forehead. He shifted my weight, letting me drop a bit, and I could feel his hardness again, the firm press of it against my right hip. And I could see into the neck of his shirt, at the neck of his other shirt, and then the dark hairs that rose up out from under the ribbed neckline, the skin there tanned and then not tanned.

I had never seen him without his shirt, although I had always wondered how he would look without it. He would roll his sleeves up high so that they cleared his biceps, the roll tight and binding and causing the veins of his arms to fill up bright and blue against the paleness of his skin. I could not imagine him without his shirt any more than I could imagine him without his pants. My mind would not endeavor such thoughts, would not entertain me with his naked hips and flanks, rosy nipples, his hooded (or not) member. In my imagination, he was fully dressed and standing by my bed, watching me pulling hard on myself, admiring my flailed cock and tensed thighs, wanting—but unable to bring himself—to run a rough hand between them and finger up inside me, prying me open.

At the trees, I could hear the noise of the brook and feel its coolness, even as hot as the day was. He was perspiring as well, and his odor, the smell of him under that cloying cologne, was stronger and more heady now, and I found myself leaning toward it, putting my face to his shirt and feeling the heat of him through it. He squeezed my arm with his one hand, my leg with the other, and I looked up to see him smiling.

"What?" I asked, feeling caught.

"Oh, it's nothing," he said. But he went on smiling, and I smiled, too, and breathed in the smell of him.

On the bank of the brook, Dan stumbled on a tree root, and we pitched forward toward the shallow water. I was sure I was going to be tossed in, but he regained his footing and stood with me in his arms, his chest heaving a bit, and we both laughed, and he said, "I almost lost you now, didn't I?"

"You sure did, almost," I said.

He set me down on grass that was long and soft and cool, like a damsel's hair. I heard the seams of his pants pop and felt the muscles of his forearms tighten. He straightened and stood looking at me, and then he squatted again, and again I heard his trouser seams protest. He went for the laces of my boots, untying their simple bows, pulling off the boots one at a time and handling my foot, fingering the damp cotton, massaging my soles, and lifting each to his face, putting his nose there, breathing through my socks, heating up my toes. He removed the right sock slowly. I watched his hands search for the sock's top, going up into my pant leg, his fingers roaming around my calf. Getting the body of the sock down around my heel, he caressed the hardened edge of it, my heel, and lifted the foot again and ran his tongue there.

He had hair that was rough-cut, hand-done, maybe by the old lady I saw living in his house with him, the one who liked to come out and chase the chickens with their feed. She would smoke a cigarette while she scattered the feed and let her robe fall open to show her lack of underclothes and her flattened titties. It tried to curl, his hair did, but she kept it short enough to undo any curl or wave, and his hair seemed to stick out of his head like the dull and stiff bristles of a whisk broom. I reached up to touch it, its oily sheen, hair the color of kiln-dried lumber and lighter than the hair on his arms and the little curls around the collar of his undershirt, lighter than the scruff shadowing his cheek and chin.

3

He started on my other foot, placing the bare one between his legs, where I felt the stump of him and the soft give of his balls. I wanted to move my foot around, but I did not want to hurt him, and I was not sure if he wanted me to move like that. So I kept still and let him strip off my other sock and stick his tongue between my toes. All the while he stroked my ankle and calf, getting his hand up as far as my pant leg would allow. And then he placed my toes into his mouth, my toes curling over the rough edges of his teeth, his tongue tickling each tiny pad of flesh, each toe-tip, and I tipped my head back. The sun splintered through the trees. He licked my instep, the knobby bone of my ankle. He wiped the spit off my foot with his fingers, slipping between my toes again and again.

He placed the foot with the other, on his crotch. My wet toe-nails shined against the dark green of his work pants. He held my ankles and worked my feet over the thick hump his cock made. He kept his eyes on mine, staring at me like something he loved or something he mistrusted. His mouth hung open, anticipating speech that did not come, except for an occasional groan that emanated from deep inside him and sounded as though it came from all over the shaded glen. I wanted to see him, more of him, the way his cock curved, the way the hair grew on him, the size and shape of his nipples, his own bared feet. I wanted to lick from the divot of his throat, just above his clavicle, then down the long center of him to the cup of his navel. I wanted to lick farther still, to his mossy pubes and fist-hard cock, to his slack and heavy purple balls and to the stink of him down between his legs. I was dizzy with it, this want, and hard with it, aching in my jeans, my own dick pressing up against the denim, darkening it with wetness. He closed his eyes and moved me faster over his huge pants-bound prick. It rolled under my heels and the balls of my feet.

"Oh," he said, shaking his head, bending over. "Oh, you," he said. "You."

I watched him shudder, gripping my ankles, forcing my feet hard against his cock, thrusting with his hips. He grimaced, his shoulders twitching. He shook me off and got to his feet unsteadily, limping toward the water, his hands in fists, his back heaving. I touched myself, the wet front of my jeans and came without a sound, my come gushing and confined. I felt the quick and urgent release and then a slack ease, an urge to nap. I closed my eyes and dozed, the sunlight dappled and playful against my eyelids, and when I opened my eyes again, he was beside me, and I was in his arms, and he said to me, "We hadn't ought to do this again, I don't think."

"Why not?" I asked him, smiling because I thought he was kidding with me, but he wouldn't smile back. He looked at the water.

"We hadn't ought to" was all he said, his eyes shaded, reflecting nothing.

I walked back through the field on my own accord. I followed him as close to his house as he allowed, but at the gate, with the house in the distance, he turned to me and said, "Not this way, Clay." His face looked pained, I thought, or so I wanted to think.

"OK," I said, and I turned right and walked along the fence, away from Dan and his gate, through the tall grass that touched my hands and dragged against my fingertips like sharkskin. *I can walk away and not look back,* I thought. But at the edge of the field, the far end, away from the house and close to where the brook comes around and there's a bridge to cross it, I turned around.

The house, his house, stood against the blue sky. It was painted a washed-out yellow—the color of the old lady's hair, it occurred to me. A shutter was missing from one of the second-floor windows, and the chimney was black-scalloped with the motionless silhouettes of crows.

"Enough is enough," I said, just low enough to be a whisper, and I put my hands in my pockets and made my way through the rest of the field and jumped the fence and crossed the bridge, walking home through the dark shade.

I saw him not so long after that day at the barbershop. The old lady was dead, I was guessing, or just stopped cutting his hair, or maybe it had always been Barker doing him injustice. I was having a shave and heard his simple voice while I was under the hot towel. Uncovered, I eyed him over my cheeks, as Barker soaped my beard. I caught him stealing glances at me as he pretended to page through an old *Sports Illustrated* as though it held some interest, but soon the magazine was curled toward the floor, unread, something to occupy the hands. He used it, furled against his knee, practicing impatience. He turned quickly to look out the window. I listened to the scratch of the straight razor against my cheek, thrilled at the warm sharpness of it against my throat, so close to my own bloody death. I smiled at the thought—and at Dan's restlessness.

When I was righted in the chair, witch hazel stinging my face and eyes, I found him staring at me.

"Well, well," I said. "Look who it is." Barker swiped at my ear and the towel was red.

"Little nick, Clay," Barker said, his eyes blue and bold. "Where's that styptic?"

I waited for Dan to speak, but he didn't, and I felt foolish suddenly and wanted something to say, something cordial and polite, and Barker pinched at my earlobe with some tissue paper. Dan sat with his hands on the arms of the chair, waiting for his turn with Barker.

"Any discount for mortal injury?" I asked, and Barker snorted.

"I coulda opened your throat for 50 cents," he said, and Dan got to his feet, his chair scraping the floor. I handed Barker a five fished from the pocket of my pants and told him to keep the change, and he flicked the bloody towel at me. I got up, and he swatted hairs off the chair and said to Dan, "Who's next?"

We traded chairs, and I pretended to be interested in the magazine Dan had set down on the seat. I opened the magazine to its middle and stared over it at the crotch of Dan's pants, making my gaze plain and noticeable until Barker blocked it with his cape. Dan stared back, trying to make his eyes hard, using his furrowed brow to tell me what I wasn't interested in hearing.

I said to Barker, "What do you hear from your brother these days?" Barker launched into a long-winded story about his brother's trailer in the Florida Keys. The trailer had been picked up by a hurricane and dropped into the ocean. Some men on a fishing boat found the trailer floating halfway to Cuba. His little dog, a miniature schnauzer, was still inside, safe and sound and a little hungry. All the while I watched Dan's face, the lines around his mouth, the hard work he made of avoiding my gaze.

"Well," I said, getting up and throwing the magazine on the table with the others. "Guess I'll be taking off now. You take it easy, Barker."

"Be seeing you, Clay," Barker said, clippers humming.

I looked at Dan. "See you around, Dan," I said, giving him a half-smile and a little wink.

"Right," Dan said, his voice tight.

I waited for him. He came out of Barker's and saw me by his truck. He stopped on the sidewalk, looking up the street, away from me. He pulled on his chin and put his other hand in his pocket, bringing out a pocket watch. He turned to me again and walked up to where I was standing, leaning on his fender. He walked past me and got into his truck. He started it up, but I wasn't moving, feeling the big rattling thing under me, feeling his eyes on my back. I waited, and so did he, until the truck was hot and he realized I wasn't going anywhere. He turned the engine off and sat there in the cab, his hands slack on the steering wheel.

I heard him say to me, "This hadn't ought to happen here, Clay."

"I guess not," I said over my shoulder. The windshield held the reflection of the sky, and I saw him through it like a vision.

He leaned out his window and said quietly, "Maybe we could do this someplace else." I shrugged.

"Like where?" I asked him, getting off the fender and coming to his door. With him sitting in the truck, we were face-to-face and on even ground. He looked straight ahead before he answered.

"Get in," he said.

He brought me back to his place. It took me by surprise, the turn he made onto the road that led to his house and nothing else. Chickens scattered as we pulled up to the front of the house. There was no yard to speak of, only scattered clumps of grass here and there, and hard brown dirt. He got out of the truck and touched the hood of it, then looked at me, still sitting inside. *You don't belong here* drifted through my head like a song.

Inside, I looked for the old lady, following Dan back to the kitchen where he pulled out a chair and motioned for me to sit down. He put some water into a pot and put the pot on the stove, but he didn't light it and went instead to the refrigerator and pulled out a bottle of something and got us two glasses and filled them with whatever was in the bottle.

"Where's that old lady?" I asked, touching the glass and leaning over to sniff it. I watched him take a small sip.

"She's over in Barstow," he said, grimacing. "Visiting."

"Is she your mother?" I asked him. He shook his head and put his foot up on a chair, his arms crossed over the back of it, swirling the contents of his glass around a bit, as if it needed stirring.

"You shouldn't be here," he said, watching me. "What are you doing here?"

"You brought me here," I said. Whatever was in the glass smelled sweet but tasted bad, like medicine or maybe poison, and my whole body shook when I drank and I wanted to spit it out. My throat burned all the way to my gut. I saw him smile so I drank the rest of it down.

"You want more?" he said.

"If you do," I said, my voice raw, making his smile even broader. He splashed more in my glass and into his own, and he sat down on the chair, putting his elbows on the table. I looked at his fresh-cut hair and realized it was indeed Barker who was responsible for the hatchet job. Didn't Dan even notice?

"Let's do it again," I said, leaning across the table, its cloth moving under my elbows, going for a button on his shirt. He let me touch it, let me undo it, as he looked down at my hands. He was wearing a T-shirt anyway, and it was sprinkled with clipped hairs. He let me undo another button, and then he lifted his glass and drank it back. He tipped away from me, his shirt hardly open, his other shirt showing how he was built, what I'd felt when he carried me across the field. He looked at the refrigerator, the sink, the stove. It was a clean kitchen, not at all what I'd expected. He looked at me again and laughed.

"You sure are something," he said, shaking his head. He poured another shot into our glasses, and the bottle was empty. I was feeling good and warm-headed and ready. I got up out of my chair and put myself on his lap. I felt his breath on my cheek and leaned against it. He put his nose in my ear and took a whiff of me. "You are really something," he told me, and he closed his arms around my waist.

I wanted our skin to touch. I worked on the rest of his shirt buttons, pulling the tails out of his pants, pushing the tattersall off his shoulders. The sleeves of his T-shirt were drawn tight around his biceps. He drank around my movements, as though I were a child at play; he indulged me, letting me tease the nipples that poked hard against the white cotton, growing harder under my fingers. He shifted me off one thigh and onto the other and leaned his forehead against my chest. Then he looked up at me, over my eyes, his own crossing from being so close, and he put a finger on my halved eyebrow.

He put an arm around my back and stood up, taking me with him. He lifted me easily, and my arms went around his shoulders, my legs around his waist, and he walked me through the house and up the stairs. I looked at the pictures hanging in the stairwell: prints, mostly, of farmhouses not unlike Dan's. There was wallpaper that was surprisingly flowered and pretty: big faded cabbage roses, all through the house, even in his room. He had a brass bed that he set me down on, its mattress sagging under me. He undid the laces of my boots, moving his lips.

Afraid he might not, I undressed myself, getting down to bare skin and shivering, although it wasn't cold. He looked at me, stripped of my shirt, my red nipples popping up in the midst of black curling hairs. I could see the jut of his hard-on, its press against the front of his pants. I put my stockinged foot against it, and he moaned. I walked my other foot up his belly and chest, all the way up to his face, fitting his cheek against my instep.

"Take your clothes off," I whispered. He kissed my sock and winked, dropping my foot. He stepped back and elbowed out of the shirt that was already bunched around his shoulders like a stole. His T-shirt was as white as paper, and he filled it impressively. He got out of that, too, pulling it out of its tuck in his pants, showing me his belly and then the rest of him, pale-skinned, beautiful. His chest was freckled, and hair grew like wreaths around his penny-colored nipples and meandered down the center of him, splitting him in two. He undid his pants, showing me that the hair grew in fuller there. He let his pants drop, and his cock swung up stiffly, like a catapult. My mouth flooded with spit.

He crawled over me, dragging his big prick against me, its blunt head smearing jizz on me. He straddled my chest, holding my arms up over my head, and humped between my tits, his dick head hitting the soft underside of my chin. And then he moved up, his knees flanking my head, his fanny coming to rest on my face, and I tasted his rank hole as he knocked his dick against my forehead. I licked his great thighs and the creamy half moons of his ass cheeks and teased his brown, haired-up sphincter with my darting tongue, making him squirm and play with himself. He eased back and pushed his cock, the wide thing, against my lips. It was stiff and immobile—so hard it would not make the downward dip into my mouth. He got to his feet unsteadily on the groaning mattress, taking care not to hit his head on the ceiling.

He licked his fingers and used them on his shaft, just under the head, watching me watching him. He stepped off the bed, shaking the house. He grabbed my feet and held them so the soles met, and he parted them, spitting there, and placed his thick cock between them, and he began to fuck my feet.

He squeezed his eyes tight, his head tipped back a bit, and he breathed hard through his nose. I felt his balls against my toes, the slack skin of them, and the long slide of his shaft between my feet. He held on to my toes and fucked between the ball and heel, and I watched his pointed dick head darting in and out of the concavity. I played with my own, working my palm over the sweaty, steadily seeping tip. My eyes memorized him—his soft middle, the line of hairs, his heavy muscled shoulders, his purple-veined and swaying scrotum—because I was thinking I might not have the chance to see him like this again, naked and sweating, fucking the soles of my feet.

He said my name quietly, and I saw him open his eyes, searching for my face. *Isn't there a way,* I wondered, *to stay here for a long time?* He grunted as he labored over his cock, his brow descending. *I could cut his hair right,* I was thinking, *and suck that cock and feed those chickens pecking and clucking outside under the window.* Dan set his shoulders and let his tongue rest between his lips. He covered me with his hot spray—a thick, gluey fountain. I strove to match his shot and make him love me forever, as he licked his come off my ankles.

GANYMEDE

Keith checked his pockets for change, for his car keys, wallet, rubbers, and then he looked at what there was to see in the mirror. He kept his thinning hair short, and had started working out again to combat, or at least slow down, time's march. He looked better now than he did when he was in his 20s, he was inclined to believe, although he really wasn't the type to admit that sort of thing, not even to himself. He was constantly reevaluating himself.

He had his torso encased in a tight gray T-shirt. *What was I thinking?* he wondered, changing into something less form-fitting. He was fretful about the slight pudge around his belly, his thin wrists. But his critical eye managed to balance everything out. *Vanity kills,* he reminded himself, remembering the song from the '80s. *Who sang that? Oh, yeah, it was ABC.* He supposed he still had the album, *Lexicon of Love,* somewhere in the back of the closet where he kept his albums now. He looked at his watch. Time marched on, indeed.

At Cupid's on Fourth Street, he nodded at the kid who sat at the register watching television instead of the screens that monitored the activity in the back rooms. The kid had long hair, compromised teeth, and a drag queen's manicure. He gave Keith 20 singles while barely taking his eyes off the television. Keith looked to see what was so fascinating—the sound was off, and techno beat throbbed in the background—and realized it was a documentary about World War I. The kid looked up when Keith said, "Thanks."

"Nothing but trolls tonight, honey. Trolls, trolls, trolls." The kid's appraisal made Keith smile and think of Billy Goat's Gruff.

He did not see an unfamiliar face, though he did not acknowledge anyone. They were all members, really, of a sort of club, an old fraternal order, like the Rotary, the Masons, or the Elks. *Here we are again,* he thought, walking up to the display of movie titles, checking to see whether they'd changed in the two days since he'd last been here. They hadn't, and the word "troll" came to his mind again when he caught his reflection in the glass that covered the video display cases. Was it the red lights they used for illumination that made him look so sallow, so much a *regular?*

He wedged himself into a booth and found the movie he'd watched two days ago, the one with the actor who reminded him of Keller. Light-colored eyes, thick thighs, freckled, lying on his back with his legs bent, looking at the camera positioned between his big pale knees. Keith unbuttoned his fly. There was a shot from another angle, handheld and amateurish, the cameraman's shadow apparent. The actor's mouth was open, and that was something else that reminded Keith of Keller, that drop of lower lip and the way his eyes emptied themselves so that it was almost like looking through the lenses of a binocular—you saw yourself doubled, whether you wanted to or not.

Keith heard and ignored the shuffle of feet outside his door, which was closed but not locked—an invitation to those bold enough to enter, for those hungry enough. He imagined he was in a confessional, or a tollbooth. He was in a state of thralldom, looking at someone who looked enough like Keller jerking off his fat, hard cock with one hand and reaching under himself to finger his butthole with the other. *I have to see him,* he thought.

Reaching into his open pants, he decided to take the drive down to see Keller. But after he'd finished the business at hand. The boy on the screen spread his legs, opening himself for the camera. Keith's hand sought out the hard-on he'd developed.

Again there were footsteps outside his door, then a pause.

The door inched open. Keith leaned against it with his shoulder; he wanted no interruption.

He twirled a fingertip around his nipple, getting himself out of his pants, his rod aching now, throbbing. The boy in the movie—Keller's twin—got up on his knees, pushing his butt close, using it to fill the screen, the hole a red wink, a plush bloom, a drawstring drawn suddenly tight. Dog tags dangled from the boy's neck, the soles of his feet shone white. Keith used his spit to smooth things out. He watched the boy's index finger disappear, the middle one, and then the ring finger, all up inside him, the hole giving, stretching to a bland pink now, his balls hauled up by his wrist and pressed flat against his inner thigh.

The door moved again—Keith felt the insistence on the other side of it. He leaned toward the crack and peeked out and to see a suit coat, a tie, the hairy wrist of someone he hadn't seen when he'd come in. Looking up, he took in the man's head—balding, congenial, and benign. Keith looked downward again, his face level with the man's crotch, and watched the man's hand work the front of his trousers, pressing his erection against the dark wool, making his need apparent.

In his car on the interstate, heading north and going home, Keith felt something—he couldn't describe it—well up inside him. He pulled over, his directional blinking, clicking like a metronome, and he wondered what happened—what had it all been for? He caught his eyes in the rearview. He felt old and tired. He palmed back his hair. "Looks like rain," he said aloud to himself in a voice that sounded strange to his ears. There were heavy gray clouds coming in from the west, outlined in orange by the setting sun.

He stopped to piss at a rest stop. It was a new one, a great mall of a bathroom. He stepped up to a long line of urinals, getting his fly open, digging around for his cock, looking left, looking right. An old man beside him fingered a slack-skinned erection, rolling it between his fingers, not pissing. He looked at Keith, who finished up, shaking himself well and still trying to keep himself hidden. Keith stepped back to zip up, as the urinal flushing magically, untouched.

The old man cleared his throat, looking over his shoulder. His nose was a Christmas bulb of broken blood vessels that looked purple in the fluorescent light overhead. His jacket was the color of Dijon mustard left out to dry. "Suck," he said, just loud enough for Keith to hear, to catch the question at the back of the old man's throat, motioning with a wag of his head to the stalls behind him. Keith looked away toward the sinks, where there was a boy wearing shorts. Dark hairs curled on the boy's calves and on the back of his neck.

The boy—18, maybe 20—stood behind Keith, as they were waiting in line at a fast-food joint to order a burger and fries to eat in the car on the way home. The boy's shorts were elastic at the waist, like boxers. The legs of them were wide but couldn't dwarf the boy's thighs, which were thick and hard. Keith watched hamstrings flex as the boy shifted his weight from one foot to the other, cocking his hip, gesturing impatience. He crossed his arms over his chest, the name of a local college on his T-shirt and just visible over the tops of his forearms. Baseball, Keith guessed, thinking the boy probably plays ball on the weekends with his buddies, a couple of beers afterward, then home to the TV and his right hand. He looked at Keith and did something with his lips that was smile-like, and he half-nodded, brothers-in-waiting.

"Alvernia," Keith said. "That's in Pennsylvania, right?"

The kid straightened up, fixing his eyes on Keith as if for the first time. "Yeah, Reading," he said.

"Outlets," Keith said, nodding. "You go there?"

"School or shopping?" the boy asked, an edge of sass in his voice, and Keith laughed.

"School," Keith replied.

"My wife did," the kid answered, leaning back against the sinks.

Wife? Keith rubbed his chin's scratchy stubble. The boy looked at him steadily, almost smiling.

Keith shook his head and went back to his car.

He pushed through the radio dial, wanting to hear anything to get the boy's voice out of his head. He finally turned it off, preferring silence, but the car's tires hummed and its engine whined, and it all sounded slightly menacing. He didn't trust the car, a 10-year-old Nova, and he thought that he probably shouldn't be driving it the 50 miles to see Keller, uninvited. He wished now that he'd rented a car with a tape player and clean upholstery. Money was tight, though, with the American Express bill a month overdue and payday a week and a half away. After a case of beer and a tank of gas, he'd had enough left over from his last paycheck to pay rent and the electric bill. *This road trip is a mistake,* he thought as he plowed through the night.

"Not right now," Keller said, rolling over and sitting up, turning his back to Keith. He pitched back and forth, a swaying mountain, and Keith put his hand on the man's shoulder blade. Keller turned, his silhouette tipped in light from the little lamp on the bedside table, his eyes half-lidded, his lips open. "I can't," he said.

"That's all right," Keith said, drawing his fingers down the deep split of Keller's back, the hot skin bearing a slick trace of sweat. "Just lie down."

Keller squinted at the dull brass headboard.

"I'll sleep in the other room," Keith offered.

"No," Keller said, shaking his head fiercely. "You stay here." He rested his chin on his chest, tired.

"Lie down," Keith said.

"I'm fucked up good," he mumbled through a hiccup.

"Me too," Keith admitted.

Wipers pushed the rain right and left. The windshield fogged around the edges. He was almost home. He watched the white dashes come at him, the red blur of taillights. It was near dawn, but still dark.

There was work tomorrow, the easy routine. He shook his

16

head, his eyes on the car in front of him; its Canadian rear plate proclaimed *JE ME SOUVIENS*.

"*Je m'appelle Keith*," he thought, shaking his head. "Should have stayed home."

What had he expected? He hadn't gone with any expectations, none that he was conscious of, anyway. Keith held the steering wheel with two hands and pictured Keller's face again—how he'd looked when he opened the front door and found Keith there with that case of beer in his hands; how Keller's mouth had moved in all sorts of directions, framed by that new close-clipped beard, before turning itself into a smile.

"What the fuck," he had said finally, opening the screen door and letting Keith in.

"That was *his* first mistake," Keith said aloud to himself.

He only had a couple of hours before his alarm would ring, but he couldn't sleep. He couldn't sleep earlier either, lying beside Keller, who snored away like a leaky bellows. He'd looked around Keller's monk-like room—a bed and a bureau and a mirror hung at an odd tilt, in which he could see himself next to Keller, arms behind his head, looking as though he belonged there. He watched Keller curl toward him.

"I sort of got a girlfriend now," he'd said to Keith earlier. Her name and number were on the back of a receipt stuck to the refrigerator door with a magnet. "Maybe we could all get a bite to eat tomorrow," he'd suggested. Keith pictured the three of them stuck in a diner booth: the girl and Keith sitting on a bench together and watching Keller as he ate, crumbs on his lips, his fingers curling through the tiny ceramic loop of a coffee cup handle, spilled coffee in the saucer.

He rolled over, facing the green glow of the clock at his bedside. He thought of the boy at the rest stop, the slouch of his socks around his thick ankles. Keith slipped a hand under himself. The boy's thighs feathered with black hairs filled the screen in his head.

17

He imagined what should have happened. He imagined the rest-stop boy turning, half-smiling, his short dark hair, arms folded across his chest, lifting the toes of his sneakers off the floor, dick playing against the front of his loose shorts. And he pictured Keller turning, both hands on Keith's head, licking his mouth, then forcing his head down into the damp, matted fur of his armpit, then farther down into the sweet funk of his crotch.

Keith's fingers curled around his shaft, the fronts of his briefs dampened. In his mind's eye he saw the boy lifting his Alvernia T-shirt up over his head, his stomach ridged with broad ribbons of muscle, his belly button a pale knot in the middle of a flare of black hairs that rise up and out of white briefs. Keller had said, "No," but it's all right for the boy.

Keith's toes curled and cracked, and he held his breath, wanting to yell at the top of his lungs. He lifted his legs, bending them, spreading them and opening his ass, underwear gone now, where he'd been fingering himself. He soaked the sheets with a spray of warm spunk. As he body slackened he wiped himself with them, too tired suddenly to clean up properly. He still heard the noise of the road in his head, and he fell asleep listening to it, driving the dark road, his hands gripping hard the wheel in his dreams.

Looking into the bathroom mirror, Keith tried to remember what he had wanted when he was 23. He looked at the skin around his eyes, the easy give of it, the loss of elasticity that seemed to have come overnight. *So old*, he thought to himself. He shaved, using an herbal shaving cream he couldn't really afford. Upstairs, he heard the old lady's grandchildren tap-dancing. The practiced their steps every Monday, Wednesday, Friday. He wondered where they were the other days of the week.

Keller was 23. His father was old, though—60-something—saving Keith from that cliché: he was not as old as Keller's father. Somewhere in between, though, and that was close enough these days. He scraped away three days' worth of stubble, lifting his chin to tighten the skin of his neck. How many times had he seen his own father like this: standing at the sink with a towel wrapped around his waist, the muscles across his shoulders moving under the skin, red lips surrounded in white, pushed out in a kiss for no one.

He'd walked in on Keller last Sunday morning in the same stance—without the towel, though. Keith stepped up to the toilet anyway; his need to pee overpowered any embarrassment about the night before or Keller's nakedness now.

"Morning," Keith said, keeping his eyes down. "Morning," Keller said back, tilting his head to get at the skin under his ear. He came out later, the strange beard gone, the old Keller back, the one Keith liked best.

Keith liked the way he looked when he was hung over, the way his blue eyes seem bluer, looking back at him in the mirror.

"You look good," Keller had said.

Keith had fought the urge to reply, "I do?"

The whole weekend had been a bust, from the moment he put his finger on the doorbell and felt the electric current of regret enter him through that extended finger. It was like playing with a light socket—and made about as much sense to him then. He regretted his tight white T-shirt he wore to accentuate the fact that he'd started going to the gym again, and he regretted not calling first, and he regretted not stopping to brush his teeth. "What are you doing here?" Keller had asked later, digging around for the next-to-last beer.

"What are *you* doing here?" Keith asked, because he couldn't answer Keller's question.

"I'm happy here," Keller said, finally, his lips moving nervously. "I chase down car parts," he said, wedging his hands in his pockets, raising his chin. "I drink coffee that comes out of a vending machine, and I give the mechanics a hard time. My uncle just closed a deal with a scrap yard that's got bins that need painting. That'll be my project for the summer."

As he spoke, Keith watched him, watched his mouth and his throat, the way his shirt lay over his body, half-unbuttoned, showing patches of skin here and there. He wore khaki cutoffs, his pale freckled thighs spread wide, and work boots but no socks. His shins shone under the light-brown hair that covered them. Keith thought about history, a night like this in his own kitchen, Keller staring him down, a shot of tequila at his lips. What happened next? Nothing happened. Keith blinked and Keller smiled. It was that tension, that electric charge, Keith was trying to recreate. *That's* what I'm doing here, he thought.

"I'm glad you're happy," Keith had said then. "It's good to be happy."

Keller washed his face, his head aching from the night before. He'd gone down to DiCarlo's after Keith left, drinking him gone or drinking him back—he wasn't sure. He wasn't sure of anything lately, except that he had another monster hangover and was going to be late for work.

His uncle's garage was about a mile away, and Keller usually walked the distance, but he wasn't up for that sort of exertion. Keller got into his pickup, an old Dodge painted orange and black with the words TONY THE TIGER painted on the driver's door—not by him: He'd never draw that kind of attention to himself. The truck was his uncle's and came with the job of parts runner.

"We'll see how you do changing the oil on Aunt Dee's Bonneville, and maybe we'll get you into the shop as a mechanic," his uncle was always saying. But Keller didn't want anything more to do with the shop than what he was doing now, driving all around town, chasing parts, drinking that terrible coffee, the promise of all those Dumpsters coming his way, sandblasting rust and old paint, and being left alone.

He got himself behind the wheel, feeling sick to his stomach all of a sudden. He sat with his forehead against the steering wheel, seeing things on the insides of his eyelids, fast-moving images that made his head spin. He saw himself with Keith, the two of them dancing, but he had never danced with Keith, or any other man for that matter. Then he saw himself with that girl

20

from last night, what was her name—Gretchen? Gretel? Gwen—
it was Gwen, and she was a...something. He drew a blank. He
lifted his head slowly, not wanting to shift the heavy brick of pain
that floated in his gray matter, and he squinted through the windshield, seeing an image of Keith up the road, walking toward him
with a case of beer on his shoulder, smiling.

Fucking ghosts, he thought, turning the key in the ignition, the
engine turning over a dozen times before catching.

Keller slept through his lunch break in the truck, parked in the
shade by the river, the radio low. He didn't dream this time, and
for that he was thankful. He woke up feeling better, his headache
just a whisper now, and he stretched his arms over his head,
pressing against the roof of the cab with his forearms. He stepped
out of the truck to piss in the brush that grew in dense clumps
along the banks of the river. He undid his jeans and pulled himself out, pulling back the meaty droop of skin that covered the
head of his prick. He hated the hood his cock wore, and the jokes
the guys in school made about it. They'd called him Jungle Boy, a
tag he'd never been able to shake.

He pinched out the last few drops, shuddering, letting the
skin slip back. The air played over him, and his cock began to
grow in his hand. It twitched and thickened, and he looked
around, making sure he was alone. He pulled back the skin and
let the sun touch his bared cock head. He felt bad—he felt bad
and he felt good in a way, too—and he worked the skin back and
forth, bringing up a sparkle of precome. He tasted some of it, liking it even though it shamed him. He pushed his jeans down
along with the old flannel boxers he'd been wearing for three days
now and put himself into a shaft of sunlight.

He jacked himself, not thinking of anything at first, then Keith
worked his way into his thoughts. He thought of Keith's T-shirt
tight across his chest, the mound of cock and balls in his pants
that was so obvious, so hard to ignore. Sitting across from Keller
the other night, Keith had splayed his legs wide, the pile of cock

21

and balls there for Keller to glance at furtively, making him drink too fast.

Then he thought about the guys he worked with, the Ripley brothers with their feathery blond mustaches and their undone coveralls, pissing with the door open, strutting around in their repair bays like sex stars. Once he had caught the younger one, Shane, watching his brother leaning over an engine he was working on. Keller looked, too, into the open coveralls, unzipped low enough to show the brand of underwear he wore that day.

The calluses across the top of his palm rasped the unsheathed glans. He played with his balls with the other hand, twisting and pulling the sack, leaning against the side of the old Dodge, letting his fingers roam down the fuzzy channel until he touched his asshole. He played around it, making it pinch and relax, and then he worked his finger in up to the first knuckle.

Keller thought about Shane and his brother and how he had always wanted a brother. They lived together, probably walked around in towels with morning wood and took dumps with the bathroom door open. They'd probably jacked off in the same room together when they were growing up, each pretending not to hear the other—that was what it would've been like if he'd had a brother.

It was going to happen: He was going to come. He gripped himself tightly at the base, wanting to prolong the feeling he was experiencing, the buzz his crotch made. Just as he was about to shoot, he looked across the river and saw someone watching him—another man—but it was too late, he was already dribbling semen, and he let himself go, the come spraying out of his fisted cock. *Enjoy the show, faggot,* he thought

The boy wanted to know how old he was. They were always *boys* around here, but this one was particularly boyish, and they were supposed to be 18, college-age, but you never really knew. Keith had found this one lying in the field on a blanket, listening to something on his Discman.

"I'm your father's age," Keith would tell him later, putting his hands into his own pockets and touching his car keys, some change, a sprig of lavender he'd plucked from a church garden where it was growing too close to the gate to ignore.

"Really," the boy said, sitting up straighter, his eyes flashing. *What is he doing there?* Keith wondered when he first saw him. *He doesn't he worry about ticks and Lyme disease, like everybody else?* Tall grass the color of hazy sunlight swirled around him. Keith walked deliberately, watching him carefully, thinking the boy's thighs reminded him of Keller's, thick and freckled, pale and big. The way the boy had his legs, Keith could see into his shorts, see the boy's underwear, cheap boxers sold three to a pack. He could see into the boxers as well, which brought him closer, coming at the boy at that angle, staring, trying to make out whatever there was to make out when the boy got up on his elbows.

"Hello," he called to Keith.

"Why here?" Keith asked a little later. The boy shrugs. His name is Cary, like Cary Grant, the actor. Personally, Cary likes the name Tab, like Tab Hunter, because, as he said, "God, that guy was beautiful."

Keith said that Cary Grant had his charms. Cary liked the more contemporary boys better—that is, if you could call Tab Hunter more contemporary.

"Most people think of the movie, though, when I tell them my name," Cary said.

Keith squinted, trying to think fast. "Sissy Spacek," he said, remembering John Travolta. The boy grinned lewdly.

Keith confessed that he used to jerk off with a copy of *Tiger Beat* he'd stolen from his younger sister, in it a centerfold of John Travolta in a red Speedo. He made his confession to see how the boy would react.

"I think he's better looking now," Cary said, and Keith cocked his head. "I like all those guys that age: Bruce Willis, Mel Gibson. They're hotter now than ever."

"What are you saying?" Keith asked. Cary opened and closed his legs, banging his knees together—he couldn't look any more boyish. As Cary moved his legs, his shorts billowed open, allowing Keith to see the package nestled in a tangle of soft hair.

"I live over there," Cary said, pointing to the dormitories across the road. This was why Keith liked cutting through this field, because behind the dormitories was the library, and after the library, the athletic field. He liked to watch the boys play football. Sometimes he'd even take a few laps around the track himself.

Cary peeled his shirt off, exposing tiny nipples, little bitten things—hardly there, they were so pale. There was no hair on him except what was creeping up out of his shorts and the little tufts growing under his arms and on his chin. It was all penny-colored, lighter than Keller's fur.

"I don't have a roommate," he said. "He left."

"He left school?" Keith asked.

"Nope," Cary replied. "He just left me. 'Cause he caught me in his bed."

He picked up his shirt and put it over his head

"And was he in it?" Keith asked.

"I wish," Cary said, sighing and meaning it. "No, I was just in it, that's all, and he caught me. I liked the way he smelled. I was after his smell. He didn't say anything. He turned around and left, and then he was gone for real—I mean, I came home from class that night and all his stuff was gone."

Keith looked at him, his coppery hair and sideburns, his green eyes. His legs were so big, so muscular—they seemed to belong to someone else. His shoulders were narrow; Keith couldn't imagine sleeping with him. But he could see himself on his knees in front of the boy, pulling down his cheap boxers and pushing his face against his milky cock, his burnt-sienna bush, cupping his swinging balls with lacy blue veins. The way he looked at Cary made the boy smile.

They didn't go back to Cary's room, but deeper into the field, where the grass grew high and they knew no one would see them.

"Except God and the birds," Cary said. "And airplanes."

Keith looked up nervously. They walked farther to the edge of the field to a stand of trees. Under cover, Keith found himself at a loss, and he didn't drop to his knees. But Cary did.

"I had boyfriends in high school," he confided, thus explaining the proficiency that soon coaxed Keith from a sluggish shyness to a full erection. Cary used his hand and his mouth together, making little noises. He came off it altogether to tell Keith he liked the way he tasted, then looked up at him earnestly, which made Keith feel particularly lecherous.

Cary fondled his balls with the other hand, cupping them and squeezing them. His fingers brushed the stiff hairs around his anus, and Keith spread his legs, making the boy look up again.

Keith stood behind the counter, by the register, looking through the wall of glass that separated him from the outside. There were things to do—labor reports, action plans, next week's schedule, and corporate numbers to crunch. He had to find a replacement for Lump, who'd given her notice yesterday. She was behind him somewhere in the store, shelving a new shipment of books, humming tunelessly along with the Muzak. He could hear her. Outside, boys on bicycles rode by, their arms tanned, heads covered with grimy baseball caps. There was someone at the magazine racks, a man with his hands in his pockets. Keith couldn't stop stealing glances at him. He didn't look like a shoplifter, but it was so hard to tell. He heard Lump walking up behind him, heard the noise her thighs made and her breathing.

"Can I have my lunch break early?" she asked. Just then Keith saw Lump's mother pull up in front of the store in her old Buick, big as a boat. She smiled in at Keith and he smiled back. She looked like Lump's worn-out twin. He turned around and looked at Lump's big moon of a face. Her name was Darlene, and that's what he called her when he spoke to her, but in his mind she was forever Lump. Her eyes shrank behind her glasses, and he saw her swallow. *I make her nervous*, he thought, wanting to smile. Or maybe she's just hungry.

He said to her, "You know, Darlene, I was just thinking how much I'm going to miss having you around this place."

Lump blinked, looking out the window at her mother who sat with her fat little arm out the window, the dimple of her elbow like some shallow pit. "I like it here," she began, not looking at Keith.

He waited. She licked her lips.

"My mother's here," she said. "She's taking me to get some contacts."

Keith smiled anyway. "Colored ones?" he wanted to know.

"Maybe," Lump answered, nodding her head, looking to the right. She rarely looked him in the eye.

And then she looked up at Keith. "Can I?" she asked.

"Go on," he said. The man at the magazine rack turned around. He'd found something to buy. Lump came behind the counter and went up to the office that was perched over the registers. The man walked slowly, looking at the remaindered books stacked on a table by the doors. *Not bad,* Keith thought.

The first thing Keith spotted was the wedding ring the man wore, the second was the magazine he was trying to purchase, and the third was his dark-shadowed chin, his terribly straight jaw. He walked up to the counter with a magazine married men don't normally buy, looking at Keith levelly, owning up to this curious fact.

Keith couldn't help it: "Did you find everything you needed?" he asked. The man's eyes went to the door. The bicycle boys were dismounting there. Probably coming in to look at the more traditional magazines Keith had on the rack, *Playboy* and *Hustler,* the usual straight fare, the stuff guys like this one usually bought. The man looked as though his son was walking in. Keith grabbed a bag and secreted the magazine into it, wanting to communicate something him, wanting to say out loud, "I understand," although he really didn't understand.

What sort of community does that man have? Keith wondered disdainfully later on at home. He had his feet up on the couch, the television on but noiseless, the man at the store imbedded into his mind like a thorn, like a sliver. He could still see the man's hands, the nervous bob of his Adam's apple.

The phone rang. When he heard Keith's voice answer, Keller said, "Keith, what's up, man?" clearing his throat, and fumbling with the receiver.

"Not much," Keith said, sounding surprised. Keller never called. "What's going on?"

Keller shrugged, feeling foolish when he realized Keith couldn't see the gesture. "Not much here, either," he answered.

Keller sat in his kitchen, using the phone that was hanging on the wall by the back door, and wished once again that he had a mobile phone he could walk around with. He played with the long curl of cord and heard Keith's breathing on the other end—the guy sounded light years away. He was still wearing his work pants, although his shirt was long gone. He pulled on the stray hairs around his nipples, careful not to touch the nipples themselves, not liking the way that felt. There was a bottle of beer on the kitchen table. He put his fingers on it but left it where it was.

"So what's going on?" he heard Keith ask again. He was afraid of that question. He didn't know what was going on—hadn't a clue, really, only an overwhelming urge to talk to Keith.

"I just thought I'd check in and say hi," he replied lamely. This was something his dad said whenever he called Keller. He knew it was just another way of saying, *I have no idea what to say to you.* Or maybe it was another way of saying, *I just wanted to hear your voice.* He had only the vaguest idea of what had happened the weekend Keith came down.

"How are the Dumpsters?" Keith asked, and Keller smiled.

"They're fine," he answered. "And how's that pile of books?"

He got to his feet, padding around on the cool linoleum, touching his chin and missing his beard.

"The books are fine," Keith said.

They were quiet then. On the other end of the line, Keith was dismayed by how little they had to say to each another. But what was there to say? He could have mentioned the man at the store, the married man with his gay porn. He could have told Keller about Lump and her Elizabeth Taylor–violet contact lenses. He could have told him about the strange ride back from their weekend together, about the Albright boy and the old man at the rest-stop, and the whining of the road that made him feel empty and alone.

"I had a good time," he said, finally, which probably wasn't what Keller wanted to hear. What did Keller want to hear? It was too hard to tell. He thought of Cary.

"Do you think I'm cute?" he'd asked Keith.

"I definitely think you're cute," Keith had answered.

"Next time, then," Cary said, "You can fuck me."

Something else he couldn't say to Keller.

He chose to think of Keller's socks falling down around his ankles, white work socks nestling themselves down into the warm stink of Keller's boots, his shins laid bare, in shorts, though the weather had turned and autumn was setting in.

"I had a good time, too," Keller replied.

Keller went back to that covered place by the river. He sat in his truck with half a six-pack and listened to the radio and waited. He watched the muddy, slow-moving water, the dip of branches, and the flight of birds until he nearly dozed off, until he closed his eyes for a moment and then opened them.

A car pulled off the road behind him. He watched it in his rearview. The car slowed; the pavement stopped, and the ruts were deep in places. He watched the car—an old Lincoln—drive past him. The man at the wheel looked older, maybe his uncle's age. He didn't look at Keller, but Keller had the impression that he was keenly aware of his presence.

He stretched his long legs, maneuvering them around the pedals, picking at a hole in the knee of his trousers that he'd not noticed before. He had come here directly from work, save for the

28

stop for beer. The sunlight trickled through the leaves, catching in the dust on the hood of the truck.

The Lincoln pulled ahead and parked. Keller saw the old man's eyes in his mirror looking back at him. Keller put his hand on the front of his jeans, on the warm spot the sun made there, slanting through the side window, making him think about getting hard, making him think about getting out of these jeans and into his shorts back home. The man watched him. Keller turned off the radio. He heard but couldn't see the cars on the highway. The water didn't make a sound.

He got out of the truck, thinking he might walk over to the bank and skip stones across the water. The old man had his window rolled down, and he stuck his arm out the window. "You can't fish these waters," he said loudly.

"How's that?" Keller asked, stopping midway, turning at the waist because he had a hard-on.

"Polluted," the man said. *Old as the hills,* Keller thought. "Can't swim in them, either."

"No," Keller said, looking at the water. It was more the color of clay than mud, he thought, almost orange, looking thinly viscous, like warmed-up motor oil. He put his hands in his pockets.

"You look like a real tiger, boy," he heard. "You look like you'd tear it up good."

"What?" Keller said, turning again, smiling.

"It ain't easy," the old man said, looking at Keller with watery blue eyes. "Tiger boy."

"What are you saying?"

The old man blinked. His hair was wet-combed, parted neatly on the side. Keller could smell his barbershop cologne. He turned himself more, showing off what he'd been trying to hide. He watched the man's eyes go hungry. It wasn't easy? It was too easy.

"Used to fish here, before we knew anything was wrong," Keller heard him say. He took his hands out of his pockets and put them under his T-shirt. He pulled on the hem of it, dragging it downward, hiding himself again.

"Sunnies," the old man was said. He dropped his arm out of the window, his hand shaking enough for Keller to notice, his fingers twitching, signaling: *Over here, over here.* Keller pressed his fists against his crotch, still covered. He stopped thinking ahead, but concentrated on the stained vinyl roof of the Continental, the hot damp press of his cock against his thigh.

"Can't eat sunnies," the man said. "Just ain't right."

Keller laughed. He stood on the hump that ran the length of the road. He didn't know where the road went. He assumed it followed the river. He asked the man.

"That's right," he said. "And then there's an old mill where the kids smoke their grass and break their beer bottles." He turned his head as best as he could, and Keller looked to see another car pulling off the highway, slowly bouncing toward them.

They look so hungry, he thought, watching this new one, younger, though not much; a handicap symbol swung from his rearview mirror. "Tiger, hey."

Keller got back into his truck. He palmed the cap off of a beer gone warm and took a sip.

"Kenny will do it," Billy said. He pushed back his ball cap and gave Cary a blue stare. They were in Billy's room, a single now that his roommate, Javier Benitez Rodriguez, had been arrested for possession of stolen merchandise.

"There goes the DVD player," Cary had said as the detectives carried out what they referred to as evidence—what Cary termed "the goods."

"Goodbye, Movado watches. Goodbye, B&O stereo," Billy said, only half glad to see his roommate marched off in cuffs.

"But he was such a hottie," Cary said. Billy had to admit that Javier was indeed *muy caliente*: the way he used to parade around in little briefs, showing off his morning-noon-and-night erections; the ease with which he'd grab a titty magazine and say to Billy, "I'm going to jack off, if anyone calls for me."

Once Billy said to him, "Oh, you don't have to go," and Rodriguez stopped in the middle of their room and gave Billy a long crooked stare. "I mean," Billy said, rushing to fill the over-heated silence, "I'll take off, if you want some privacy."

Rodriguez cocked his head and did something with his lips. He had a goatee that framed his full mouth. "I kind of like the crapper," he said. "Reminds me of my days in the service." And as soon as the door was shut, Billy was having one of his own service days, albeit *self*-service, pulling hard on his sudden boner and jacking off into one of Rodriguez's gym socks, holding its mate under his nose.

"Kenny won't," Cary said now. "Kenny doesn't suck dick."

"Well, come on then," Billy said, throwing himself on the bed alongside Cary. "I *need* this," he said, whining. He was hard already—had been hard for hours, it seemed to him—and he was sick, just plain sick, of his own solo efforts. What he wanted was a good old-fashioned blow job.

He finger-walked up Cary's inseam. "Isn't it too hot for long pants," he asked coyly. Cary hitched his shoulders, watching Billy's hand coming to rest on his lap. His dick shrugged. Billy wasn't exactly his athlete of choice. While he certainly looked like, say, a wrestler or some other little brute, Billy lacked the hovering height that Cary adored. Cary longed for the long arms of Bennett Clark on the basketball team, or the freckled thighs of his lacrosse player who, at six foot two, fulfilled all of Cary's criteria head to toe, but especially midway, where hung the most beautiful penis Cary had ever seen.

"Really," Cary told Billy after seeing it for the first time. "It was photogenic! He could make the fucker smile! And what a beautiful smile."

"Oh, my," Cary said now. "Look at the time." He got himself off the bed that used to belong to Javier Benitez Rodriguez. Billy's hand fell open and empty on the bare mattress. He looked at the map of stained fabric, wondering which were Javier's vital fluids and to whom the rest belonged, imaging a long line of sturdy boys with wet dreams and errant hand-driven ejaculations. He was worked up now.

"Come on," he said. He stuck his hand down the front of his shorts, digging around for his boner, not that it was hard to find. He gave himself a squeeze and felt a gush seep out.

Cary faked a yawn. "I have to go," he said.

"You can't help a guy out?" Billy griped.

"Isn't that what girlfriends are for?" Cary said, waving his hand. "Besides, I have rehearsals. I have to nap."

"Yeah, whatever," Billy said. He contemplated a quick jack-off session with one of Javier's leftover girlie mags, but the idea of it wasn't doing anything for him. He thought about Kenny. "Kenny'll do it," he said to himself, and he picked up the phone and called down to Kenny's room.

"You got anything?" he asked—shorthand for "You got any weed to smoke?" Billy knew this much about Kenny—that Kenny got the horns whenever he smoked. He'd light up a bowl, and the next thing you knew, he'd be pulling pics off the Internet of guys and girls fucking, and he was sitting there feeling up the front of his pants, palming a hefty hard. He wasn't gay, but he didn't mind sucking dick every now and then, so long as you kept your mouth shut about it, which was why Cary was clueless. *That would be like telling the school newspaper,* Billy was thinking, bounding down the stairs to Kenny's basement room.

Kenny Kyle was wasted. He opened the door barefoot, wearing flannel boxers and an Abercrombie long-sleeved tee. A red lightbulb glowed in the lamp beside Kenny's bed. Phish was on the stereo.

"Dude!" Kenny said, closing the door fast. "You're letting the secondhand smoke out." They shook hands loosely, and Kenny pulled Billy close for a brotha's hug. "Peace, dude," he said.

"Who do you think you are—Biggie Smalls?" Billy asked.

"Yo, Gee—peeps are peeps, black or white," Kenny said lazily, playing with the pale little chin beard he'd grown over the weekend. He hopped onto his bed and sat cross-legged, and Billy spotted the sly droop of Kenny's uncut buddy.

"Sorry to hear about your love dog Benitez. The brotha got fucked over," Kenny said, leaning over to the plastic milk crate beside his bed, retrieving his pipe.

Billy licked his lips. "The brotha had brothas mopping Nordstrom, man—he fucked himself over," he said, taking the bowl Kenny held out. Billy smiled; the bowl was packed. He heard Kenny say that the lighter was on the desk. *Wouldn't be long,* he was thinking, looking again at the pale drop of Kenny's dick, the shirred end of it against the dark hairs of his thighs. The butane flame warmed his face. He inhaled and held the smoke. He squinted into Kenny's shorts and saw that Kenny was getting a chubby, hanging a little longer, a little fatter, taking a late-afternoon stroll down to the ragged hem of Kenny's boxers. And then Kenny shifted his legs, getting them uncrossed, stretching them out, flexing his feet and cracking his toes. His dick was trapped and obvious under the plaid flannel. He put a hand near it and gave Billy a look.

"You wanna bust a nut?" he asked.

Billy choked on the smoke.

"That's what you usually want, isn't it, dog?" Kenny said. "I mean, it ain't just the dope, is it?"

Billy shook his head, still unable to talk. He tried hard not to cough, but managed only to hack and wheeze like an old man. His eyes got teary and he couldn't catch his breath. He passed the pipe to Kenny and then the lighter, hacking away some more.

"You want some water?" Kenny asked, one-eyed at the pipe. He leaned back after his hit and smiled at Billy.

Billy, without the pretense of hetero Internet porn, was frozen. He liked the way they usually got around to it, paging through cunts getting it, enjoying the process of Kenny building his own excitement to a level of not caring what he had to do to get off—boy, girl, pussy fucking, dick sucking. So he was not altogether prepared for Kenny handing him the bowl with one hand and reaching out for the hardened front of Kenny's khaki shorts with the other. He jumped back, and Kenny laughed.

"Dude, don't tell me you're shy now," he said, and Billy laughed, too, but too loudly, with too much gusto. He was stoned. Kenny was staring at the front of his shorts, and Billy looked down at his own rocky poke, and his cock suddenly felt breakable, it was so hard. When Kenny reached for it again, Billy moved closer. There was no give to the thing. It jutted out like a tree branch. Kenny undid the fly.

With his shorts around his ankles and his cock stuck through the fly of his briefs, he let Kenny lick the tender tip. Kenny's fist

covered half the shaft, and the rest of it enjoyed the manipulations of Kenny's buttery lips. He slurped around the head, keeping a tight grip on Billy, making the split end red and swollen.
Billy did not know what to do with his hands, so he crossed them
over his chest, blocking the view he had of Kenny's mouth working on him. He moved them up over his head, but felt silly, like
an aerobics instructor or something. Finally, he placed his hands
on his hips, which made him feel like a posing porn star getting
his due.

"Suck it," he said silently, writing his own script, directing his
own movie. "Suck that big dick."

Kenny shrugged out of his T-shirt, his shoulders bony. His
skin was pale, and he had the long sinewy muscles of a skate-
boarder, no heaviness to him anywhere but his cock and balls.
He had hair down the front of him, shaggy around his nipples
and navel. He had a long torso, and his hipbones were girlish. He
was not exactly Billy's type, but Billy wasn't all too sure he had a
type yet. This was what he liked—so far, anyway. He closed his
eyes, and it could have been anyone down there: his girlfriend
back home or Cary or even Rodriguez or—fucking why not!—
Gwyneth Paltrow, for Christ's sake.

Kenny played with his balls, stroking them, pulling them
downward. This was, Billy, decided, probably the best blow job
he'd ever had. *I thought Cary was decent,* he said to himself, feeling his nuts start to shrink up despite Kenny's tugging. He let
himself moan a little, enjoying the noisy suck of Kenny's hard-
at-work mouth, spit dropping down between them, and Kenny
working his fingers back behind Billy's balls and poking around
his butthole.

"Whoah," he said, opening his eyes. *This definitely ain't
Gwyneth Paltrow,* he thought, backing up. His cock dripped
between them, and Kenny looked up at him with his battered lips
all wet.

"Whaa?" he wondered.

"Just, um…" Billy stammered, "uh, chill. I'm getting close."

Kenny smiled up at him. "That's the whole fucking idea, dude," he said. He slipped off his boxers. His cock slapped his hairy belly. It was wide and white, and the droopy foreskin had lost its droop and was a tight turtleneck around Kenny's pink head. He pumped the skin back and forth, cuffing the head and banging his balls between his thighs. He brought his head closer to the fallen head of Billy's dick.

"You taking a nap?" he asked the fat leaking head. He licked a dewy drop that had settled in the slotted end of Billy's drooped dick and then he took the whole thing in his mouth, his jaw seeming to dislocate itself to accommodate the girth at Billy's base. He chewed on the hairs there and let the plump head settle deep in his throat. And he went back to the stiff curling hairs around Billy's asshole, only this time Billy wasn't in any condition to protest, regardless of who was doing the probing.

Billy grabbed hold of Kenny's hair, keeping himself at the back of his buddy's throat, the sensation of his constricting esophagus unlike anything he'd ever experienced. He fucked himself into Kenny's mouth, enjoying the scraping teeth, the useless tongue, the yielding gag. Kenny moaned, giving himself a rough pounding. He fingered into Billy's tight little pucker, making him yelp and hold Kenny's head like a football he was on the verge of fumbling. He stuffed his mouth with Billy's dick and Billy held on for dear life as Kenny choked and poked and made a hot mess of himself all over Billy's shins just as Billy was about to bust his nut. Billy pushed Kenny off and grabbed hold of his quivering shaft and gave himself two hard tugs that unleashed a white flow of come all over Kenny's bearded chin and slim, hairy chest.

Billy's phone rang—it wasn't late, but he was sleeping anyway, still pretty buzzed from Kenny's pipe. "It's me," he heard Cary say. "Hey, can I come over?"

"What for?" Billy asked.

"You know," Cary said. "Your problem."

Billy smiled, his eyes closing, the television a blue glow against his eyelids. "Mmm," he said. "I'm all right, bud, all taken care of."

He heard Cary sigh. "Whatever," Cary said, miffed. "Everyone was talking about Rodriguez tonight—your little jailbird. You must miss him terribly."

Billy slid a hand under the sheets, finding himself twitching to life, conjuring a beautiful image of Rodriguez up at dawn, the front pouch of his little bikini filled to the brim, his erection in a space-saving double fold that looked painful. Billy squeezed his own boner hard enough to hurt, and he stifled a sigh and said into the phone, "What the fuck. Come on over. Just don't wake me, OK?"

He said, "My wife was going to throw this shirt out. I caught her using it as a dust rag once. It's my favorite. She just doesn't get it." He pulled off his trousers. "Yeah, it's got some holes in it, but it still works—it's not too worn out. I can still wear it, right?"

He was tall, sold pharmaceuticals. Shawn knew this because just as he'd parked his Montero in the gym's lot he'd seen the guy retrieve a gym bag out of a car trunk packed with cases of pharmaceutical samples. Shawn now was watching him pull warm-up pants up his long legs, covering his boxers, which were distracting because of their simple design and low cut, barely covering his hipbones. He had Kennedy looks.

He wasn't talking to Shawn, but to the man on the other side of him, the semipro wrestler, whom Shawn recognized from an article in the local paper. Shawn stared into his gym bag, its contents not nearly as interesting as the tall one's upcurled toes. He grabbed his shorts and undid the fastenings of his jeans and stood a while in his briefs. He suspected that the semipro wrestler was lingering over the conversation in order to watch the pharm rep take off his Brooks Brothers oxford and put on the favorite shirt, the one wrested from the mean old wife. Shawn got into his shorts and tried to pick a CD to listen to, going through a comprehensive collection of circuit party discs: *White, Black, Blue.* The pharm rep elbowed his way out of his crisp white tee, laying bare the beautiful geography of his torso, hairless save for a few errant curlies around his butterscotch nipples. Shawn did his best not to stare, but he was unable not to pause in his movements at the sight of such fucking sweetness.

Shawn had been a member of this gym for over five years, and crushes came and went. He had to admire his own tenacity, if nothing else. The membership did not always provide much eye candy, but he did not see the sense in switching gyms, because it really was about fitness, wasn't it? He began to think of the whole experience as a kind of living magazine to be perused— the muscle growth was an added bonus for his subscription! He came to the gym to flip some pages and do some bench presses. He wasn't much of a reader these days. He liked, rather, just to look at the pretty pictures.

The semipro did some lazy stretches, always a giveaway in a locker-room setting, and the pharm rep glanced down toward Shawn's end of the bench. He had just pulled "the Shirt" down over his beautiful head when he said, "Now isn't this perfect?"

Unable to restrain himself, Shawn tried to stifle a little snort and keep his eyes off the dimple that sat smugly and righteously under the pharm rep's fat lower lip. He glanced cursorily at the rep's shoulders, at the Shirt's alleged holes there.

"That is…" Shawn struggled to find the word. "Ah…perfect," he said, feeling as though he'd aced something.

"Damn straight," the rep said, slapping his own pecs hard to emphasize his point. "It's a guy thing," he said proudly.

"Perfect," Shawn said to himself later, walking past the rep doing chin-ups, his shirt rising and baring the married man's beautiful gut. "I hate this fucking place."

Shawn showered afterward, embarrassingly alone—the general notion at this gym was that only "the fags" showered here. Everyone else took his dirty, sweaty body home to clean up. Shawn scrubbed himself with a plastic loofah but was unable to rid himself of the horniness that clung to him as a result of his workout. His cock kept bobbing upward, threatening fullness, an awkward hard-on no towel could cover. He turned down the hot water until he was shivering and goose-fleshed, but there was no dousing the fire down below. He kept his back to the shower-room door and waited until the locker room sounded empty. He turned off the water and grabbed his towel, wrapping it around his waist and binding his rigid prick up against his belly. He looked as though he was trying to hide a bottle of wine.

He opened the shower curtain and there was Dean the Queen. Who else would be sitting right in front of the shower, tying and retying the laces of his sneakers? Dean looked infinite-ly disappointed to see Shawn, although it was plain that he did not miss Shawn's gut-bound hard-on.

"You sure know how to make cleaning up fun," he lisped. "And you're all alone!"

"Yup," Shawn muttered, making his way to his locker. Keeping his towel on, he prudishly stepped into his underwear and, back turned, got himself into his jeans. He heard Dean the Queen sigh and turned to see him picking up his gloves and belt and heading out to the gym floor.

In his car, Shawn readjusted his erection and played with the radio. His SHeDAISY disc was in his bag in the backseat. The effort required to retrieve it was enough of a pain in the ass to make him settle on the disc already in the CD player: *The Best of the Ohio Players*.

"Fi-yah!" he sang along with them; "Fi-yah!"

It was desire that made Shawn drive to the library at Aubrey College. He walked past the checkout desk, manned by a stoned Deadhead with snaky, unclean-looking dreads and a washed-out tie-dyed T-shirt. He headed straight for the back stairs, past the periodicals, past the card catalogs. He walk-ran down the steps, down to the basement men's room. It was empty, and he placed himself in his favorite stall, taking his pants down and sitting on the cold toilet seat. He could see through the gaps on either side of the stall door the urinals situated directly across from him.

There were two reasons boys came down here to use this

particular bathroom—the need to void and the need to void, the former involving the complex plumbing of the bowel and bladder, the latter making use of the equally complex plumbing of the seminal vessel. Shawn waited patiently. Despite the fact that it was only Monday, usually an off-night for getting off, he was hopeful. And then the outside door squeaked open and then the inner door, and Shawn saw the lanky frame of a boy in baggy jeans and an Old Navy T-shirt step up to the urinals. The boy glanced behind himself at Shawn's sneakered feet before unzipping his fly and letting a ringing blast of piss flow into the porcelain receptacle. He was gone before Shawn could work up an erection, his earlier gym lust turning into something more cerebral and thoughtful and somehow less interesting. He was ready to pull his pants up and cut his losses. *There's always Dirk Yates,* he was thinking. The door opened again.

This boy was big and tight-shouldered. He looked permanently flexed, walking with his knuckles facing forward. He had a buzzed head, a heavy chin, and small sharp nose. He stepped up to a urinal toward the back of the bathroom, to Shawn's right, and Shawn leaned forward to peer through the gap. The boy was out of sight for the most part—there was just the edge of his body showing, his thigh, his scabbed elbow, and then his face, looking in Shawn's direction. He made a side step toward the door, turning a bit to show Shawn what Shawn wanted to see.

The boy's cock dangled heavily. It was milky white, its head pink-rimmed—*A milkmaid's prick,* Shawn was thinking, his mouth going thick, his tongue sliding over his lips. His own cock, pinched between his legs, bulged into bent hardness, wedged against the rim of the toilet. With sanitary issues forgotten, Shawn froze on his seat as the college boy began a very slow and deliberate tug on his creamy shaft. His eyes, Shawn could see, shifted between the stall door and the bathroom door, then down to his cock, which was fat and firm but not quite hard. He took another step toward Shawn. His T-shirt was tight: the muscles of his arms fought the fabric. He lifted his chin, and Shawn stood. He opened his door slowly.

He remembered the last time he'd had any luck here—it had been a Thursday night, right before the library closed. It was with a tall skinny boy with an enormous prick, a salami prick, super-sized, nearly ridiculous in its excess. The boy had knelt on the floor, spreading his knees wide, and dipping his hips to get his crotch-bound monolith under the partition and into Shawn's mouth. He'd come quickly and too loudly for a library bathroom and, Shawn thought, tasted sulfurous. Still, Shawn had thought then, it was quite a good time.

This was looking like a good time, too, Shawn thought. The boy gave him a needful, vulnerable look, his cock quivering in his grip. He motioned toward the back of the john, where more toilets were situated. *Why so many pissers?* Shawn wanted to know. There must have been 10 urinals there. What was it about books and studying that made boys have to pee so? In his thinking the ingestion of so many words would more likely lead to the need to take a dump. Leastwise, that had always been Shawn's experience in college, where he had first discovered the hidden joys of library basement johns.

In the back corner, out of sight of the door and under a frosted window, the boy said, "Suck me." His cock hung out of his fist, a thick droop.

He had fuzzy sideburns dropping below his ears, tight white Hanes briefs, straight fair hairs around the base of his dick, and old and frayed Calvin Klein jeans. His T-shirt read STUBBY'S MUFFLERS. Shawn took mental snapshots of all of this on his way down to kiss the blunt head of the boy's cock. He licked under it, taking it into his mouth, just the pink end of it, the piss slit drooling pearly dewdrops. It was rubbery and chewable, toy-like. He heard the boy sigh, relaxing his grip, allowing Shawn the entire piece. Shawn, instead, dropped his head to lick the full ball bag, the boy's low-hanging danglers. They filled Shawn's mouth, rolling over his tongue and stopping his throat. The skin they bobbed in was silky and tasty and smooth. He pulled down the Calvins and the Hanes, baring the boy's beefy thighs, hairy-blond, hard as tombstones. He gurgled on the boy's nuts, gargled the nut sac, his own spit turning to something like glue.

Back at the knob, the meaty chewy head, he stuck his tongue into the end and drew out what there was to draw out—salty honey. He put his hands on the boy's uncovered glutes, twin rocky orbs that squeezed tight but so very smooth. He took in half of the boy's hardening cock. He worked the rest with his hand. The boy let out a groan, his hands useless over Shawn's head, fingers flexing and knuckles cracking. Shawn lipped the buttered cap, licking the fleshy underside, making the boy's gut ripple. Reaching up under his shirt, Shawn played with the boy's nipples, little baby dots. The boy registered unease unappreciatively—tits are for chicks. But Shawn liked the thick muscled-plates of pec, despite their ill-proportioned decorations. He focused on the cock, because that was all that mattered, as the boy was concerned anyway. His cock was central right now—*crucial:* It throbbed like his heart, possessing all of his energies, vibrating on Shawn's roaming tongue. He took the length of it to the back of his throat, wishing now that the boy would touch him. Shawn looked up to see the boy had struck a manly pose, arms across his chest, reciprocation clearly out of the question. He swallowed the head, sputtering a little for show, and he thought he saw the boy smile.

"Fuck, man," Shawn heard, voice disconnected, floating above his head. It was a grunt, a warning. The balls against Shawn's chin shrunk up hard and densely textured, bristling with newly cut hairs. The boy held his breath then, and Shawn waited for the flow. It came hard and thick, ropy blasts coating the inside of Shawn's mouth and throat.

The boy stepped back, grappling for his jeans and under-clothes, covering himself. His cock, log-like, encased in tight white cotton, looked bigger than Shawn managed to remember, his jaw aching, his own cock sputtering, spraying hot bursts of come all over the boy's Pumas, making a mess.

43

"Sorry," Shawn said, and the boy shrugged.

"Whatever," he said, zipping up, repositioning his dick to make it less obvious. He stepped up to the sinks, trying to fix his bristle of unruly hair in the mirror. Shawn got off his knees. He wasn't much older than the boy at the mirror—five, maybe six years his senior—but he felt old suddenly. The door opened. Shawn went to the sinks. A slight boy with fat lips eyed them both, his gaze lingering on the ass of the boy beside Shawn. He turned on the taps, making too long a job of washing his hands. Shawn waited, too, as the new boy entered the stall Shawn had occupied. He waited for the sound of the door locking, but the sound never came. The boy beside Shawn pumped out some more soap. Not up for the competition, Shawn turned off his water, dried his hands, and left the two of them to their own devices.

He saw the pharm rep again—this time out at a bar called the Spruce. The rep was by himself and so was Shawn. Their eyes met in the mirror behind the bar, and Shawn saw him trying to register the familiarity.

He leaned over then, looking down at Shawn, and said, "Long time, no see."

Shawn smiled and said, "Yeah."

The rep nodded, smiling, too, and Shawn felt as though he were missing something, some piece of information that was vital to this small exchange. It felt coded, indecipherable, until the rep moved down a couple of stools, maneuvering himself beside Shawn, and ordered shots for the two of them. He grinned into Shawn's face, his breath boozy, and said with hushed gruffness, "You thought I forgot you, didn't you? Yeah, I'm sorry I didn't call like I said I would, but you know how it goes."

Shawn gave a vague shrug that seemed meaningful to the rep.

"I even remember your name," the rep said, pointing. "Billy. No, umm…"

"It's Shawn."

The rep's face dulled; he looked momentarily stupid. *Funny*

44

what bourbon does to a man's features, Shawn thought. A glint of bar light bounced off the man's wedding ring, catching Shawn's eye. The man started twisting the ring then, watching Shawn's face. "I remember you," he said again.

"I bet you don't," Shawn said, playing along. Whatever the game was, Shawn was all for it, remembering the man's bare torso, his long, thick-muscled legs, his beautiful proportions.

The man grinned hard, leaning toward Shawn. "Up on the hill," he whispered, nodding.

"Yeah?" Shawn said.

The rep stopped grinning. "You're the one who don't remember," he said.

"Sure, I do, sure," Shawn said. "You sell drugs."

He had to figure out whether or not Shawn was being funny, explaining the delayed laugh. "Yeah, right!"

"But your name," Shawn said, shaking his head. "I just can't—"

He lifted his glass and looked over the rim of it at Shawn. "Look, I can't remember what name I gave you, either." He paused, taking a drink. "It's Paul." He set his glass down hard. "Damn glad to know you, Shawn," he said brightly, holding out his hand for Shawn to shake.

"Yeah," Shawn said, taking the offered hand in his. It was big and warm, slender-fingered, and gripped Shawn's tightly.

"What was that I just ordered for us—them shots?"

Shawn had to think about it. He shrugged his shoulders. "Couldn't tell you," he said.

Paul grinned lewdly, leaning in toward Shawn for a moment before straightening up and giving the clientele at the bar a quick inspection. "I fucking know everyone here," he said disdainfully, his mouth rigid and smug. "Ever feel like you're living in a fucking fishbowl?"

Shawn shook his head. He wasn't a native, but he'd learned that most of the men and women had come here first when they were teenagers and returned once they'd finished college, moving back to live not far from their parents. There was something about this town, some charm, some hold, but Shawn was blind to whatever it was. He was hitting the road as soon as the next best thing came along.

"We should get the fuck outta here, know what I mean?"

Shawn nodded, knowing.

"The old lady, she's not bad—don't get me wrong. She's fine, she's real fine," Paul was saying, his hands running though his curling dirty-blond hair. His eyes were green, his face long, and he'd lumbered ahead of Shawn like a basketball player bereft of his ball, heading for the showers—not altogether a bad combination. "Chemistry!" he shouted suddenly. "What happened to the fucking chemistry?"

They sat in Shawn's Montero, which was parked behind a cement building that might have been a garage, might have been an office building. The SUV's windows were down—it was the first real warm night of the season. The radio was on low, playing songs Shawn knew by heart—songs by Shelby Lynne and Aimee Mann. He watched as Paul undid the fastenings of his pants, pushing them down his thighs—also known to Shawn by heart. Paul's cock stood through the gaping fly of his boxers, a stony monument. He put his thumb and forefinger to his mouth and then to the end of his tall prick.

"She's all right," Paul said, closing his eyes for a second, maybe imagining her, Shawn was thinking. Paul undid the first few bottom buttons of his shirt, baring his stomach, its tautness obvious. Shawn swallowed, looking out the windows of the SUV.

"Are you sure it's cool here?" he asked.

"It was cool enough last time," Paul said, smirking.

"Last time?" Shawn said. "There wasn't a last time, except maybe this time."

Paul froze, his hand arrested mid-stroke. He made an "oops" face. "You know, I was wondering what happened to your Jetta," he said.

"So you're saying I have a queer twin?"

"No," Paul said, resuming his jacking off. "You don't look like him at all, now that I think about it. He had red hair and was, like, six foot three. I could have looked him in the eye if I'd wanted to."

He leaned over then and kissed Shawn, who tasted the bourbon and a mint Paul had managed to suck on without Shawn's knowing. His free hand kneaded the front of Shawn's jeans.

"I know you from somewhere, though," Paul said, his mouth still on Shawn's, tongue swirling and confusing the words.

"The gym" Shawn garbled back.

"Shweet," Paul said, nodding, finding the fly of Shawn's jeans and tugging on the obstinate zipper. After much digging he found Shawn's prick—solid and fat and half-curled—nestled in moist pubes. He hauled it out and went down on it, lapping the tapered end. Shawn placed one hand on the back of Paul's head and the other on the headrest behind him. His cock buzzed into the hot mouth, guided by Paul's tight grip, making it pulse and throb. He forced Paul all the way down, eliminating his fist, wanting to feel the man's lips against his pubes and balls. Paul came up choking, his smiling lips rimmed with hairs and shining with spit.

"Easy, pal," he said, tugging on his own prick for a while, leaning back to look Shawn over. "I remember you now," he said.

"Yeah, right," Shawn said, stroking his lonely prick. He watched a bubble or two of precome drool from the split head of Paul's cock. "I still don't think this is such a great place."

"Don't worry about it," Paul replied. "I own this building—nobody's gonna come back here unless I ask 'em to."

In the back of the Montero with the seats down, there was room to roll around, room to grapple and undress. The sun was setting fast, and in the dusky light Shawn licked remembered nipples, narrow hips, and a tightened ball sac, as he fingered Paul's knotted butthole, tight at first, then giving gently, opening like some secret door. Paul moaned and used his hips to feed Shawn more of his dick, riding the mouth, forcing his prick deeper into Shawn's widened throat, muttering praise for Shawn's cocksucking skills.

"You're fucking awesome, man, fucking awesome."

Paul slid his pole in and out, his hands on either side of Shawn's hips, dropping his head to lick Shawn's slick shaft and aching, eager balls.

"You like to fuck?" Shawn heard. He made an affirmative grunt with his mouth full of dick.

"Cool," Paul said, leaning back, squatting on Shawn's face, filling his mouth with cock, balls cascading over his stubbled chin. "Finger fuck me, dude."

Shawn's finger was already planted, so he added a second, and uncorked Paul's long prong from his mouth and went to work on his dangling balls instead, liking the way they stopped his throat and nose simultaneously, the bag suede-like and luxurious and breathtaking. He probed around Paul's insides, making the man squirm and giggle, his dick bopping Shawn's forehead and leaving sticky little kisses.

Paul shifted and pivoted, straddling Shawn's hips. He held on to Shawn's prick firmly and pushed it up into his asshole, and he squatted lower and took more. He had no trouble with Shawn's length or thickness; he was a regular pro, Shawn saw appreciatively, as he watch Paul dip his ass and fill himself with quick sighs. Paul sat himself down, resting his butt cheeks on Shawn's hipbones. There wasn't enough dick to fill him, it seemed—he took the ample supply Shawn could give him, and still he wanted more. He fingered Shawn's little nipples, twisting and pulling them until Shawn yelped. He bounced against Shawn's pelvis and leaned back, moving his feet up toward Shawn's armpits, making himself crab-like and more feisty, giving himself a nasty fuck on Shawn's back-bent prick.

"Oh, man," he said, sweating, winking at Shawn. "You sure know how to fuck."

"No," Shawn said. "*You* know how to fuck."

"You don't like?" Paul asked, slowing down, but not much.

"Oh, I like, I like."

Paul pushed his fanny forward. "Aw, you feel that?" he asked.

Shawn felt something, the beginnings of something. It roiled around his groin and tickled his nuts up tight and swirled up his shaft and circled the knob of his cock. Paul continued his fanny slams and Shawn's breathing stopped. He opened his mouth, wanting to say something meaningful, but only nasty words came to his mind, nothing nobler than "Ride me, you fucking cock jockey!"

Shawn watched Paul's face freeze, as his own prick waving stiffly, untouched up until then. Paul managed to continue, positioned like a tripod while jerking himself roughly, his breathing hoarse, his language coarse, and he banged himself on Shawn's exploding prick, sucking up every last drop and spraying Shawn and the felt ceiling of his Montero with a proud and copious load worthy of a porn star. Shawn had never seen so much jizz come out of one man at one time. He took a deep breath and licked the corner of his mouth. He put his hands over his head, stretching, liking the way his cock felt up inside Paul. He closed his eyes for a second, and Paul leaned forward finally, putting his face on Shawn's come-spattered shoulder.

"I messed you up," he said quietly.

Shawn smiled. "Oh, boy, I'll say you did."

Shawn holds up the Shirt. "I swear to God, Paul, I'm throwing this away."

Paul glances up from the television and squints at the tattered T-shirt Shawn is dangling by a ragged sleeve. "Aw, hon," he says, "it's not that bad."

"You can't wear this at the gym—your nipples would show." Shawne watches Paul grin and play distractedly playing with the absent wedding ring on his finger. Shawn bunches up the shirt then and holds it under his nose, breathing in the smell of his lover, thinking—and not for the first time: *Sweet.*

Fitz Is 25

Fitz didn't think it was going to happen. He checked his watch. It read quarter to eight, and Knowles said he'd be there at eight. But it wasn't likely, Fitz was thinking. *Not too likely, not a guy like Knowles.* Fitz wasn't even sure why he'd asked the boy for a drink the day he'd run into him at the campus mail center. Buildings and Grounds had sent Fitz there to work on an HVAC call. It was seeing him again, he decided—the way Knowles had jumped up out of the seat where he was reading his mail to shake Fitz's hand.

"You fixed the heat in my room a while ago," Knowles had said, not that Fitz had needed the memory jog. He remembered Knowles clearly: the way the kid had looked in a wife beater and the pair of filmy shorts he'd chosen to wear, despite the malfunctioning radiator. He'd imagined later that he'd have blown him if the kid were into it. But, no, he decided then and now: *Not a guy like Knowles.*

Fitz sunk lower in his seat, a bottle of beer before him. He looked at the bar—at the long row of plaid and working-man blue backs of the men who labored at the paint factory around the corner, not far from the college where Fitz worked and Knowles lived some seven months of the year. Fitz could have gotten a position at Glide-On Paints, but the college offered full tuition, not that he'd had occasion to take any classes yet. *Plenty of time,* he was thinking, checking his watch again. *Nothing but time.* He was 25. He had all the time in the world.

Behind him the door opened, and Fitz turned in his seat. Knowles stood in the doorway a moment, looking down the row of men at the bar. Fitz raised a hand, and Jason Knowles nodded. He was wearing a Deacon College T-shirt that fit tightly across his chest and shoulders. He settled in at the table across from Fitz, who suddenly felt skittish and girly. He pressed his palms flat on the table, displaying nicked knuckles and dirt under one of his nails, and the two men grinned at one another, and Knowles turned his head, surveying the place, and Fitz looked at the tall blond's jaw-line, sandy-stubbled and sharp.

"You wanna beer?" he asked him, and Knowles shrugged. And then he leaned over the table, blue-eyed and grinning.

"I'm not 21 yet," he said softly. "I've got my brother's card, but he's like 35. It works at the Boiler Room downtown, and that's pretty much it." Fitz stopped looking at the boy's mouth.

"Don't worry about it," Fitz said. "You want one of these?" He tipped his bottle on its side, and Knowles nodded, and Fitz went up to the bar and brought two bottles and two shots back to the table.

At quarter to two, Knowles grabbed Fitz's wrist and turned it, trying to get a better look at the watch there. "Oh, man," he said, shaking his head. He had hair that fell over his eyes, hair like boys had in the '60s, surfer boys, and his blue-green eyes were the color of the ocean. "There is no way I am doing crew tomorrow morning."

His hand was still on Fitz's wrist, and Fitz regarded it. They were buds now, hanging buds. They had talked about high school and campus shit and what they were planning to do with their lives. Knowles listened carefully when Fitz told him about his broken engagement. "It just…" Fitz said, trailing off and cracking his knuckles and trying to find the right words.

"Wasn't right?" Knowles had offered, and Fitz nodded. That was it exactly, he told his friend.

"Closing time," Fitz said now, and Knowles made a face,

pouting his full pink lips. "Done all ready?" he asked. "C'mon. Let's get a six to go."

Fitz grimaced. "Looks like you're going to make me use my last sick day," he said, and Knowles lifted his bottle, knocking it against Fitz's.

Outside, each of them swinging a six-pack that neither really needed, they wondered aloud where to go. Knowles's room was closer, but his roommate was a "real prick," he said. Fitz lived in town only about 10 blocks away, but it had just started to rain. They stood under the canopy, debating, cursing the drizzle.

"Yours. It'll be better," Knowles said, and Fitz agreed.

"Mine," he said. They knocked into each other like old pals and started walking, their shoulders hunched against the warm rain, and Fitz wondered what "better" meant.

"I live here," Fitz said, stopping in front of a three-story brick building. The first floor housed a chiropractor. The rest of it was Fitz's. They went through an alley and were out of the rain that had started falling harder. He felt Knowles on his heels and then they were at the back door in the rain again, and Fitz fumbled with the keys. Knowles stepped close behind him, getting under the little roof over the door, his breath on Fitz's neck.

In the living room, there was a sofa left by the last tenant. Knowles sat there and palmed a cap off a beer. Fitz shifted inside his wet clothes. "We're soaked," he said.

"Yeah, and it's fucking cold in here," Knowles laughed. His T-shirt stuck to him. His nipples showed through, their brownness a sharp contrast under the white wet cotton.

Fitz watched as Knowles wrestled out of his shirt. He had a narrow drift of hair that sneaked up his belly like creeping phlox. The rest of him was smooth and defined. He was all shoulders and back and impossibly slender at the waist. He raised his hands up over his head, showing off twin dark patches of hair at his armpits. Then he stood and pulled on the buttons of his jeans, opening them and revealing gray boxer-briefs.

"You got something dry for me, right?" he said, working to hide a grin.

Fitz blinked once, then twice. "Yeah," he said. "Sure." He shook his head a little to clear it, and he put down the six-pack he was still holding, the plastic bag strangling his fingers, and he got out of his own wet clothes.

Knowles stared. He swallowed. He looked down at the beer he was holding and took a drink, his eyes drifting back to Fitz's bared torso, his fuzz-covered legs and dumb plaid boxers. He licked his lips, wet with beer.

"I'll get us some clothes," Fitz said slowly, unsure. *That sounded pretty queer,* he was thinking. He went up to the bedroom, and Knowles followed closely behind him on the stairs, which were narrow and steep. Knowles hit his head on an overhang, and Fitz said, "Sorry," and Knowles laughed, saying "Ouch."

Turning on the overhead light, Fitz went to his dresser and started pulling things out and throwing them on the bed. Knowles leaned against the doorway, watching. "What do you want to wear?" Fitz asked. "I've got, like, jeans or some sweats or whatever, and here's a shirt. Everything should fit. We're about the same size, right?"

Knowles walked across the room, and Fitz saw the bobbing front of Knowles's underwear, heavy with a growing cock. He took the shirt from Fitz's hand and put it back in the dresser drawer. He put his face close to Fitz's.

"I fucked up the heater that day," Knowles said. "I did it on purpose." That was how they'd met, when Fitz answered a complaint early in the semester about a lack of heat in one of the rooms of Byerly Hall. Knowles's room.

"They could've sent anyone," Fitz mumbled, unable to break the long stare into Knowles's blue eyes. "Dan White's better at heating. So's Dave Cannelli. I'm, uh, A.C., usually."

Knowles put a warm hand on Fitz's shoulder. "You're hard to figure out," he said, getting closer. He pushed Fitz toward the bed, nudging him gently onto the mattress. Fitz was all too aware of his cock, hard and juicy, jutting up through the fly of his shorts. He wondered whether to tuck it in, and just then Knowles touched it, taking it in his hand, going to his knees between Fitz's legs. He licked up one side of the thick shaft and down the other, gripping it tightly, his fist hard against Fitz's balls. His hair swung into his eyes and he flicked it back, tonguing around the pink-rimmed cock head, giving Fitz the chills. He lay back for a minute but didn't like not seeing what Knowles was doing to him.

When Fritz sat up, Knowles was getting to his feet, his dick pointing at Fitz's face, making a little twist to the left. It was short and lean, its head flared and shining. Knowles fisted it, getting up on the bed and kneeling beside Fitz's head, dipping into the man's open mouth. Fitz sucked the end of it and then all of it, sticking out his tongue to swab the boy's fat, heavy balls. Knowles leaned over him, using his hips to fill Fitz's mouth again and again, pulling out, going back in. He fucked himself into Fitz's tightened lips, against Fitz's sliding tongue. He played with one of Fitz's tits, poking it with his finger, then getting it into a pinch and pulling hard. Fitz's dick jumped with each touch, pull, and tweak.

Knowles dragged his palm across his mouth and then wiped his ass with it, working his fingers up inside himself, letting Fitz watch and jack off. Knowles got a leg up, still kneeling on the other, and Fitz moved up, getting his face behind Knowles's nuts and going for the fuzzy pucker, competing with the boy's fuck-finger. He sucked on the dark knot and tongued into the softened slit, making his tongue hard and pointed, going into the hot inside of Jason Knowles.

"Aw, jeez, man," Knowles said.

Fitz pushed his nose into the dank hairs and used his whole mouth, chinning Knowles's balls. He felt Knowles's grip on his cock, yanking up on the sensitive stalk. He used the other hand on the back of Fitz's head, holding him tightly, smothering him in the wet stink of his crotch, his butt cheeks clenching and relaxing in self-determined spasms. There was no air for Fitz to breathe but Knowles's own ass-breath. For the time being, it was all he needed. It made him dizzy, and he gulped it down and used his rough chin against Knowles's puckered lips, and Fitz heard him cry out somewhere far above him. He felt the boy's balls pounding against his throat and his own cock's strangled eruptions that made Knowles cry out again. He stood up quickly, and his face seemed different somehow to Fitz: it was red and lined, his brow wet and heavy, his eyes intent. Maybe it was the face he made when he was in his crew shell, rowing atop the Schuylkill, skimming across the water. He put his fingers into Fitz's mouth. They dripped with his own come. He sucked them and watched Knowles aim his first shot over his knuckles and into Fitz's mouth, the rest coating his chin and throat and chest.

"I was waiting for you," Knowles confessed. Fitz stared at the ceiling. Loud police lights ripped across it as a silent cruiser tore down the street. Knowles's hand was next to Fitz's head. The boy was staring at him in the dark.

We're not supposed to say anything, Fitz was thinking. *We're not supposed to say anything at all. We're not supposed to stay either, not like this.* He was not comfortable in his own bed, sharing it like this.

He wasn't drunk anymore, and he didn't like the way his head felt, and he didn't like the way Knowles touched him now, his face, his chest, his cock. *Stop it!* he wanted to yell. *Cut it out!*

Knowles lay his head on Fitz's only pillow. He was thinking, too—about the next time and what his roommate was going to say if he didn't come back tonight and what he was going to say in return, and Jason Knowles started making up stories, making up excuses, and Fitz did the same.

"What time is it?" Knowles asked, his voice a thick whisper.

"Late," Fitz answered just as quietly. "It's late."

Nova Scotia Sucks My Ass

I want to fuck his brains out. I want to fuck him blind, but I'm worried about the Canadians. I am always worrying about the Canadians. Who doesn't around here? This is fucking Buffalo, dude.

I gave Jeff a lift because he said he'd be late if I didn't, and I didn't want him to be late for his first day on the job. He's just gotten hooked up at Shoes R Us. I've had a job for a while at U R Cool. We sell T-shirts with Farrah Fawcett pictures on them, and Skechers and Fubu jeans. It's a good place to work because you get a 40% discount and there isn't anything to do but fold the Farrah Fawcett T-shirts and ask people if they want to buy "some socks to go with that outfit" or a "really cool hemp necklace."

Jeff looks like the guy in Third Eye Blind. I think it's that guy, the one that sings. Or maybe it's the Better Than Ezra guy. I can't remember. I only know that I saw Jeff in his boxers once and sprouted myself some mighty wood and had to cover it with my dad's golf-club towel, which seemed kind of appropriate at the time.

So I like guys, but I don't like to talk about it, you know? I don't go around saying I'm gay or anything, because I'm really not too sure about that right now anyway, and my mom thinks I should make sure before I march in any gay pride parade. I think she's offering some good advice. But there's something about Jeff that would make me march down the middle of Main Street in my mom's bra and panties if I knew I was marching toward him. I can just see it—me marching toward Jeff with his Abercrombie boxers around his ankles, ass flying high like any proud rainbow fucking flag, ready for some major plowing.

I've got a fattie, a cock like a third fucking arm, which would make a great name for a band, I'm thinking. Once I was fucking around in the store after hours with this guy, Bryan, who said he was the district manager of one of our biggest competitors—We Be Phat. He'd been on my shit all day, telling me how he was going to get me my own store and how he liked the way my hair looked because I had the tips bleached. He wanted to know how much I benched—like 210 at the time, by the way, and practically 250 now. He hung out after nine because he said he wanted to compare our closing procedures to the ones at his stores, and I was like, *Whatever*. The lights went out and he had me back in the office, his hands all over me.

"You look so tense," he said, massaging my pecs, dropping down to my crotch, where I'd sprung a leak, if you know what I mean.

And I'm saying, "Tense? You don't know tense."

Then he starts undoing my jeans and digging around in my boxers, getting my man in two hands and bringing it out into the open.

"At last," was all he said.

Jeff was playing with the radio, and now he's playing with the end of his shirt. He has to wear this completely gay shirt that says YO! SHOES R US!—which I think is totally offensive, but there's marketing for you, and I'm thinking of majoring in that next semester at Buff U., and then I could get a job—uh, nowhere, you know what I mean? He looks better in a wife beater, because then you can see his Superman tat and the hand-sampled heart he drew himself in sixth grade, long before I ever met him.

He digs at himself, getting a good handful of his crotch and squeezing it hard, grinding the heel of his hand into himself, making me wince, thinking he might have crabs or something—

scabies—whatever. I'm watching the road because my car isn't exactly insured, but whatever he's doing or whatever he's trying to kill down there has my attention. I got a bone myself that's stuck up against the steering wheel. It's making my driving skills strictly retarded. I'm thinking I shouldn't have worn the warm-ups without some protection, but I'm looking forward to the next turn I'm going to make, my dick head wedged nicely.

Jeff said, "Dude, I am so not into this. Wouldn't it be cool if you could just keep on going? Why don't we drive to California—I hear everyone is cooler out there."

"Who told you that?" I asked.

"Some dude from L.A."

That district manager is from California. I like thinking about him. I haven't done anybody since him, and I'm feeling kind of backed up, which is why I nearly got off on the steering wheel, seeing Jeff scratch himself. I like thinking about Bryan and Jeff together, what they might do. I like thinking about Jeff bending himself over for this guy who isn't much older than we are and letting him fuck him. I'm thinking that Jeff could like lean over a chair or something and completely open his ass for this guy, who's hot, really—a fucking sketchy hottie, all tall and black-haired, like some *Vogue Homme* model. His hair's always getting into his eyes and his buzzed little goatee is itching him all the time, making him look thoughtful yet completely fuckable, which he was.

When he opened my jeans and pulled out my pole, he looked a little pale, a little beyond happy. Like I said, he held me with both hands and moaned, staring at my cock's single eye, "At last." Considering the dime-sized opening of my piss slot, I was about to consider this guy a bit gone. I've never known anyone to praise the beast so highly. It's a daunting piece—so said my history professor—a dick to fear, according to some of the other guys. It's an ass-stretcher, a mouth-wrecker. I'd come to think of hand jobs as the only way I would ever get off—haven't ever met a girl or guy willing to actually insert it. I've heard it all when it comes to my dick, but never "At last."

The next thing he said was: "We need some lube," his voice strangled. He flicked my dick head with his finger and I nearly came. Lube? I was finally going to get some. I watched him undress, undoing his Gucci belt for him, unknotting his Hermes tie. He was too cool for this shithole store, but that didn't make much difference to me. He let his pants drop and I eyeballed his hairy thighs and wanted to feel them against mine, and I stepped toward him.

Jeff says, "I need some Gatorade—I think I'm dehydrated."

I stop at 7-Eleven and stare at his ass as he walks into the store. That's one thing I haven't ever seen—his bare butt—but it's something I'm very interested in, like it's a hobby, something of a pursuit. In his jeans it's a sweet bubble. Naked—who knows? Smooth cheeks? Fuzz-covered? It's a crap shoot, this second-guessing, but crap I wouldn't mind shooting, if you know what I mean.

"Get me something not—you know," I yell out through the window.

"Canadian?" he calls back.

Exactly, I think.

The DM didn't really have hair that got into his eyes or a little goatee, and he'd have never made the pages of any fashion mag. He was actually kind of balding and a little on the fat side. And his clothes were all from, like, the Polo outlet. It didn't matter to me, though, because he was married and had two kids and used to play football in college. All of that was like some sort of aphrodisiac for me. I was the one that pawed him from the start, letting him know from minute one that he could do whatever he wanted to me, that I was his for the taking. He was crazy about my cock, though, cock-crazy like you wouldn't believe, throwing himself on it, first his mouth and then his ass. He was fired up and wanted to be torn up—wasn't like the old lady was going to notice or any-thing, he said to me. He took off his tasseled Cole Haans.

"Do me a favor," he said, holding out a shoe for me. "Smell this and tell me what you think."

I took the shoe and took a big whiff. My cock dripped like a honeycomb. "I think you fucking stink," I said.

"Damn straight," he said, smiling hard and punching my arm.

He started sucking my knob. It's a big old red thing, like a tomato hanging from a fucking thick-ass vine. He made some gur-gling noises, some choking noises, then some more gurgling nois-es. I saw him whip his own out, a nice looking piece of meat, very pink, very straight, very long, rising up out of a thick patch of red-dish hair. He swung it around like a bullwhip, and it sprayed out a golden thread of leakage that marked up his Ralph Lauren chinos. He got his mouth close to my halfway mark, a bulge in a vein that pretty much marked the 4.5 inches of dick, with that much to go to get to the base. He handled my nads hard, like a man should, and I stayed quiet, enjoying the soft slip of his tongue, the firm grip of his lips. He tugged on my prick for a while, banging his nose into to my bush, his fingers moving up toward my butthole.

The one time I saw Jeff in his boxers, in his room at his par-ents' house, before he got kicked out for selling acid to his cousins, I was drawn to the swinging bob of his cock as he walked across the room. He was fresh from a shower and in pursuit of something to put on, probably to cover that swinging bob, that juicy hang. He has a nice body, his stomach all boxed up with muscle, with tits not big like mine, but there, enough to want to put your mouth on them. He's not into bulk, isn't bulky himself, no interest in fat hard tits or big wagging quads, but boasting some sweet ass cheeks and knuckle-biting thighs—sweet things, those thighs, fucking sweet.

We were listening to Ben Folds and getting ready to go see *Armageddon*. I have a secret bone for Ben Affleck because I figure *he* has a secret bone for Matt Damon, but I forgot about it, seeing Jeff in his shorts. He put his hands inside them, as if I wasn't there. "Dude," he said, running his hands through his perfect fucking hair, "What am I going to wear?"

He comes back to the car with a bottle of water for me and a can of Canada Dry for himself. This is his idea of a joke. "Don't even," I say, not letting him into the car with the ginger ale. "Just get it the fuck out of here." He takes it to a garbage can, holding it like a grenade or a turd.

"Dude," he says. "You are totally fixated on this Canadian thing. What is up with that?" He looks at me like I'm fucking Winona Ryder, and I feel like a complete asshole, but what am I going to say? How can I explain myself?

"Fuck, man," I say, putting my face in my hands, feeling like Johnny Depp for a minute. "I don't even fucking know," which is about as close to the truth as I care to go.

He has such sweet-colored hair, kind of blond, kind of not. Like how I wanted my own hair to look, but can't, not really anyway. I want to touch his hair, to put my nose into it, to smell him and lick his scalp and his neck and all the rest of him. All the fucking rest of him. He's narrow but thick, a guy with meat on his bones. He knows that Post Office was a game his parents used to play as an excuse to make out. He said to me once, "Dude, you ever hear of Post Office?" I shook my head, and he said, "It's like this excuse to make out. You go to the post office to get your letter, and the post office is like someone's bedroom, and the letter is swacked, man, sealed with a kiss? You never heard of that?"

"Never ever," I said, but I would have like to have. I would have liked to play Post Office with Jeff.

One of the things about Jeff that bothers me is that he has no idea about my cock, none that I know of anyway. Like I said, not everyone says, "At last!"—like my dick is a fire hydrant in the middle of a desert.

But all Jeff can say about it at this point is "What about it?" because he hasn't seen it. Now Bryan, he's still talking about it, catching me online, calling me up every once in a while for some pretty hot phone sex. I can still see his squirming hairy ass, blond fuzzy cheeks, grinding and chewing, eating up my fat cock slowly, taking the whole thing slowly the way a boa swallows up an armadillo. I was thinking then that he was going to take all of me into him that way. I leaned back in the chair I was sitting on, this dilapidated office chair from like the '40s or something, and watched his ass drop lower and lower, and more of me disappeared, ready to be sucked up into his ass like some sort of birth in reverse. He had his shirt off by then, and I was playing with the hairs on his back, which I always thought would gross me out, but found a little more than kind of sexy, like I was thinking, *This is a GUY, man—a fucking GUY!*

"I feel like I'm trying to fit someone's knee up my ass," he said over his shoulder, and I saw beads of sweat on his forehead and across his scalp, clinging to the sparse little hairs there like dew. "You are fucking big, babe," he said.

Later, when I was fucking him, the two of us standing and him holding on to a wall because I was wailing on his ass, he kept calling me "Big Man." "Come on, Big Man," he hollered, "fuck my ass, yeah, fuck it, Big Man."

"Tell me about your wife," I said, my voice all hoarse and shit, and he started telling me about her tits and how often he fucked her and how she gave the best head. I started getting dizzy, and my cock felt dizzy, too, and I grabbed his titties, these huge fucking red nips—fucking *cherries,* dude—and I started slamming him, and he said, "Give it to me, Big Man, give it to me." And I did.

He let me squirt off into him, his big shoulders heaving under me. When I was done, shaking like a weasel, laying all sweaty across his big back, he shook me off and uncorked himself—the noise we made was fucking gross, I'll tell you—and told me to get down on my knees. I opened my mouth, ready for him, and he blasted my face. It wasn't excessive, though—just enough to get me off again, hosing his ankles with a meager but still respectable amount of what I call the reserves.

We're outside of the mall, and Jeff's shift starts in like 20 minutes. He says to me, turning in his seat, bringing one leg up and putting his chin on his knee, "This is so fucking stupid."

I ask what, and he says, "Everything, man, everything."

I'm wondering if he's scared, because he sounds kind of scared. He looks out at the parking lot. Security drives by, making me feel safe. It's some fucked-up looking dude who looks like he's looking for his Siamese twin, and I start thinking about winter because what the fuck does this guy do in the snow without his Siamese twin? Jeff leans back in his seat, throwing his head back. He makes a noise that sounds like *ahhh*.

"What's up?" I say, because he's scaring me and I don't feel safe anymore.

"I can't say," he says, looking at me with these eyes that like rip out my heart, they look so sad and wet. I want to reach out and grab him and hold him and I want to tongue-kiss him until we both die and the moment is so intense that I just sit there like a fucking mushroom.

"Who killed Kenny this time?" I ask.

"Not funny," he answers.

I decide to be bold for a change. I put my hand on the back of the seat in the general vicinity of his shoulder, close enough to be *around* him, and I ask him, all sincere and shit, "Dude, are you all right?"

He plays with the scuffed hem of his stovepipe jeans and whispers something I can't hear.

"What was that?" I ask.

"Never mind," he says quietly again, but this time I hear him. He licks the knee of his pants. I feel my thighs through my warm-ups, loving the feel of the nylon. My dick rests against my belly, hot and fucking engorged, which is a pretty decent description as far as I am concerned.

"Will you pick me up after work?" he asks me.

I say, "Sure, no problem." He gets out of my car, not really closing the door. He looks like a kid going to the principal's office. He disappears behind a Jeep Wagoneer and is gone.

I'll tell you about this Canadian thing. When I was a kid, I had this dream that the U.S. was going to be invaded by Canada, and it was so fucking real that I woke up screaming. And every winter afterwards, when the lake froze up, I'd think about that dream and how easy it would be for them to just walk across the ice and take over the whole fucking country. Then there'd be all these Canucks telling us what to do and making us pay more for cigarettes, changing the way we talked and shit. It's stupid, but it has stayed with me. And then one day my dad had this job selling fruit juices, and he crossed the border and I never saw him again, and now he's like some Canadian or something. It's like they grabbed him and washed his brain so that he forgot about us, me and my mom. Once I was drinking a beer and found out it was a Labatt's and I spit it out. That's how much I hate the Canadians.

Stupid, huh?

I wait for Jeff at 9:30. He comes out the doors with all the other mall workers, looking fried. "I ate dinner at Chick-fil-A," he says by way of an explanation.

I head for home, and we almost get there, but he stops me. "I've got to piss," he says.

"We're almost there," I tell him, looking at him, wondering if really wants me to stop.

"Dude," he says. "Don't make me wet myself."

I pull over—what else can I do?—and he steps off to the side of the road and starts pissing. I find a song we like on the radio and turn it up, mostly to drown out the sound of him pissing, which has given me another bone, making me feel simple and a little like Pavlov's dog, something I learned about my one semester at Buff. U. He turns around when he's finished and puts himself away, and I see everything—his fucking cock, a drip of pee, his darker-than-his-head pubes, the slow zip of his stoves, and a trail of sparks from his fly.

When he gets back into the car, he moves in close to me, closer than he needs to, and I'm wondering what's up with that when he tells me he has to talk.

"Go ahead, dude," I say, fingering the keys in the ignition, not intending to go anywhere until he says so.

"Maybe we could go to your place," he says, because he's living at home again and feels kind of wussed-out as a result.

"Sure," I say. "Whatever."

At my place, he flops down on the couch and I run around throwing shit out of sight, trying not to look like half the pig I really am. Like anything that's food and moldy goes right in the trash, and the dirty clothes go into the coat closet, and the porn magazines—not many!—are all bundled up like old newspapers and thrown behind the bedroom door. I put Rufus Wainwright on the CD player, followed by the new Luscious Jackson, and try to chill, but can't. Jeff's looking at the toes of his Skechers and making me nervous, looking all *Party of Five*'d–out.

"What's up," I say, wanting to put my arm around him again, as if I'd actually done it before. "Do you want to lie down?"

"What?" he says, looking at me as though I'd asked to eat his liver. And he's lying down already.

"I don't know," I say. I don't. It's Jeff, here in my living room and in some kind of emotional turmoil. I feed on it and turn it into my own. Jeff with the perfect hair, the cute body, the best ass.

"This music," he says, making a face.

"You don't like it?"

"I want to die," he says.

"I can change it," I say back. "But I don't have any Foreigner, dude."

"This guy is totally Canadian, you know."

I go pale, feeling it. I could faint.

"No way," I say. "Don't fuck with me."

"I swear to God," Jeff says. "I have a friend at Discs 4 U. He fucking told me."

"Not true, not true."

"And one of the girls in Hole."

"Shut up," I say. "I can't hear you anymore." I put my hands over my ears.

He wiggles his fingers, some dumb kind of sign language I don't get, and he says something I don't hear, so I say, "What?"

And he says, "I said I fucking love you."

"Shut the fuck up," I say.

"Whatever," he says, getting up.

"Where are you going?" I ask.

"Home, dude, I'm walking home."

"Why?"

He turns around. "I guess because you haven't asked me to stay."

It's weird because it's Jeff, but he lets me undress him, and I get a hard-on that like oozes my pants. He doesn't want any lights on, but I get him to let me at least light a candle I have from the Bath and Body Works, a gift from an ex-girlfriend. His skin is beautiful, his shoulders so pretty. I kiss them feeling kind of stupid, but what the fuck, and I see myself as a total Chester, all close and touchy and gross, the kind of friend you don't want to find yourself alone with.

"We could take a bath," Jeff says.

"Yeah," I say. "Sure."

He still has his boxers on, but I can see he has a boner, too. He walks to the bathroom, and I follow him, flicking on the switch.

"No lights," he says, so I run back for the candle that smells like my fucking grandmother and reminds me of a girl I never want to see again.

I just want to jump ahead here because I have to say what I like best about the whole thing. Even though he like completely changes his mind the next day. That minor detail aside, the thing

I like best is the way, when it's over and we're dripping onto sheets that smell a little too much of me (if you know what I mean), Jeff puts his arms around me. He puts his arms around me and holds my head to his chest where I listen to the bass-beat of his heart. I listen to that deep thump, and the fill and empty of his lungs, and the little squeaks and gurgles your stomach makes after you eat something at Chick-fil-A.

Anyway, I fill the bath, squirting in some shampoo for bubbles, and Jeff gets himself out of his boxers and I see his hard-on for the first time. It's white and beautiful, banana-curved, a righteous sword. His balls dangle low, dark-skinned, almost red in the light of the candle. He steps into the sudsy water and laughs.

"It's fucking hot, dude," he says. "You trying to cook us?"

I still have my clothes on, although I'm desperate to be naked. He squats slowly into the foam until he can tolerate the heat. I just stand there watching him. He's like something out of a fucking movie, naked like that and beautiful the way he's always been beautiful, and I feel like such a fag and I don't even care, first of all because he said I love you first.

I take off my shirt, Jeff staring at me. I feel like a stripper but am completely self-conscious. I run my hand over my pecs because I can't help it, wanting to feel how full they are and to touch my nipples which always gives me a little rush anyway.

"You're big and shit," Jeff says.

And I say, "Yeah."

"It's cool, though," he says, playing with the candle.

I play with the waistband of my warm-ups—that's all I have left on. Jeff is completely engrossed with trying to burn himself and dripping hot wax into the water. I reach into my pants and tug my woody, letting him know that I am totally hung and wicked hard, but he's too busy making the bath bubbles disappear.

"Dude," I say, turning sideways casually, wanting him to get the full effect before I set the beast free, changing things forever between us. "Are you into this or what?" I guess I sound kind of annoyed, because he drops the candle into the bath.

"Shit!" he says. "Fucking clocked my nuts, man."

I play with the cords that tighten my pants, thinking this is fucked up, feeling as though my dick is going to burn through the nylon that covers it. I see him glance at it once, twice—the third time, he starts staring, and his mouth opens but he doesn't say anything. It's time—I have his attention. I take off my pants, turning away from him, showing my bare ass first, giving him back. When I turn around again, the breath leaves him.

"Dude," he says airlessly. I step toward him, the big stick wagging at him. I kneel on the tub's edge, the heavy sappy head dipping at his face. He looks around it at me. "Fucking amazing," he says.

"I guess," I say, shrugging. I've seen bigger, actually, and more than once. Up on Skyline Drive, I once saw this guy jacking off in his car, fucking whacking his dick against the steering wheel and making the horn blow. And then there was Donny Hays, this Indian kid I worked with at U R Cool, before he got caught blowing a security guard in the public toilets. He was huge!

What I have going for me is thickness and a huge fucking knob. I grip the base and swing the hose around a little until I start pulling on my pubes, which kind of hurts. Jeff's mouth is close, and it's open, but he isn't doing anything with it. He plays with himself underwater.

"Awesome dick, man," he says, sounding all sincere.

"You want me to come in?" I ask. I bob myself in front of him, feeling buzzed and juicy, ready for anything.

Jeff shrugs his shoulders.

"What do you feel like doing?" I say, and he shrugs again, staring at my prick.

"Lick it," I tell him, dropping my voice, making it sound— I hope—sexy. "Lick my dick, dude," I say.

I'm shocked when I see his tongue, more shocked when I feel it. It's hot like a flame, swirling into the fat piss slit then dragging around the head. He turns his head and has my balls in his mouth and sucks them hard, making me feel queasy and real turned on. He takes his wet hands out of the tub and grabs my hips, holding them hard, and he gets the head of me into his mouth, tongue dancing wild.

What the fuck! I'm thinking. *What the fucking fuck!* Everything's normal one minute—as normal as things get with me— and then this shit happens. It's too much like a dream, too unreal, too good to be true. I start thinking about all those times I was laid up with an aching boner because he let his pants drop low on his ass. Or because he reached up under his shirt to play with the feathery hairs there, or grabbed my tit and pinched the hell out of it just for the hell of it, or pissed right next to me, like I wasn't there at all. And here he is now, struggling with my swollen knob, two-fisting it, giving me the chills and sweats all at once.

He rises up out of the tub, all shiny and wet, suds dripping off him the way I want to, and he lets my dick swing from his mouth. "Ever get fucked?" he wants to know.

"Only once," I say, a painful confession and a lie, too. I've gotten rammed a few times, up on Skyline on those afternoons I had off, guys with pickups and dirty fingernails and little bent dicks wanting to pop my cherry—as if.

"Let me see it," he says, and I turn around and bend over for him. I put my hands on my cheeks and spread them for him, giving him an excellent view of my pink hole, knowing this because of the breeze he blew over it.

He licks me there—now that's a first, for real—and wiggles his tongue into the wrinkled opening, which he then fills with his finger. He grabs my balls through my legs and starts sucking on them at the same time, and I'm ready to die because what else is there, man, what else?

When he slaps the head of his own pointy pecker against my pucker, I open up big time, leaning back against him and trying to get him inside me fast. I want all of him in me, as much as I can get, and he puts his hands on my shoulders and slides in slow, until I can feel his hips against my ass and his dick-end somewhere in my guts. "How is it?" I want to know.

"You tell me," he says.

"Excellent?"

"Fucking right," he says, shoving it in, his body taking over mine like I never imagined. His hands go all over my chest, squeezing my tits until they hurt and fucking me harder all the while. He roams over my abs until he gets hold of my big cock, taking it with both hands again and pulling on it, thumbing the sticky head, causing some serious leakage.

"You leak as much as I come," he says, laughing, and I bang my ass against him.

"Easy," he whispers. "Easy, easy, easy." But I don't want it easy. I fuck myself on his bone, grooving on the fiery slide it makes up into my asshole, digging his wild balls bucking against my own wet skin-bag sticking between my legs. I reach behind me and take one of his pale nips into an easy pinch, tugging on it and making him moan. "Oh, fuck," he says, warning me, and I steady myself, ready for whatever he's about to give up.

"Dude," he says. "I'm going to—"

"Whatever, man, whatever."

"It's cool?" he asks, missing a beat, and I help him pick it up, sliding my butt down his shiny pole. "Fuck," he breathes and starts ripping me apart, shredding my ass with power thrusts, gripping my dick like it was what's keeping him alive, and I feel myself gel, my ass cheeks puffing as cock cream flies out from his fist.

Like I said, he holds me later on in my bed, doing it all over again—this time by hand, which is cool, too—and I have my head against his chest and it's like fucking beautiful, just fucking beautiful.

And like I said, he changes his fucking mind the next day, waking up straight again and totally not into guys. We stay friends for a while, but it's fucking strange, you know, having had his dick up my ass. It's kind of hard looking at him and not dropping a wasted load into my shorts.

One day I go to the lake and look across it. You can't see Canada, and that kind of makes me feel better. I know I'm going to find someone I like as much as Jeff; it's just going to take some time. In the meantime, the new guy at U R Cool is giving me some dirty vibes and staring at my crotch, like every time we close, so who knows?

CHUBBY

Kyle says it isn't right, and he's right: It isn't right. It's wrong. "Jesus knows it, and I know it," Kyle says.

He's always bringing Jesus into everything. Tonight, though, he's whispering Skip's name from across the cabin they share.

He says, "Skip? Skip?"

Skip pretends to be asleep—they're supposed to be asleep—and he pretends he can't hear him. He pretends to toss and turn and even moans a little and smacks his lips together before he settles again, on his side this time, getting his dick in his hand because it's worked its way out of the fly of his boxers. He holds and squeezes it, thinking of Kyle and then of Blake, squeezing himself again, a tight clench, the kind you'd use on a cow's teat. He thinks of Blake grinning, his shirt nowhere to be found, and he's squeezing himself, too, and he hears Kyle say his name again—maybe he knows what Skip is doing, and maybe Jesus isn't looking now and he'd like some himself.

"Skip," he whispers sharply, one last time, and Skip almost expects to hear the papery shuffle of his bare feet across the cabin floorboards, and it makes him harder, rougher, handling himself with short sharp tugs, hand hardly moving, but moving just enough. "I like it," he wants to hear Blake say. "I like it just like that."

He holds his breath and lets go, and there's this rushing up from between his legs, a blind spray and wet sheets. He's still holding his breath, though he wants to pant and sigh. He's made a mess. The sheets cling to his relaxed fist, and he lets himself breathe again when he feels the pulse in his throat, and he tries to breathe normally, deeply, because after all, he's supposed to be asleep, and Kyle is quiet now, quiet and listening, probably.

In the morning, he's up first and down to the showers. Blake is there, and so is Shawn, another camp counselor like Skip. Blake is their boss, the counselor supervisor. Skip looks over at Shawn, who is wearing sandals—*Pussy,* Skip thinks—for fear of athlete's foot. It's a small room with six showerheads and no dividers, the kind of showers that freaked Skip out in high school. Shawn shampoos his hair. *Maybe he'll be done soon,* Skip is thinking, hoping. Blake is just standing, turned toward the water, letting it run off of him. He holds on to the shower nozzle with one hand, while the other wanders his belly and chest lazily. When he turns, Skip thinks he has been caught staring, but Blake's eyes are closed, so Skip studies the straight lines of hair on his boss's chest and thighs, the way he lifts his toes off the tiled floor. He has soccer legs and a funny tan line and longish blond hair that looks darker now, its curl straightened, sodden. He wears a cross on a chain as well as a hemp necklace.

When Shawn walks through, his wet sandals slapping at the soles of his feet, Blake yawns, looking at Skip for the first time, and Skip is thinking that he probably shouldn't have taken this space directly in front of him. Blake spits pointedly, though his point is lost on Skip. Together they listen to Shawn's blow dryer— blow dryer!—and the fall of water on skin and tile, the raining splash of it.

"Do you like it here?" Blake asks out of the blue. Skip wants to say *Huh?* Even though he's heard and understands Blake perfectly. He blinks at Shawn and his mouth opens.

"Yes," he answers, eyes downward, his voice echoing dully. The grout between the tiles is stained a strange green. Maybe Shawn isn't so dumb after all. "It's cool here," he adds, aiming for casual disregard. He comes off lamely, he feels, reaching finally for his soap, ready to get this washing-up business out of the way, ready to get away from Blake's naked body and supervisory air.

He ignores, or tries to ignore, Blake's penis. It is hugely pen-
dulous and horse-big. It hangs dumbly like a too-thick, misplaced
tail, barely moving, hanging almost to mid thigh. It says simply,
"Ignore me," knowing full well it's impossible to ignore.

"That's great," Blake says, nodding absently, turning to the
water again, washing himself with his hands.

He goes back to his cabin, sneaking in quietly. Kyle is sleeping still, his legs hanging out of the blankets, his shoulders uncovered, too. He has a swimmer's back, lats and deltoids bordering
on overdevelopment. They are what Skip likes best about him.

He kneels at the foot of Kyle's bed and leans close to smell his
sleeping skin, the warmth of him, his fuzzy black-haired calves.
He puts his tongue on the heel of one of Kyle's feet, tasting salt.
He licks upward, along the slender tendon to the thick calf to the
pale and hairless cup behind Kyle's knee. The blanket slides easily, and Skip bares the muscled back of Kyle's thigh, hairier still,
up to the starkly white half-moons of his ass cheeks. It's there he
wants to be, in the dark split—Kyle's shame, his dirty ditch.

Skip watches his friend flex his butt as he grinds his dick
against the mattress. Kyle's no longer asleep, Skip figures. He
reaches for that brushy hole, pushing his thumb against it, into
its wrinkled opening. Kyle wriggles ass-ward, reminding Skip of
a boxer pup his family had. Kyle's legs are spread, but otherwise
he stays still as Skip opens the pale split and faces the hole, getting his tongue into it. Quietly, he eats Kyle out, working in and
out of the pulsing squint. He kneads the boy's butt—the two of
them are cheek to cheek, as it were—and he tickles his thighs
and works a hand underneath them, wanting to get at his cock.
Kyle's balls peek out from between his thighs, and Skip brings
out his long, stiff shaft, its head leaking, smearing the sheets
with its snot. From the hole to the pole, Skip chins the mattress
in an endeavor to suck Kyle's boner. The prone boy protests with
a moan. "You're going to break it," he says into the mattress.

"So roll over, then."

The boy twists and Skip gets out of his way. Kyle scissors his legs and tangles himself in his sheets and peers at Skip sleepily.

"Good morning," he says, uncovering himself, revealing his erection. *Breakfast,* Skip is thinking, going down on the boy, gripping his balls and cock in the same motion. Kyle moans. His legs bend and hug Skip's head. Skip slurps down to the black-trimmed bush, his fingers spreading into it. He uses his teeth with no little finesse as his chin drops onto the suede nut sac and Kyle flutters beneath him. His balls tighten, and he arches his back under Skip's determined tongue, which he stills long enough to enunciate his wish to fuck Kyle's ass.

"Oh, Jesus, no," Kyle whispers.

"Figures," Skip says as he is called back to Kyle's urgent prong, which bubbles a greasy seep that makes Skip's mouth water. With the help of Kyle's heavy hands, he swallows the prick entirely, gagging on the blunt end of it. Kyle holds him there, throat-fucking him, calling out to Jesus again and pumping a load into Skip that is too deep to spit out, and it slides down his gullet like thickened salt water.

Skip gets to his knees quickly and pulls down his shorts, hauling out his hefty cock, already mattress-buzzed and trigger-happy. Kyle wipes himself off with a handful of his bedclothes, looking out the window, ignoring Skip's need.

"Jesus, I'm starving," he says, getting out of bed and walking over to the pile of clothes he keeps in a corner of the cabin, his dick flopping stiffly still, refusing to deflate.

"What about me?" Skip complains. He plays with himself, chucking a cocked finger against the sensitive underside of his prick. He watches Kyle shrug, stepping into soccer shorts.

"I'm gonna miss breakfast," is all he says, leaving Skip high and dry.

After lunch, Blake taps Skip in the crafts tent, leaning close to whisper, "I need to see you in my cabin before dinner." It is a supervisor's whisper, not conspiratorial, closer to menacing. And all through crafts, Skip's thinking, *Shit, shit, shit, shit.* He's heard that there are a lot of no-show campers this time around—and too many counselors—and it's only too likely that he was tapped for dismissal, chosen for his bad attitude and slack management skills. His team is the worst. As a group they've gained 35 pounds since coming to Camp Fataway. His mini-interview in the shower this morning, he's thinking—if only he hadn't been so fucking blasé. *On the other hand, maybe Blake liked what he saw,* Skip wonders, then shakes his head. *Whatever!* Or maybe the meeting with Blake would go like this: "The kids hate you, Skip—I'm sorry, but you'll have to go." And he needs this job, or else he'll have to go back home to Watertown with his mother and her NASCAR racer boyfriend. He cringes at the thought of trying to find work at the Admiral Halsey Mall, which is dying its own slow death. He'd only be another nail in its coffin.

One of them throws clay, one of his team. Horseplay hurts. He tells them to pack it up because they're done. They're toast, he tells them, even though there's a good 40 minutes left. He decides to have them sit with their hands folded for the duration. It's a little extreme and very boring, but they have to learn who's boss, who's calling the shots, who's running this show. *The boss,* he's thinking, *is me.* Blake would agree. Blake would back me up, Blake would have them under house arrest, denying them their wienie roast privileges and feeding them rice cakes and water.

Skip leaves them to their collective misery. *So they hate me. What-the-fuck-ever.* He sits on the steps and listens to what they think he can't hear—or maybe they don't care either. *Fuck them,* he's thinking. *They're fat and unloved, embarrassments to their families. Fuck them all. I'm fucked anyway.*

Blake has his own cabin because of his position. Skip knocks on the dark green–painted screen door, hearing the new R.E.M.

CD playing. "Just a minute," Blake calls, and Skip tries to make him out through the screen, but the cabin is dark and the screen as thick as a blanket. But then he appears, walking toward the door and pulling on a blue broadcloth shirt—Brooks Brothers, probably—and his green and blue ribbon belt is undone.

"Oh, good," he says, looking at Skip and smiling. He pushes open the screen door with his bare foot as he does up his belt. The cabin is small and dark, blinds drawn, the evening sun not up anyway to the task of penetrating the thick pine canopy. There's this smell, a strange combination of patchouli and something else—Hugo Boss, maybe. It is intoxicating, and so is Blake in his unbuttoned shirt, his wet hair combed darkly to his head. Has he had another shower? Skip's fear of displacement shrinks. He stares at a shadowed nipple as Blake sits on his bed to put on his Birkenstock sandals.

"Sit down," Blake says, "Please." There's a chair at a desk on top of which the boom box is playing. Skip turns the chair away from the desk and sits. Blake has golden hairs on his stomach.

"I've been thinking," he starts, standing now and pacing in front of Skip, his shirttails floating in his wake. *He's too close,* Skip is thinking; too close, but distant nonetheless. *There could be miles between us. I would not know what to do with my hands— how I could touch him.* He thinks of Kyle and his cool, rubbery hands, tentative and stuttering. Blake has elegant fingers. Skip's own are rough and stubby: pickax-swinging, fence-mending hands. Hands like his father's.

"I was wondering if you're happy here, Skip," Blake says, stopping in front of him, his shirt settling, riding the outer reaches of his shoulders, his collarbone bared. Some of his drying hair has lightened and lifted from the comb-trained rest.

"I'm happy here," Skip answers.

Blake sucks his lips into his mouth thoughtfully. "It's just that we all need to project a certain…" he pauses for the right word to come. "Attitude," he says after a half a second.

"A happy attitude?" Skip suggests.

chubby

"That's it exactly!" Blake says, his hands fisting. "For the campers' sakes, yes. I mean, we're thin and we're happy, right?"

Skip nods.

"And they're…" Blake pauses again.

Fat? Skip thinks. *They're lard-asses?* "Tubulent" was the current "fat" euphemism passed around by the counselors.

"Hefty," Blake concludes.

"And miserable?" Skip offers helpfully.

Blake nods hard. "Exactly," he almost shouts, his hands in fists again, stiff-armed at his sides. His nipples are barely covered now. "So you see, we're role models here. We need to lead by example. Thin people are happy people. You understand what I'm saying here?"

Skip does and he doesn't.

"I love these kids," he says anyway. "I want to help them." And Blake walks up to him and puts his hand on Skip's shoulder.

"I know you do, Skip, I know you do." His hand stays on Skip's shoulder, and there was his half-clad torso. It seems like an invitation. But still, Skip feels tense, wary. Was this an OK? Permission from ground control? Would running his hand over the muscled terrain of Blake's stomach be acceptable? Skip was paralyzed.

"This morning," Blake says, "I felt as though…" He stops. His hand slides off Skip's shoulder. It's darker now, the sun all but set. He switches on the small lamp on his desk, casting a gold light on himself. His dried hair has lifted off his head, twisting and turning—he has no control over it. He tries to keep it behind his ears like a girl, like Skip's sister.

"Hmm," Blake says, seeming to scrutinize Skip's face.

And because he is not sure what Blake is getting at, because he offers no plain direction—not like Kyle, who was very straightforward about what he wanted—because of all this, Skip stays dumb.

Blake lifts his chin. He walks to the screen door. "You monitor the wienie roast tonight, don't you?"

"I do," Skip says, pushing the cheerful envelope. Everything he says from now on will be punctuated by an exclamation point, brimming with cheer.

"Good then," Blake says. "Let's go."

There is a small uprising when the campers discover their long-awaited wienies are actually tofu dogs. The insurrection is held in check thanks to the ingenuity of counselor Clark, who runs to the lock-up cabin where contraband is held until the end of the season. Chips and candy bars and, yes, even cans of warm beer are tossed frantically to the angry rotund mob. "Quick!" another quick-thinking counselor shouted,

"Put on some Britney Spears!" What else could a 12-year-old ask for?

The riot quelled, Skip watches Blake walk over to his side of the fire. Wordlessly, he forces Skip back into the shadows, and shoulder to shoulder they walk down one of the many paths to the lake. Ranks of crickets go silent as they pass, only to start up again. Blake's arm brushes Skip's arm again and again.

There's a moon and some chalk-sketched clouds. Blake's hand slips around Skip's waist, up under his shirt, and they turn toward one another, lips finding lips, firmly pressed, opening as tongues meet. Skip wonders how long he can go without breathing. He unbuttons Blake's shirt, wanting him like he wanted him earlier in the evening. He touches his warm belly—it is hard and six-packed, only lightly fuzzy. Skip pushes the shirt off Blake's shoulders and steps back, the moon bright as streetlight. Blake has an odd smile on his face.

"What?" Skip asks.

"I used to be fat," Blake says.

"No way," Skip says. He presses his thumbs against the muscled ridges of Blake's abdomen.

Blake steps back. "No really," he says. "I used to be a camper here."

"You look awesome," Skip says, not needing to lie.

"Oh, my legs are huge," Blake says, "and I've got these things here." He twists and pinches what may or may not be a very small deposit of fat. "Love handles," he informs Skip.

"Here's your love handle," Skip says, groping the front if Blake's chinos, finding him thick and doughy there. "Now that's a chubby."

It takes a bit of work, but Skip manages to undo the strange ribbon belt and the many-buttoned trousers. Blake is wearing jersey briefs that bear the impress of his long, thick member. It is excessive, really, Skip decides—too much dick for one guy. It doesn't seem fair. Skip cannot help but compare, having approximately half of what this guy swings with, although Blake does not seem to mind as he digs into Skip's shorts with the kind of relish pigs have for truffles.

He encloses Skip's cock in his fist—*Oh, this is going to be no trouble at all,* Skip is thinking—and smears their mouths together. "Skip," he says, only it's not exactly clear and sounds more like Miff. He takes Skip's head with both hands, which become heavy and insistent, and Skip finds himself directed to the locus of their mutual desire—the stiff upward poke of Blake's massive cock.

Skip struggles with its girth at first—it is way more than a mouthful. He takes what he can and leaves the rest for his hand. Blake has an odd sweetness, a creamy sort of ooze. He hits the back of Skip's throat with ease and the smallest of hip thrusts. Skip can hear Blake breathing through his mouth, a loud panting Skip finds erotic and most encouraging. He hadn't ever imagined this scene, not like this, on his knees in the wet sand after a wienie roast for 40 overweight preteens. Either he'd lacked the imagination or the confidence. Blake fucks his mouth as though he were born to do nothing else.

Blake has a big bag of balls, rivaling something hanging from rearview mirrors, and just as fun to tug and twist. His fingers knead the back of Skip's head, digging into his scalp. He fills his mouth with his dick and leaves it there, making Skip swallow, making his eyes tear up, and Skip feels the slide of Blake's dick past his tonsils, and he doesn't taste him until he pulls out, head oozing over Skip's tongue.

"You're good," he says, and Skip nods, looking up at him. He's not thinking about him, though, or about what he's doing. He's thinking instead about Kyle and his blue eyes and what's right and what's wrong. Blake sticks a finger in his ear, his dick going deep in his throat. Kyle, when he's sleeping, has leg twitches and it's as if he's running, having running dreams, and he always reminds Skip of the dog he used to have. The dog would let out these tiny barks while he slept. Skip's dad would say, "Scout's having one of his rabbit dreams again."

Blake says, "I'm coming," warning Skip, and he's ready to replace Skip's mouth with his own hand. But Skip stays on him and tightens his lips and puts his arms around Blake's thighs, and he drinks him down, all that he has, and they stay that way until Blake twitches and moans, and Skip swallows and swallows until there's nothing left but his own thick spit. It isn't until the taste of him has left his mouth that he touches himself, and all it takes, all it ever takes, is a few short tugs, and Skip closes his eyes and empties himself onto the sand, as Blake stands over him, playing with Skip's nipples through his shirt.

They'll have Tang for breakfast and dry toast and plain old oatmeal without anything to make it taste better than wallpaper paste. And maybe Skip will sit at Blake's table, and maybe he won't; maybe he'll sit with Kyle like always because, after all, it's his voice Skip hears again, like always—Kyle's voice saying his name, coming up behind him, soft sand muffling his steps.

Killian or Welch

I didn't mind listening to what they did together. I used to sit up waiting for them, listening for their footfalls in the hall, the two of them loudly drunk again, voices booming, and I could imagine them shouldering between the narrow liver-colored walls, lumbering against one another, muttering fuck this and fuck that.

I liked the one with the light-colored hair, the one with the Gulf War Vet license plate, the one with the scar under his left eye, the bigger one. His name was Killian or Welch: he was one or the other, according to the names under the buzzer to their apartment in the tight foyer downstairs.

They were always drunk. I wondered how they got anything done—their jobs, their workouts, all of the other things they did. It seemed to me that they spent every night and every spare dollar they had at the bar around the corner, the one called the Monk's Robe. I'd seen them there, slump-shouldered at the bar, watching the Flyers on the TV in the corner, waiting for the next fight on the ice to set straight their shoulders, stretching their arms up over their heads in unison, like indifferent twins unable to help themselves.

I made my own noise from time to time, giving Welch and Killian something to listen to if they were so inclined. I played party to some infrequent guests who, if not as athletic as the two next door, certainly were as loud and uninhibited. Kevin, for instance, would come close to something like hyperventilation upon ejaculation, crying and gasping as if he were drowning. "My little death," Kevin would remind me, quoting something he'd undoubtedly picked up from Colette or Anais Nin or his wife. And Barry, who loved to recite every expletive he'd ever come across at the top of his voice, which was very deep and booming, operatic, really, and actually quite sexy. Often enough he was able to make me spout off a couple of "Goddamn motherfucking bitches" myself.

I'd see my favorite, Welch or Killian, carrying cases of empties out to the trash, ignoring the recycling bins and tossing them clattering into the Dumpster. It's amazing what you can forgive a boy with double-wide shoulders and shaved forearms.

I imagined they thought they had a secret, something no one would ever guess. I imagined they never realized how thin the walls were, never realized—and this was most likely, given their sexy dopiness—that despite being privy to many of my own, shall we say, escapades, anyone could possibly hear *them*. Dumb as doorknobs, these boys, and every bit as useful, I should think.

Kevin put himself in my doorway. He was as big as those boys next door, though a few years older. He looked past me into my apartment and said, "Hey, am I interrupting anything?"—as if he'd surprised me or caught me, as if he hadn't rung the bell to get in, hadn't announced his own arrival. He accepted the beer I offered and sat down on the couch. He picked up a book from the coffee table, a novel I was reading.

"Is this any good?" he asked, making a face, judging a book by its cover.

I shrugged. "Haven't started it yet," I said. "I'm still working on the Bacon biography you bought me," I added, to flatter him. I'd not yet started that one either, drawn instead to the dull TV screen at night or to the antics of my horny neighbors. He dropped the book and gave his attention to the small painting I'd hung on the wall across from the sofa.

"That's new, isn't it?" he asked, and I said it was, and he asked if it was one of my own, and I told him it was, but he didn't get up to look at it more closely. He simply nodded and said that it was nice.

I liked Kevin for his self-interest; it made him more intriguing, I thought. It was fun to watch him struggle for a topic of conversation that was not centered on him.

"I saw Jared at the gym today," he said. "He looks at me as if I don't have clothes on. It's kind of embarrassing—he's so obvious. Is he like that with you?"

"He's like that with his own mother, Kevin," I told him, watching his face register what I'd just said. His eyes glazed snakelike, going hazy blue. He tipped his beer bottle up to his lips and drank and ignored me. The bottle was empty when he placed it on the coffee table. I got up to get him another. He carried it to the bedroom.

I watched him getting undressed. He hurried, his back to me, and got himself under the bedclothes, even though he was beautiful naked. He did not enjoy my scrutiny and had said so more than once. I knew the source of his embarrassment—a sloppy circumcision that pulled his prick to the right and marred the beauty of his cock head. He'd been left with an asymmetrical bob that he seemed never to grow comfortable with, the way some will (or won't) grow accustomed to, say, a missing finger, or a mole under an eye. I was not uncomfortable with it—it was long and lean and shot like a pistol. He came the way most porn stars aspire to and fail—money shots that flew across his partners, across mattresses, onto walls, just missing ceilings.

He was on his stomach in bed, meaning he wanted me to fuck him. I got myself undressed, folding my things as if I was the guest, as if I were in a hotel room and would eventually need to be on my way. He watched me from the corners of his eyes and rested his head on his folded arms, the hair of them darkening his skin more deeply than a tan. He caught my eye and winked at me. At least, I thought he was winking—it could have been a blink for all I knew. I was thinking, in the way I thought about every man and boy who passed under these sheets, that I might possibly be in love with him. What I loved about Kevin, what I loved about all of them, really, was that they were here at all.

I lay on top of him, my dick in the tight crease of his ass cheeks. I had my arms around his enormous shoulders, holding him the way I'd always wanted to hold my father. Once, he'd taken a fall and broken his collarbone and I had to wash his back in the tub. I stroked the breadth of him with a washcloth, staring at the sunburned skin of his shoulders. It was hard to see any man from behind and not think of my father.

Kevin sighed and relaxed his tensed buttocks, allowing me a deeper slide. He turned his head as much as he was able, getting his head off the pillow, attempting to kiss me. He was a famous kisser, famous in these parts, anyway. I'd not met anyone so into kissing, save for my grandmother Lil and her papery lips covered with fuchsia. It was almost unnerving to be smooched so enthusiastically. Sometimes I thought he might rather kiss than fuck.

I knelt between his knees, spreading his great ass cheeks with my prying hands, laying bare the dark pout of his butthole, the region around it recently cleared and just beginning to stubble. I put my face into that charming ditch and ran my tongue over the brown plug drawn priggishly taut. He squirmed, rubbing my cheeks with his own. "That's nice," he said, lifting himself to me, his pinch becoming less tight. He was coming around finally, going slack and pliable. He sighed into the pillow, as my hands roamed the vast and muscled terrain of his backside. I was feeling scholarly and adroit and eager to please. I was feeling scrappy and cocky, my hair just cut, another workout under my belt, still buzzing from a protein shake and 50-pound dumbbell curls. I was a wrestler today, and I had Kevin in my favorite hold.

He liked it the way I liked it, with our feet on the floor. He wasn't much taller than I am, but I still felt dwarfed and ridiculous behind him, all but jumping to get my hot-wired prick up his bum. Regardless, it was my favorite position, even though we were poorly matched for it. He did his best, dropping into a deep squat—much like the guy I'd seen at the gym today, his big bubbled butt straining the worn seams of his sweats, making them translucent and showing the white glow of his briefs underneath and the huge package of scrotum they contained.

I thumbed my cock in the general direction of Kevin's stink hole. He grunted with anticipation, looking ready for scrimmage. He was going to get scrimmage indeed.

The first thrust caused him to take a steadying step forward. "Christ almighty, Forster," he griped, sneering over his shoulder, wanting me to think he didn't like it. I pulled back slowly, drawing my dick through him like a knife through butter, sucking the foul wind out of him, and giving him something else to complain about. I left his hole opened like a screen door. He farted to let me know how he really felt, but I ignored him and used my dick like a nightstick against the complaining pucker, slapping the luscious ridged cunt. He growled then, and his anus twitched, and I went into him again, more courteously this time, stroking his spine and the little patch of dark hair that grew spade-shaped up over his ass.

I said to him, "Hey, baby, how's it feel?" as I pushed into him, getting my hips to slap his muscled cheeks and liking the noises we made together. He held on to the foot of the bed, gritting his teeth, his hair falling over his forehead and into his eyes.

"You little fucker," he said over his shoulder. "You're going to get it one of these days." I was slamming into him by then, forcing every other word he was saying to rush out of his mouth in little grunts. I was looking forward to that day.

I held on to his hips, and Kevin reached down between his legs and mine to play with my balls and push his finger up into my own hole. Not far from us, a mattress-length away, the thin wall of my bedroom rattled with the fucking I was giving him, driving him against the foot of the bed again and again.

"It's good like that," he said over his shoulder, leaving me alone to worry his own cock with one hand, since he needed the other hand to continue to stay on his feet, to steady himself from my butt-slapping thrusts. With each thrust the bed banged the wall, and I wondered about my neighbors, Welch and Killian. I wondered whether they were home yet from whatever they did on Saturday afternoons, whether they could even identify the wall-banging with what Kevin and I were doing in here. Would they look at one another with "Hmm" raising their eyebrows and a couple of quick rising biscuits in their shorts. *Imagine inciting them that way,* I was thinking. Imagine getting them all riled up and off the couch to do some wall-banging of their own.

I started slapping Kevin's ass, wanting to elicit some of his sweet little moans and barks. He growled back at me, sweat making him squint.

"You moth-er-fuck-er," he said, the syllables gusting out of him with each syncopated thrust. He straightened his torso, pressing back against me, twisting to get his mouth on mine, his tongue going up my nose. He ate my chin and much of my face, and I ate back and slid in and out of him, his hole greased and easy now. He butted my hips and grabbed one of my hands, getting it on his hot pole, begging me to bring him off. I held him firmly and chucked the thick shaft just under the head, giving him the willies, and feeling my own resolve building as his hole sucked me off.

I felt my own first blast go nowhere in that black cavern and witnessed Kevin's single-barreled shot arc over the bedclothes. A dollop of it landed in a white curl on the wall between the brass posts of the headboard, though the rest of it was not so high-flying. Kevin had made a prodigious mess nonetheless, and I pushed him into it so that it stuck to his face and chest, and then I licked it off him and reveled in the musky stink of it, the gluey, savory goo that was distinctly Kevin. And then there was none.

We lay together a while—he had a wife at home; a kittenish burden, I imagined—and listened to the boys next door.

"What are they doing?" Kevin asked coyly, his lips unable to keep from grinning.

"Jesus," I said. They were raising quite a ruckus. "When one of them says 'Take it out, it hurts,' I think they're fucking."

"They don't fuck," Kevin said resolutely. "Guys like that don't fuck. At least not each other," he added.

Whatever it was—horseplay, wrestling, roughhousing—it made my dick hard. I swatted the stinking thing, trying to attract Kevin's attention, but he was already up and dressing, already on the road, heading home for some roast beef and mashed potatoes and canned peas. (I liked to imagine the old lady as pretty but a terrible cook.) I watched him leave, tossing me a wave over his head, saying, "I'll call you."

"You do that," I said when the door slammed shut.

The boys continued, and it was hard not to imagine them, the way their muscles strained for leverage, for greater purchase, for the upper hand. It was hard not to imagine that upper hand and the stroking it did of haired-up shin, of sweat-slicked backside, stubbled cranium, pulling full-lipped face closer to kiss. Killian and Welch scrambled together, attached at the hips, yet shying away from crotches, each possessing length and girth that had often caused teammates envy, and neither was willing to bank on his fortune—not yet, anyway. Horseplay, indeed.

One of them yelled out, a great bellow of giving in, of losing, and in my mind he took it like a man, enduring the huge plunge that my Killian (or Welch) was giving him. It was easy to play along, to get myself in a hard grip, to join in, so to speak, and take part in the grapple. In my mind I was with them, standing ringside, watching them floor-crawl, all white-assed and brown-shouldered, scabbed-kneed and cursing.

"Fuck you, Welch! Fuck you, man," I heard clearly, and it was over. Killian had succumbed, he'd come, and Welch—so *that's* his name—had won after all. Afterward there was the sound of pissing and some softer mutterings and then their door slamming shut and their walking down the hall, past my door, talking about darts and somebody named Fried Egg.

It's Friday night and I'm at the Monk's Robe. Killian and Welch are at the bar elbow to elbow. Flyers losing to Pittsburgh. They moan, rapt, lift pint glasses to lips absently. Lindross receives his 25th concussion. The boys look up at the ice-thrown Lindross the way I look at them—wistfully.

"Poor fucking bastard," one of them says, I can't tell which. One of them, the one I call Welch now, wears a gray T-shirt with navy trim at the neck and sleeves, number 28 on the back, and somebody's name. His ass is in jean shorts that gape at the small of his back and reveal a wealth of bare skin and hair and the white tops of his ass cheeks—he is clearly without underwear. He pushes his ass back toward me and hitches up the right sleeve of his shirt, bringing the arm up to scratch his neck, flexing his biceps, sniffing secretly under his arm. He turns slowly and looks at me. I can see clearly that small sickle-shaped scar under his left eye. He looks at me like, I think, I hope, I imagine, *Can you fucking believe this?*

I shrug my shoulders to say, *I wish I fucking could.*

PATRIA

She says, "It's your dad." She's got the phone at the end of her hand, held out like a vowel I just scored from Vanna White. I don't want to talk to him, but she's already tipped him off that I'm here, so I take the phone from her with a look that is clearly displeased. She tromps back into the kitchen where she was making brownies, singing to me, telling me to go fuck myself.

"Hey, Dad," I say.

"Look," he starts, and it's already too much, what will inevitably follow, so I put the phone back in its cradle quietly and end the conversation that way.

"You're a fuck for doing that," I tell her. She is stirring batter, looking innocent. "You know I don't want to talk to him."

She shrugs and brings the spoon to her mouth, unleashing a tongue that drags through the fudge obscenely.

Jeremy is fucking me, massaging my shoulders as he works his thick cock in and out of my asshole. My back is arched and my legs stick straight out behind me. My butt cheeks are so tensed they barely allow him to move. "I fucked a dancer with a butt like yours once. It was like slamming an encyclopedia closed on your hard-on," he says. He puts his face between my shoulder blades, and I spread my legs a little. My cock is jizzing up my navy blue sheets, leaving stains that will go chalky and might not wash out later.

His body is tight and wet, overheated. Sex turns him into an engine, a furnace—he's too hot to lie with afterward. He presses his slick belly against the small of my back, pushing deeply into me, and it is this way we fit best, I always think. He wraps his arms around my shoulders and rolls me over so that I am on top now, so that I can get to myself, my dick, which is thrusting upward and very red and very much wanting to be up inside Jeremy's behind. *Not this time,* I tell myself, but maybe later, when it's dark, after we've eaten and maybe had a few beers, gotten a little languid together on the sofa, and I've gotten him aroused again with my restless hands.

He fills me up. I bend my legs, heels on either side of his knees, and pump my ass up and down on his cock. My cheek rests against his, and he kisses me again and again, his tongue dragging across the beard on my chin, the new little tickler I've cultivated over the weekend. He grips my hips and then his hands slide upward, his fingers finding my nipples, which he bothers to pain because he knows I like it. Each rough twist elicits a moaning thrust and I see across my closed eyelids: *I AM YOURS.* It does not bother me that he's managed to purchase me so cheaply.

"I love being in your ass," he tells me, making me dance on the head of him. He pushes up into me, nailing me, and I am playing the end of my cock with my fingertips. His lips find my ear, tonguing into it, and I am a goner—there's no stopping it now— and I pound my pole, roaring to a finish; wet fireworks scatter over me and land everywhere, ember-warm.

He makes a few last plunges and scrambles out of my slackened hole. On his knees, he aims his load at my mouth because he's come to know that I love this most about him, the almost ridiculous amount of ejaculate he blows, not to mention the force with which it's released. It hits the inside of my mouth, sounding not unlike the stream from a cow's udder or a beer-drinking man's prick. And there's enough of it to drink.

He collapses over me, sweating all over. I can feel his heart, the pounding of it, reminding me again of his age, which is 15 years past mine, although there is very little that points to this fact. He is youthful in dress and action, a regular at his gym, down in the weight room with the boys. And while lines crowd around his eyes, it's only when he smiles. Jeremy could pass for my older brother, but never, never my father, of whom I am reminded every time we fuck. And every time my phone rings.

We both freeze as it bleeps beside us on the table next to the bed. It could be anybody, but we always seem to have the same thought: It's him.

It's not. It's not even for me. Someone leaves a meandering message for my roommate, punctuated with the phrase "You know what I'm saying," using it as a comma and semicolon.

"It's her crack dealer," I tell Jeremy, whose mouth goes slack. He likes Meredith much more than I do. He wraps his arms around me and shimmies beside me. Only a shower will cool him off. Our skins stick together, and he blows into my ear.

"What am I going to do with you?" he asks, as if I am some unwieldy parcel or problem. And maybe I am. We both look at my ceiling, which is blankly unresponsive. Indeed, I am feeling slightly problematic.

Jeremy has told me that I can fuck whomever I want, that while he had no intention of sleeping with anyone else, I was free to do as I pleased. "I mean it," he said. "Party up. Do your thing." His face had a slack earnestness that was unconvincing. Still, I follow this boy out of the mall and up to his Pathfinder. He is maybe in his twenties, a civilian with a military haircut. His jeans fit him well, showing off his ass, and his T-shirt's sleeves reveal tattooed guns.

I say, "What's up?" and watch him rub his crotch through his jeans. *Old school,* I am thinking, and he says that up the street is an old camp road. I am familiar with it—know it pretty well, in fact.

Smiling a little, I say, "Is there?"

He opens his door and looks at me. He has brown eyes, an intense kind of stare. He is probably scared shitless. He has one leg up on his running board. I let my eyes drop to his ass, letting him know what I want.

"Get in," he says.

The camp road is overgrown. Twin ruts lead deeper into the woods. Pine boughs slap at the windows as we bounce by. He doesn't say anything but keeps his eyes on the trail, his hand on the gearshift. He pulls around a deserted cabin and cuts the engine. He moves his seat back. I'm not even going to learn his name.

I touch his fly and he moans, closing his eyes. He is hard beneath. I pull his shirt out of its tuck in his jeans. He has a feathery trail that spreads all over his chest, dark chocolate-colored nipples, white milky skin. I lick him from navel to tit then up over his shirt to his throat and all around his mouth, which opens for me, tongue wagging across his full lips. He sucks on my mouth, groaning into it, pushing his hips at me, undoing his pants and freeing up a slick-headed cock, enough for two men to share. He grips it like an ax handle, squeezing up precome that bubbles out of the fat coin-size piss hole, then pushes my head down to introduce us, and I get the wide chewy head in my mouth and that's about it, which seems to suit him just fine. I suck hard on the end of him, circling my tongue around the underside of the head, and he bucks his hips slightly and plays his fingers through my hair, telling me how fucking sweet I am. I've been here before, again and again.

I play under his balls, digging into the trap of his underwear, searching out his hot insides and encountering only brush and resistance. I can smell it; I just can't find it. I poke around some more, finding a fold of flesh that seems to yield, and there it is. I finger the pursed lips and he cradles my head, forcing his cock deeper into my mouth. Its girth stretches my lips.

I sit up for a moment, startling him. His eyes dart—his head practically spins. I am staking out the back of his SUV: The seats are down and there's room to fuck. I suggest we move to the back, and he agrees, panting. He hops out of the truck, pants down to his ankles, and he opens the tailgate, getting in, and I join him. He takes off his sneakers, not wanting to mark the ceiling. I free up one of his legs from his jeans and get myself up to his hole. He watches me pull my cock from my pants, and his face registers a certain amount of relief when he sees that I am not nearly as hung as he is. He polishes his thick shaft lovingly, spiraling his palm up and down, and I spit on myself for lube and push my prick-end against his little brown anus. It gives, but tightly, and he winces. I've got his ankles, spreading his legs, and I bend over and nip at his tits.

He is lean-muscled and resistant. His thighs protest against me, but he begs for it, and I give it to him the way he wants it. "Easy, easy, easy," he pleads. But then I forget about him and concentrate instead on the grip he has on my cock, and I want more resistance, his cunt dragging my shaft, and I fuck deeper than he wants me to. He lets me anyway because I tell him I love being inside him—I love what his ass is doing to my cock. I lean over him again and smear my lips against his throat, his fist slamming my belly as he jerks off. I fuck him with short thrusts, down to the pubes, letting him wrap his legs around my waist. His free hand takes hold of my neck, and he gets my lips on his, his tongue dashing in and out, and he snorts into my mouth and tells me he's going to come. He starts yelling—fucking bellowing—and I feel my own nut rising, and I try to pull out, but he holds me fast. I feel the first wave rippling up my gut, and I pump my come into him as he dispenses his own sloppy load all over my belly.

At home, Meredith is on the couch watching *The Price Is Right*. "Your sugar daddy called," she says, "And your other daddy called, too."

She stops eating chips and looks up long enough to tell me, "He cried. It totally freaked me out."

I walk slowly to my room, undress, and fall across my bed. I can smell the afternoon on me, the boy's tight asshole, and my stomach is flaked with his dried come. On the nightstand there is a girlie magazine my father sent me last week, all the models' cunts circled with vivid black ink. I can see him in our little brick house on Richmond Avenue, sitting at the kitchen table with a Magic Marker and outlining cunt after cunt, saying with each circle, "Dick goes here, dick goes here." The last time I saw my father, he held his hands in fists. The last time I saw my father, he wouldn't look at me.

Meredith calls my name from the living room. "I'm going to McDonald's. You need anything?"

"Fries," I yell, covering myself instinctively, "and something else."

"Like what?" she asks, appearing at my door like I knew she would.

"You pick," I tell her because I just don't know.

ANARKY

They each give Devitry a dollar. "You guys are gonna love this," he says, unbuttoning his shirt. Nate is still wondering why he and Bumpy had to pay a dollar to see what Devitry was about to show them, but then Devitry doesn't have a job, and he needs money for cigarettes now that his mom is on the patch. He watches Devitry shrug off his flannel shirt, getting down to a skinny wife beater. He can see the boy's nipples through the filmy fabric.

"You taking your pants off, too?" Bumpy asks.

"You'd like that too much," says Devitry, but Nate is the one whose palms go sweaty, his cheeks heating up so that he has to look away, pretending interest in the tank of fish Devitry keeps in a dark corner of his room. But he turns to watch Devitry lift his shirt, baring a patch of medical gauze across his stomach, and Nate feels a snaky twist in his own gut, this turning over inside, signaling something like panic. Devitry arches his back and exposes a strip of pale flesh between his Wranglers and the gauze that is dotted black and red in spots. He pulls up the tank top, and it curls over his nipples like a lip, and he picks gingerly at the bandage across his belly. It sticks to him, to whatever's underneath it, his wound, but he pulls it anyway. In dark Gothic letters he's had ANARKY tattooed over the middle of him.

Nate blinks. "Anarky?" Bumpy laughs. "That's in New Jersey, isn't it? I think my Aunt Lou lives in Anarky."

Devitry looks at Nate. "It's a joke, isn't it?" Nate asks because he doesn't know any better, but then he does—it was no joke.

Devitry looks down at himself. Ink and blood have mixed, and the effect is a beautiful dark purple that will fade to steely blue in a few days, but right now it's welted and awesome and beautiful even if it is misspelled, rising up from his skin like Braille.

Bumpy's got a curfew. "See ya," he says as he shuffles out of the room, sounding like he expects to bump into them tomorrow at school, but Bumpy's always playing hooky. His brother opened a garage in Bristol and that's where Bumpy spends his time when he's not sniffing Pam.

Devitry looks up from his belly. "Later," he says to Bumpy, not quite there, still trying to figure out what was wrong with his tattoo. If he had a dictionary, he'd check it. Nate watches his friend shrug and reach for a crumpled cigarette pack, blowing it open and digging out a bent, twisted butt. Before he lights it, though, he covers his tattoo again with the spotted gauze. The guy at the tattoo parlor had cut a swath through the thick black hair that covers Devitry's stomach. Nate is thinking about the hair growing back and obscuring the letters, the way ivy grows over things, over walls and fences, the way the hair right now covers Devitry's nipples, fat red dots all shadowy under a web of black.

"Does it hurt?" Nate asks, not really wanting to know, but wanting an excuse to stay. He watches Devitry shake his head and roll over onto his side. He blows smoke into the air between them, and Nate drags the toe of his sneaker through the shag carpeting. He's got homework piled like bricks in his backpack, and laundry to do if he's going to have anything clean to wear to school tomorrow. He stands there anyway, looking at the hole in the knee of Devitry's jeans. *It's not going to happen,* he's thinking, seeing Devitry's toes curl in the dirty end of his socks. He feels stupid standing there with his hands under his armpits, surveying Devitry like a new car. But there's something about having Devitry alone and distracted that makes Nate feel both invisible and entitled. He stares at his shoulder, its rounded thickness, the muscle of that arm, the pale inside of his wrist as he holds the cigarette to his lips and inhales. Devitry looks down at himself, doubling his chin and frowning again, pulling at the hairs on his chest. Nate sees the dirt under his nails.

"I gotta get a job," he says after a while. He looks up at Nate. "You think your stepdad'll take me on?"

Nate shakes his head, a thought rattling around in it like a shotgun pellet. His stepdad has his own construction business. Nate did some odd jobs for him one summer, but it didn't work out. He doesn't even like to think about it. He lets his eyes linger too long on the front of Devitry's jeans.

Devitry stretches, arching his back. His shirt slides upward, and the gauze falls off. ANARKY. "I'm fucking beat," he says, and Nate knows it's time to go home, that nothing is going to happen now.

"It's getting late," he says, not wanting to be there when Mrs. Devitry comes home anyway, not liking the way she looks at him, like she knows something about him, like something about him stinks.

He walks home in the dark. His breath mists under the street-lights. He pretends Devitry is with him, talking to him. He speaks for them both.

I thought you were tired.

I am tired. It's fuckin' cold.

No shit.

Nate passes Bumpy's house. He can see through the windows right to the back of the house where Bumpy's mom is doing dishes. He breathes hard, his breath foggy. He shoves his hands deep into his pockets. He'll wake up to frost tomorrow morning. He looks over his shoulder and sees circles of light on the road behind him as a car comes his way. He moves to the gravelly side of the street, and the car slows. It's Devitry's mom's old Bonneville. Devitry leans over and opens the door and says, "Hop in," like he's fucking Richie Cunningham, and Nate laughs because Devitry's got this look on his face, all wide-eyed and earnest, his

Boy Scout face, his "Gee, Mom, this roast beef sure is good" face.

As Nate gets in the car, he smells something off, a bad-meat smell. Devitry's got the heat going full blast because he isn't wearing a coat, and there's shit all over the front seat.

"The old lady needs milk," Devitry says, tapping the accelerator. Nate slips down in the seat, trying to identify the things that lay at his feet: bottles and more bottles.

Devitry doesn't take Nate home, not right away. He turns the wrong way—away from home, away from the mini mart—and Nate knows they're headed for Flygate Farms. Nate plays with the radio, happier now—things are looking up. He finds the new R.E.M. song playing and he likes it and he leaves it on, even though Devitry thinks they're all gay—Nate wouldn't say anything about it now, not on their way to Flygate Farms. He looks at Devitry's driving face, all eyes-on-the-road, all serious about what he sees through the windshield. He turns at the sign for the new development.

The houses here are huge, with fireplaces and sunrooms and in-ground pools out back. They have three-car garages—to be used for cars and not made into extra rooms, as Bumpy's dad did when he fixed up the attached garage. Now it's called the rumpus room.

These places are all lit up from the outside—like banks, like Burger King, as if to say, *Look at fucking us!* Nate looks into windows swagged with curtains that never close—*they want you to look,* he's thinking, as he catches glimpses of paintings, portraits, all kinds of art. But you never see anyone in these places—isn't anyone ever home? He wants to say these things to Devitry, but he doesn't want to sound stupid. He looks at him, though, dash-lit, his skin and shirt taking on a green glow. He's leaning on the stack of newspapers that separates them, leaning toward Nate, and Nate can smell the smell of him, a little like sweat, a little like cologne.

They drive past the big occupied houses and turn onto a street that doesn't have a name yet. The houses here are two-by-four shells, skeletons. Devitry turns into the would-be driveway of a soon-to-be-house.

This never happens. That's what Nate likes the best about Flygate Farms, that they come here and do this, and it never happens, not as far as either of them are concerned. It's a non-event, like lost time. It's like huffing, but better.

Devitry pushes his pants down. He likes to be able to spread his legs, setting his knees far apart so that his balls lay on the seat. He keeps his underwear up, playing with himself through the fabric, rubbing himself, getting hard and watching himself. He has a cock that Nate envies. Soft, it's stumpy and fat with a long sleeve of skin that puckers and curls at the end, reminding Nate of a turkey's wattle, and it all but disappears when he gets it hard—it gets so big. Devitry presses his palm against the roll of flesh firming up, snaking into the upper regions of his briefs, pressing up under the waistband in the general vicinity of his left hip. He gets to see this all by the dashboard light. Nate is hard, too—a steely span over his belly despite the restriction of clothes. He gets his own pants open, a little down, his dick coming through the fly of his boxers. He is more than hard; he's superhard. It leaks an oily thread of precome he finds with his finger and takes to his lips. He likes this taste better than any other taste. But maybe not as much as he would like the taste of Devitry.

Devitry finally uncovers his prick. Its size is always a surprise to Nate, a shock that anyone could carry around something that looks so cumbersome. Nate longs to touch it, to hold it, to grip its baseball-bat circumference, but that is not allowed. He can look and he can touch himself, but they are separate, not together, and this is not happening anyway.

Nate watches Devitry spit into his palm and apply the self-made lube to the thick shaft of his cock. He grips himself, his fist firm against his pubes. Veins bulge. Nate swallows. He reminds himself this is not happening. Devitry clears his throat—he's a lit-

100

tle nervous—and Nate jacks himself, his callused palm rasping against the soft skin of his hard-on. Devitry lifts his own shirt. The bandage looks worse in the strange light. Devitry touches his nipple with his thumb. It pops up hard like a little cock, the dark skin around it shrinking. He turns up the heat.

They are jerking off—Devitry watching himself, Nate watching Devitry. Their noisy breathing fills the car—they are not quiet, especially not Devitry, who moans like a porn star. He's good with the sex sounds and the fuck faces, too. He looks as though he's getting the best head of his life, staring at his hand as though it were the mouth of a hundred-dollar whore. Nate has to stop, his stick quivering, as the blast begins to build. His cock throbs haltingly, come bubbling under his balls, wanting to spill. He measures his breath, waiting for Devitry to catch up, watching the Devitry pole glisten.

Nate wants that frilled end in his mouth, his tongue poking around, lost in pink darkness. He wants Devitry's bowling bag of balls in his hand, and the brownish stink of his butthole on his fingers, sucking on the fat head and receiving the blast of the boy's squiggling sperm, a potent mouthful. The thought is like a stroke along his cock head and he cannot wait for his friend any longer, and just then Devitry's mouth falls agape and he pisses out a gush of come that drapes itself languidly over the steering wheel. Nate squints through his own blinding orgasm, his jizz spraying wetly across his own face, red and proud. He even gets a little on Devitry, who bitches but doesn't really mind.

Bumpy wants a Milky Way, so they cut class. They walk down to the mini mart in the midday sun, Nate touching the dollar bill in his pocket, his fingers curled around it and the warm roll of his not-quite-soft cock. He's been horny all day, and even Bumpy's ass in his falling-down jeans is of some interest to him, the way his black boxer-briefs are exposed, name-brand waistband extolling Bumpy's designer fetish.

"That shit's phat," he says

Nate says, "Uh-huh," agreeing distractedly. He looks up from Bumpy's rear end.

"What shit?" he asks.

"Where the fuck are you?" Bumpy wants to know, pulling up his pants and walking like a drunk. It's warm again, maybe the last warm day of the year. The trees are holding on to their green leaves, and it is all going to change in a day. The air smells of apples, and Nate is holding his hard-on in the dark of his pocket, disturbed that he is finding Bumpy not altogether unattractive. He thinks about his new favorite song, the one by Patty Griffin, about summer and love, hearing it in his head, looking at Bumpy and wishing it was summer all over again.

"Do you think," he asks, "that it's hot in California right now?"

"Dude," Bumpy replies, "It's always hot in California."

"How come your stepdad won't hire me?" Devitry wants to know. He can't find a job anywhere, and he's starting to act like Nate's mom's husband owes it to him to help him out. "I'll do anything, man. You know I will. Why don't you say something to him? Hook me up, dude."

Devitry's smoking a cigarette—"Mom fell off the patch"—and he's got the other hand in his pants casually, as if that's where it belongs, driving Nate crazy. He's lying on his bed and looking like that fucking poster hanging behind Nate's art teacher's desk—Monet, Manet, whatever. Devitry looks better.

"How come you don't work for him anymore?" he asks. He's got his sneakered feet on his bed, fingering the lettering of his ANARKY tattoo with the hand that holds the cigarette. The hair has started to grow back and it looks funny, sprouting up through the lettering. He plays with it, stroking it one way and then the other. Nate doesn't want to answer the question Devitry asked. "He thinks I'm a dumb fucking fag" just doesn't sound so good.

"I thought you were going to the movies with Bumpy," he asks instead.

"Fuck that faggot," Devitry says. "He can't now because his grandmom's dog got hit by a car." He looks at Nate, his hand quiet in his pants. "What are you doing tonight?" he wants to know.

Nate shrugs. He was going to go down to the rec center to see what was going on. He says that much. Devitry toes off his sneakers. Nate stands, staring as his friend pulls off one sock and then the other. It just doesn't make any sense to him why he pops an instant rod, seeing Devitry's long naked toes, the blue veins that run across the tops of his feet, the powdery white callused heels. If he could put his tongue anywhere on Devitry, he thinks now, it would be between any two of his finger-like toes.

"Dude," Devitry says lazily. He leaves it at that—he doesn't need to say anything else—he has Nate's undivided attention. When he's with Devitry, Nate's seldom aware of anything else.

They go to the mall—Devitry's mom driving. She gives them a twenty, telling them she'll be back at 9:30 when the mall closes. "She's being nice," Nate says as she pulls away.

"I think she got laid last night," Devitry laughs. "I'm not shitting."

They pass some girls, and Nate watches Devitry's eyes narrow. He practically turns around and follows them out into the parking lot. Nate holds the door open, waiting, looking at Devitry's shoes. "Any day now," he says, letting the door close.

It's cold in the mall, and Nate feels his nipples shrivel like little raisins that poke hard against the front of his shirt. He's walking slow now and staying a little behind Devitry so that he can watch his ass. Devitry's got a great ass, small and round, not flat or flabby, but high and tight. Nate imagined putting his hand on those warm, smooth cheeks, his fingers just fitting into the crack. He can't even think beyond that point, the point in time when Devitry spreads his legs, opening his ass. Nate's own crack is overgrown with hair. He thinks about shaving it bald but can't bring himself to use a razor down there, afraid someone will notice and make fun, but who is looking at him down there? He wishes Devitry would look.

They piss together in the rest room, ignoring the old men shuffling by the sinks. "Lose something, fellas?" Devitry asks, stepping away from the pisser before he's zipped up all the way. "Fucking fags," he says, halfway through the door, and the men flutter like washed-out banners. Nate looks beyond them into the mirror toward his future. He's afraid, but he's riding Devitry's tow, and hoping maybe there's some way to avoid a sad end. Get a girl. Get a job. Refuse the rides to Flygate Farms. Clean up his room, do his homework. Visit his grandmother in the nursing home more often. What's it going to take? Who does he have to be?

He watches Devitry's ass anyway, and they go into the Gap and try on clothes. Devitry takes off his shirt right on the sales floor to try on one of theirs. He likes his new tattoo—even if it isn't spelled right. He doesn't look for a mirror, though—he asks Nate: *How's it look?* It's tight on his arms and across his chest and doesn't cover a lot of him. If it's too small, it doesn't matter—it looks right on him, perfectly right. He walks away, though, not wanting Devitry to see the buzz he was getting.

Nate dodges squirts of Curve at the Bon Ton and ignores the Calvin Klein underwear display, and can't shake the feeling that he is doing something bad, his fingers in his pockets touching his semi as if it were something lucky, like a rabbit's foot or an Indian-head nickel. They are stepping out of the entrance, shuffling like homeys, when security stops them.

"Guys," Nate hears through a giggle—he feels so stupid, so stoned—and there's a hand on his shoulder. He turns around and there's this mountain behind him, some huge-ass Steve Austin–looking motherfucker with a shaved head and arms like railroad ties.

"I'm looking for a bottle of Curve—wondering if maybe you might have seen it." he says, and Nate looks and sees it as plain as anything in Devitry's pocket. *Fucking A!* he's thinking, when Devitry pulls a slick one and tries to make a break for it. He doesn't get very far because Steve Austin, catching Nate up in one arm, starts after him and practically tackles Devitry right in

104

front of a Christian bookstore. *What would Jesus do?* Nate wonders as he's being bundled up in the manly arms of the store security guard, who smells a little like the Curve he is trying to keep Devitry from pilfering.

Steve Austin has a sterling hoop in his ear and a black T-shirt that might just as well have been sprayed on. He gets them both by the scruffs of their necks like a couple of naughty kindergartners and hauls their asses back into the store. "Got 'em," he tells the made-up old lady behind the scent counter. He hauls them up the escalator and through the bedding department, where they pass openmouthed Mary Beth Pasternak from Nate's biology class. He pushes them down a dull-colored corridor, past closed offices and empty racks, throwing them into a room with a bunch of really ugly mannequins. He closes the door behind him and leans heavily against it, and Nate is thinking there's going to be a little more trouble than he had first anticipated. He glances over at Devitry who looks like he would love a cigarette.

"You boys know how much it costs the consumer every time you rip off a bottle of cologne?" Steve Austin looks at Devitry and then at Nate, not blinking or even breathing, it seems. He's a killer, Nate thought, terrified, one of the avenging angels of retail. He folds his arms across his chest. "What are you looking at?" he asks Nate

"Nothing," Nate mumbles, dropping his gaze to the floor, wishing he could pluck out his eyes. He'd been looking at the fist-like lump to the left of the guy's fly.

"'Nothing,'" he mimics as he narrows his eyes at Nate and puts on a pained expression. "I know what you were looking at." He touches it then, shoving it more to the left under the tight skin of denim. He looks over at Devitry. "This your suck buddy? You two fags?"

"Fuck no," Devitry stammers. "No fucking way."

Whatever, Nate thinks.

"Caught myself a couple of cocksucking shoplifters," Steve Austin says, grinning. He thumbs his package again, and Nate swallows the large amount of saliva that has suddenly flooded his mouth. "I should get a fucking bonus for this one."

"Look," Devitry says, "Just call the cops or my mom or whatever it is you're supposed to do, man." He looks at Nate then, only a glance, and says, "Hey, bud, we'll do anything you want. Anything."

Steve Austin takes a deep breath and draws himself up. His elbows point menacingly. "You know, boys," he says, lisping, "the judicial system just ain't what it used to be, you know what I mean? I'll call the cops, and they'll hold you for a little while, and then your parents will take you home, and maybe they'll beat your asses, and then you'll turn around and sue them for abuse—and you'll end up fucking millionaires, so what kind of lesson is that?"

Nate says, "No way—like, my stepdad will probably definitely kill me. No shit—like dead and I mean it."

"Yeah," Devitry says, "My mom straps me all the time for the stupidest shit—she broke my arm once, too, didn't she, Nate?"

"No shit. She really did, man." Nate says, nodding his head frantically.

"Dude," Devitry says, putting a hand on his own crotch. "Do we look like shoplifters, man? We saw your shit in the Calvin aisle. Nate here popped a boner looking at your pecs, so I figured the only way to get with you would be to mop something, you know?"

Nate is in awe, glowing in Devitry's brilliance.

Steve Austin smiles. "I thought so, you sexy little fuckers. I'm getting hungry just looking at you," he says. He eyes up Nate. "I bet you do all the sucking. I'm betting he just lays back and lets you do all the work. Pretty mouth, real pretty." His cock is creeping upwards. Nate can't help but stare.

"He'll suck the hair off your balls," Devitry says. Nate turns, wide-eyed. "He's fucking awesome, man. Best head I've ever had."

"That right?"

"Fuck, yeah."

Nate shakes his head "No," he says, "No."

"I'm inclined to take your buddy's recommendation, but here's the thing: I'm here to teach you boys a lesson. That's my job here—I teach lessons. So here's how things are gonna go from here on in—you guys are gonna do exactly what I tell you to do— *exactly.* Know what I mean? I say do *this,* you're ass better be doing *this.* Am I clear here? Are we understanding each other?"

Lessons? Nate is thinking, *Like I need them.* He says "yes" anyway, but Devitry stalls. Nate sees him chew the inside of his lip. He's playing him, Nate thinks.

Steve Austin steps up to Devitry, looking down from six and a half feet. "Have I made myself clear?" he asks.

"I want to see my lawyer," Devitry says, losing his cool. Steve Austin looks very amused.

"You know what, kid? Your lawyer just happens to be on the end of my dick—you're going to see plenty of him."

"Fine with me," Devitry says, feigning disinterest.

Nate thinks about passing out when Steve Austin starts taking off his shirt. He is buff and packed, skin all tanning-bed brown, nipples as big around as little pancakes and the color of chocolate. There's no hair on him that Nate can see, not even under his arms. He busts a couple of gunshots, showing off, hands curled into fists by his ears, setting the veins in his arms on edge.

"What's your name?" Devitry asks. He doesn't sound tough anymore, and he doesn't sound scared, either. His voice is breathy and not under his control—Nate can hear his friend's heartbeat in his throat.

"My name, princess, is Sean. You want my badge number, too? Or just my phone number?"

Sean undoes the button of his jeans and unzips his fly. Nate sees the little dark mustache of pubes and fights the urge to put his hands in his pockets. He sees that Devitry is interested, too, his mouth hanging open, a wet spot on the front of his khakis. There is no underwear, just a big roll of flesh under the tiny bangs of his crotch hair. He walks between Nate and Devitry, getting his ass out of his tight jeans, shaking out his long stiffy and giving them both smoldering looks.

"Here's your lesson today, boys—and you've each got a different one so there won't be any copying, if you know what I mean." He looks at Nate. "Now, I'm going to do you a favor here and teach your selfish friend how to suck dick like a pro." Then he looks over at Devitry, who is having a hard time keeping a happy, buzzed grin off his face. "And then I'm going to teach your buddy how to fuck some butt."

Sean's butt is gigantic, white and tight and high, monster cheeks that make Nate hungry. He reaches out for the fleshy globes, and his hand is swatted away. Sean sneers smilingly. "Wait your turn," he says.

He stands in front of Devitry. "Ready?" he asks.

Devitry stays quiet, but he's staring at the thick prong inches away from his face. Its head, as far as Nate can see, is wide and rubbery, a huge cap atop a really fat cock. It's bulbous and heavy, too big for anything but ruin. He wonders how Devitry will manage.

"Open up," Sean says. "And open wide."

Nate watches his friend's lips part enough to spit a nickel. His tongue slips out tentatively, a bit of pink welcome mat. Sean puts his fingers there, and the tongue becomes bolder, slides over the digits, taking the fingers into his mouth, down to the crotch of them until he gags and spits them out, thick with saliva.

"That ain't nothing, boy," Sean says, wagging his beef-stick under Devitry's nose. The boy licks at it, catching the balled end and covering it with his mouth. His eyes find Nate's, and they're as wide as his mouth.

"Just go easy," Sean says, towering over Devitry, who slips off the chair and gets on his knees. "Now you," he says to Nate, "You're going to get behind me and start eating my ass. You think you can manage that?"

Nate nods, hypnotized, rubbing the front of his pants. He's ready to strip and lay himself out on the desk and let Sean teach him anything he wants. If he can teach trigonometry with his cock, Nate is willing to learn. Nate all but crawls the six feet of linoleum to Sean's shining butt. He puts his hands on them first, surprised to find the flesh quite warm and very hard. He licks one and then the other, smelling his fragrance—Curve and soap and the familiar scent of Devitry's spit emanating from up front.

"Now, what you're doing back there," Sean says, "is just the beginning, you know—the foreplay, I guess you call it. Usually, I don't go in for much of that shit—a lot of wasted time. You got a nut to bust, you don't want to dilly-dally and eat someone out first? But I want to teach you right—yeah, that's right, right there."

Nate slides into the crack, which is as bald as Sean's head, although a little gritty with stubble, not so freshly shaved. He finds the tight wrinkle, the little blinking pucker, and pushes his tongue into it. It tastes pungent, like something he's eaten before and didn't much care for, like trout, not that Sean tasted like trout, but the experience was the same. When you're hungry enough, you'll eat anything and probably like it. And Nate likes it now, lapping up the hard-ridged hole and teaching Sean a thing or two about rim jobs.

"Damn, boy," he says, turning around. "That's good eating."

Devitry, on the other hand, on the other side, isn't doing so well. "Cover the teeth with your lips—you're messing up my dick, man. Shit."

Nate takes hold of the tanned globes on either side of his face and grips them hard. He chews a little on the pucker, making Sean wiggle his ass like a 16-year-old cheerleader, a pretty sight from Nate's perspective, if only his eyes weren't screwed shut.

"Oh, man, that's sweet," Nate hears Sean say, and Devitry gulps and slurps, and Nate reaches through the sweating arch of Sean's legs and pokes at Devitry's chest, fingering into his shirt and touching the hair patch between his pecs. Every once in a while Sean relaxes his sphincter, and Nate works a bit of his tongue up into the brown wink and wiggles it around. Sean reaches behind himself and puts his hand on Nate's head, holding it tight against the crack. It's hard for him to breathe that way, but it feels fucking excellent. He snorts, licks, and chews, and Sean's butt dances all over his face, and then his hole goes tight, and there's no getting in. Nate backs off, dismissed, turning the corner of Sean's bucking hip, finding Devitry impaled, Sean's snake banging into him, spit dripping, cheeks puffing out. Devitry's got his buddy out, big pink cap blinking, and is cuffing it dry.

"You finished or something?" he hears Sean ask, and he looks up at the dick.

"Couldn't get in," Nate says, feeling stupid, palming the front of his pants, his boner sore.

"Use your finger," Sean says, grim as shit. He's got this strange look on his face—one half killer, the other half pussy. His blue-green eyes are slitted. Nate returns to Sean's ass and gets his hand into the tight crack and pokes into the little cunt. Sean's butt tips back, sucking on Nate's digit. Devitry chokes. He looks around at Nate, red-faced, sweating. He shakes his cock. Pre-jizz flies

"You swallow?" Nate hears Sean ask, and Devitry says something cock-mouthed and unintelligible that must mean "yes," and Sean, doing something rigorous to his own nipples, starts fucking himself into Devitry's face. Nate digs into his drawers for his sticky handful, watching the artful glide of Sean's monster shaft sliding into Devitry's swollen lips. *It'll come out the back of his head,* he's thinking while palming himself and getting out of his jeans and stretching out on the cold linoleum.

"Fuck, yeah," Sean moans quietly, ruthless in Devitry's wide gape. He freezes up, clamping tightly on Nate's finger, and Nate sees Devitry's over-filled mouth, come spilling out, white goo that slides down his chin and hangs in stringy drops to his chest. Sean pulls out and sprays even more across his face. It glues Devitry's eyes shut.

"Now, that, my man, is how you suck cock, and I have to say that you did a fine job there."

Devitry smiles up at him, looking a little weak-kneed and very horny. Sean turns to Nate.

"And that was fine ass-licking, excellent foreplay, bud, but now it's time for the rest of your lesson."

Nate swallows hard.

Sean pokes himself back into his pants. "Don't do it," he says, his mouth turning up on one side.

"What?" Nate says, a little dumbfounded.

"Crack kills, man," Sean says, trying hard not to laugh. He pets his big half-hard prick and turns to walk to the door.

"Wait a minute," Devitry says. "What about us?"

Sean looks over his shoulder. "What about you?" he asks.

"Well," Devitry stammers, "Aren't you at least going to like get us off or anything?"

Sean shakes his head. "You little fuckers just don't get it, do you—you just paid your debt to society—" he points at Devitry— " And you—" stabbing his finger at Nate—"are fucking lucky because I would have disemboweled you. Now get your asses home and don't let me catch you in my store again."

"Dude," Devitry says when they can no longer hear Sean's Skechers on the funny, liver-colored linoleum in the hallway. "Did he notch his eyebrows or what?"

Flygate Farms again. Nothing changes, Nate decides. Devitry doesn't mention Sean, or that he's started to hang out at the men's room at the mall these days. Nate lives out of an Abercrombie and Fitch catalogue, jerking off to guys in First-String Jerseys and Power Play Shorts that bare their hipbones and make Nate bony. He has decided that he's going to move to California when he graduates. He's going to bring his lawn chair and his long hair and wait for big love. *It'll be fucking cool,* he thinks, his fingers sliding over the purpled letters of Devitry's ANARKY tattoo, smearing come over the ink.

Stop and Go

Clay steps out of the steam of the shower and wraps himself in a towel, shy suddenly, not at all as comfortable with his nakedness as Bingham, who loiters nude at the bank of lockers, dripping still, his towel nowhere in sight.

"Forgot it," he says, grinning. "Borrow yours?" And in a moment Clay finds himself uncovered again, digging through his gym bag for fresh underwear and trying to be oblivious to the luxurious drag of his towel across Bingham's chest. He tries to ignore the rough ball of it between Bingham's legs, realizing he'd be once again in possession of that towel and that it would become, he's decided, infinitely more valuable. He steps into boxers, finds his deodorant, glances at the white cheeks of Bingham's ass, tightly muscled and flexing like coy winks.

"You look hung over," Bingham says, and Clay blinks himself back into consciousness, having taken a little side trip, wandering through the thick brush around Bingham's balls.

"What?" he says, dumbly as he feels himself blushing.

"You're like a fucking retard," Bingham says, throwing the towel at his friend. It lands around Clay's face and he freezes, his dick wobbling. He quickly grabs the soggy towel, sniffing and smelling nothing but his own soap, but imagining something else, and it's like an aphrodisiac, and he has to hurry into his jeans, pulling them up before his excitement shows, fumbling with the buttons, a breeze from nowhere fluttering across his nipples.

Bingham, naked still, turns toward the mirror at the other end of the locker room. "Fucking shoulders, man" he says as he examines himself in the mirror. "Where the fuck do they go?"

"They haven't gone anywhere," Clay mutters, examining things just as closely. Someone's going to come in, he thinks, and he doesn't even care. Clay watches Bingham's ass, the smooth white flesh, the dark split, the squat backs of his thighs, the pale behinds of his knees and his over-muscled calves. Clay elbows into his shirt, retrieves his dropped towel and sprays cologne on himself, ignoring the fact that his cock has engorged, thick as a brick. Bingham leaves his reflection and comes back to their shared bench, his dick fattened and unacknowledged, but not by Clay, who watches the slow ascent until it is tucked away in Structure briefs, an arrested semi that Bingham smooths out before he steps into his jeans. Clay gets a shudder of chills.

"What are you doing tonight?" Bingham asks.

Clay shrugs. He shoulders his gym bag.

"Give me a call," Bingham says. He's still in his briefs. They are dark blue and cling mid thigh. His shaved smooth belly rises up from the waistband, and his navel is perpetually popped out like a sweet roll. He is stalled, stalling. He goes through his bag but pulls nothing from it. He glances in the mirror again and then down at his own pecs. Then he looks at Clay.

"OK," Clay says, and Bingham just stares at him.

Clay is at the mall in the men's room on the lower level near the garage. There's a note written on the inside of the stall door, saying the shit goes down at four, and Clay is waiting. He sits on the toilet, listening to the pound of his heart. The rest room door opens, hinges screaming, and Clay's eyes go wide. He freezes. He listens to the footsteps and to the sounds this man is making, his breathing and noises, the drag of his zipper, his breath held now and the long wait for piss to splash in the toilet.

And in the waiting, Clay goes hard. He pulls himself out of his jeans and pinches the head of his cock, thumbing the slit that oozes, and he tugs quietly on the head, again and again and again, waiting for anything to happen, not sure how these things go. The man—Clay can see the side of one of his Adidas athletic shoes— doesn't pee and he doesn't move, but he's breathing again, and his leather coat pulls loudly, and still there's nothing.

Clay is pulling harder on himself, and picturing Bingham's shower scene earlier that afternoon at the gym. In his mind's eye Clay sees Bingham turning into his spray of water, twisting his body, his stomach tightening into neatly sectioned muscle, the hair there turning into a black ribbon that unfurls down to his thick stubby cock, curling around it and spreading down over his big pink balls. Clay licks his thumb and forefinger and works them over his cock head. He wedges his fingers into his jeans to search for his balls, bringing them out, rubbing them with his left hand. They are big balls, bigger than Bingham's, only not as hairy, and he strokes them through the easy give of the sack. Taking himself in a fist, he leans over and drops a gob of spit on his palm, not caring about the obvious noise this produces.

The sneakered foot remains unmoving, its trio of black stripes going nowhere. In Clay's fantasy Bingham is showering, spitting, squinting through the spray, legs spread, water falling from his dick like piss, the expression on his face unreadable. He looks at Clay. Who knows what he sees? Clay squeezes up on his shaft. Behind his closed eyes he sees Bingham's hand, soaped, between ass cheeks, making his hole clean.

Clay's nylon sleeve is loud and telltale, each swish clearly defining the action of his arm, each stroke of his prick. He doesn't care because the man at the urinal has come over to the stall door and is peering through the crack, watching Clay jacking off. He is an eye and some shoes and then a voice telling Clay to stand up, to take down his jeans. Clay pushes his jeans down his thighs, the air cool on his skin, and his cock is electric, harder, he thinks, than it's ever been, but he can't touch it, because it's already humming, dribbling, twitching with pulse and want. The voice tells him to lift up his shirt and he does, offering his belly, his pink nipples that are tight as spring peas and just as small. The eye darts up and down. Then the voice commands him to turn around, and Clay turns and bends over. He holds on to the seat of the toilet and he smells the rim heady with the scent of many men and he swears he can feel the eye on his tight little hole. His head reels from the smell of old piss, from the sight of curling dropped hairs of men and boys before him. He pushes his cock and balls between his thighs because the voice tells him.

"I'm coming," Clay says in a perfectly normal voice, and the voice that belongs to the eye, still whispering, tells him to turn around. Clay turns and sprays the walls of the stall. He comes until he begins to think he will never stop coming. He hears the man's harsh breathing and sees light glinting off the eye that never blinks until the end, when the man holds his breath and comes between the door crack, his semen thick and yellow and dripping, adding to the mess of the rest room floor.

Bingham's flannel shirt is undone. He's wearing a wife beater underneath it with a dragged-out neck and a hole under his right arm. His shirt has slipped off one shoulder, revealing the hard-balled deltoids. Clay wants to know where they're going, but it doesn't really matter. He's not sure what matters anymore. He used to think it was baseball and girls and PlayStation 2 and a fake I.D. to get beer on the weekend and maybe getting promoted at the paper mill, maybe going to college someday. They're heading toward Glens Falls, and then they get off at the South Glens Falls exit and get back on the Northway, heading south again. Winter is over, but it's still cold and there's still snow, though not much, and Clay is not cold, but he settles into his coat, and Bingham lifts his arm to slip his shirt back where it belongs. They pull into a rest stop, and Bingham cuts the engine. He looks through the windshield at the trees at the edge of the grass.

"It's all fenced in now," he says, "but you used to be able to come here and walk the trails back there." He turns to Clay. "Mad shit, back there on those trails, man," he says, smiling.

Clay understands. It's like the mall rest room, and it's like the county park after dark. Men with their hands shoved deep in their pockets staring holes through you. He starts the car again.

Neither one talks. Clay watches his breath when he gets out of Bingham's car. The driveway is empty; Bingham's parents have gone to Vermont for the weekend. Bingham was supposed to work today, but he called in to take the day off.

In his bedroom, Bingham takes off his flannel shirt. Clay sits at the desk, going through Bingham's CDs, but he watches his friend flex his biceps as though he can't help himself. There are sketches—Bingham's tattoo designs—on scraps of paper littering the desk. Among them are tribal bands, barbed wire, and entwined Celtic intricacies. He's staring at Clay, and Clay quickly realizes that there won't be any talk, no discussion. There's no need for words now. Bingham has a hand over his fly, gently strumming the front of his jeans. Talk would define, and definition would bring a false sense of meaning to what can only be, for Bingham, a meaningless act. Clay can see it in Bingham's expression, he can read already the raw need with nothing more behind it. It's the eye again—and its hunger.

Clay stands and touches the front of his own jeans. He's hard, has been hard for some time. His cock is hot and flat against his belly, hidden beneath layers of clothing. Bingham's is much more obvious—it presses up to the left of his fly and makes a widening wet spot. He steps backward and sits down on his bed, leaning back on his elbows, his white tank riding up his belly, baring his navel and the dark trail of hair there. He doesn't have to say anything to make Clay walk over to him and touch the damp stiffness, swirling his finger against the leaking head beneath. At this, Bingham exhales—it is almost a moan. His eyes close and his head tilts back, and Clay leans in to put his lips on the boy's throat, just over his Adam's apple, and Bingham groans and pushes up with his hips against Clay's hand and forearm. Clay tongues the soft skin under his bristly chin and accepts the hand that grabs the back of his head, moving it gently but insistently down. His lips press against the dampened jeans, and Bingham's hips arc upward to meet his embrace.

Clay struggles with button and fly and then the tangle of underwear until he actually touches the firm hot flesh of Bingham's pole, the humid bush. Wetness is everywhere. Clay wrestles the jeans off Bingham's hips, baring his cock. It is thick and hovering, a slimy drip leaking from the pale end, its deep slit. Clay tastes him then, and Bingham writhes beneath him, pressing toward Clay's eager maw.

Bingham's cock hits the back of Clay's mouth and Bingham lets out a pained grunt. He grips Clay's head tightly and fucks his thick shaft into the boy's mouth. Clay snorts and chokes but stays on the prick, his lips stretched, kissing curling pubes with each beat. His fingers roam Bingham's torso finally, the plaited belly, the slabs of his pecs. He tears at the wife beater and it comes apart easily, making Bingham groan again.

"Holy shit," he whispers roughly, jacking his hips. He rolls over, never breaking contact with Clay's mouth, and gets him on his back and continues to fuck his face. He gropes the front of Clay's jeans, the bone-hard, covered stump. He squeezes it tightly, repeating the motion ever more quickly until Clay is moaning. Clay is close to release, swallowing the salty leak of Bingham's dick, his jaw aching but still hungry. His back arches and his throat constricts and his cock blows in his pants under Bingham's heavy grip. Bingham shudders above him and drags his prick from Clay's throat and tries to hold off, clutching each breath, his balls tucking upward, and he blows his load across Clay's face, leaving clotted chugs of warm white on his cheeks and nose and lips.

This will happen again or maybe not. It's up to Bingham to make it happen. Clay lingers on the bed. He has wiped his face clean with a towel. He holds the towel over his crotch, watching Bingham walk over to the window and look out through the blinds, his cock still hard and shining. Clay watches and waits. He has all the time in the world.

Virtual Virgin

Malcolm filtered through the crowd in Letitia Blaze's living room. More than anything, Letitia had wanted a loft, but she hadn't been able to find one she could afford. So she rented a place with a big living room and moved all her furniture into it. She called the bedrooms closets. Guests positioned themselves between her bed and her kitchen table.

"Where's the toilet?" Malcolm heard someone inquire of another guest.

"I'm afraid to ask" was the reply.

There was some beer somewhere, and Malcolm was looking for it. He didn't look at anything but elbows and shoulders. The lighting was bad anyway. He heard Letitia's laughter and the marching-band music that seemed oddly appropriate to the scene. "Where did you get that?" he asked someone tall, pointing to the beer bottle the man was holding.

The beer was in the bathroom. Letitia had turned the tub into a makeshift ice bucket. Someone stood by the door, just out of the light. "Are you going to be long?" he asked Malcolm. "I'm expecting a call."

Malcolm got himself a beer. "That long," he said, lingering to open the bottle. "So who's calling?"

The man smiled, looking away. "My mother, actually," he answered. "Her dog died today."

"I'm sorry," Malcolm said, feeling as though he'd put his foot in it. The man was tall, in tight black clothes. He looked a little

118

like a mime, Malcolm thought. He had a mime's face: expressive, animated. It made him seem loud, even though he spoke very quietly. Malcolm had stumbled across an attractive mime.

"What's with the music?" the tall man asked.

"Letitia used to be a drum major," Malcolm replied.

"Oh," the man said, looking puzzled. "You can major in drum?"

Malcolm made room for Simon Devray, who wanted to get into the bathroom. They'd dated once, he and Malcolm, and now they weren't speaking to one another, each pretending not to remember the other. Simon brushed past the two of them and into the bathroom, not saying a word.

"What's *your* major?" the tall man asked after Simon had gone. Malcolm shrugged, grinning. The tall one smiled back. He was very handsome, Malcolm decided. He liked the man's hair because it moved freely, unencumbered by gel. It caught the stray light from the bathroom when Simon stepped out, air-drying his hands. He winced at Malcolm, who winced back.

"I'm a poet," Malcolm lied.

"Really?" the tall man said, holding his beer to his temple and regarding Malcolm in a new light. They both heard Simon snort his way down the hall. "So you've probably read Jewel's new book—just kidding."

"So was she, I hope," Malcolm said.

"My name's Tom Curry," the tall man said, extending his hand Malcolm took it. "Letitia's new personal trainer?"

"Uh, no," Curry said, "But thank you. I'll take that as a compliment."

"It was," Malcolm replied.

"I'm thinking this is risky," Curry said. He was getting himself out of his black turtleneck.

"I've got condoms," Malcolm said, his feelings a little hurt.

"Not what I meant at all," Curry said, setting his hands on Malcolm's shoulders. "I meant doing this here in Letitia's bedroom."

"I told you—this is her closet."

"Someone's going to come in," Curry whispered, running his tongue along Malcolm's jaw. He undid the fastenings of Malcolm's trousers, and they fell quickly to the ground. Malcolm lifted Curry's T-shirt and put his mouth on a dark rubbery nipple. He felt Curry's hand wander the breadth of his back, dipping low, sliding under the waistband of his briefs, grabbing his ass cheeks. Malcolm fingered the tab of Curry's zipper. He could already feel the thick bulge of Curry's prick. He thought about his not having wanted to come to Letitia's party tonight. He had dreaded the ride up in her prissy little elevator and the prospect of schmoozing with the "eclectic" mix of people she'd promised. And, strangely, Letitia had a habit of not putting out finger food for her guests.

That was, until now.

Not that Tom Curry's dick could have been considered finger food.

"I'm sorry," Malcolm said, turning on the lights. "I have to see this."

Tom Curry's ass, bared, was hairy enough to comb. The bottom half of him was in fact goat-like, furry. He appeared to be half-dressed for Halloween, waiting for the rest of his gorilla suit, which appealed to Malcolm, who had grown weary of stubble-covered boys trying to cheat their hirsute fates with razors and waxes and depilatories. He tugged off Curry's white briefs, making room for the heavy swing of his oversize prick.

The rest of him—his chest, arms, and back—was remarkably devoid of hair. Malcolm pushed him toward the bed, where he fell easily onto the dark cushion of coats. Malcolm could smell Simon's Drakar-soaked cashmere car coat, which he intended to adorn with some egg-white streaks of come. He knelt shakily, ankles bound by his trousers, and kissed Curry's red mouth, lips like pillows, eyes sparkling despite the dull low-wattage lamp on the bureau.

"You're tall," Malcolm said.

"Thank you," Curry replied.

"I usually don't like tall men."

"I see."

They kissed again, and Malcolm stretched out over the tall, half-furry Curry, feeling the bulk of him coming between them. *It's like a misplaced arm,* Malcolm thought, dragging his belly across it. He moved down the smooth torso, tonguing into the belly button, beside which lay Curry's log. He licked the whole thing from top to bottom, getting it very wet, very slippery. He repositioned himself atop Curry and humped his own dick against Curry's huge piece, sharing spit and mixing it with pre-come—a very pleasant combination, he was thinking. Maybe too pleasant, he began to realize. He watched Curry tip his head back, chin to the ceiling, mouth open, his whole demeanor ecstatic. *Houston, we have a problem,* he thought as Curry gurgled sexily, tensing his long thighs, stretching cruciform across the coat-covered mattress. He felt the first shot like a wet bullet— all the rest gushed out like what's left in a fire hose when the water's turned off. There seemed to be buckets of it.

They both held their breaths.

"I don't—" Curry began.

Malcolm felt the warm wetness spread between their bellies.

"I can't even—" Curry began again.

"No problem," Malcolm said easily. "It's fine. It's fine." He eased himself up, glancing at the thick white puddle on Curry's belly. There was enough of it on Malcolm's cock to make him at least *look* as though he'd been satisfied.

"It's not fine," Curry said. He got up on his elbows, and his come slid down a sudden ravine, dripping glutinously onto someone's—perhaps Simon's—dark coat. Malcolm, on his haunches, was not so much disappointed as surprised. He waited for an excuse, a logical explanation—"Haven't had sex in three months." "Been jacking off all day without coming." "I'm taking these vitamins."

"We could always," Curry said. "I mean, I could…"

Malcolm pressed his palms between his own thighs. He had huge thighs. He was a squat powerhouse, a little fireplug— compact and muscled, one of those guys who usually seems to have a chip on his shoulder. He would have wrestled in school, but he'd hated the thought of cauliflower ears and mistrusted his ability to separate sex from sport, especially a sport that seemed more like thinly disguised sex. He contented himself with taped collegiate wrestling events on public television, whacking off to them as if they were his favorite fuck films.

And then the excuse: "I'm kind of a virgin," Tom Curry said quietly. "Ostensibly, anyway."

"An ostensible virgin," Malcolm said a little too loudly. He was actually thinking of his wrestling tapes now. He liked the short guys the best, the little ones who weighed in at 170 or 180, the little bruisers. It was a form of self-love, he realized, straddling the elongated thighs of Tom Curry. He looked at his own thighs, doubled in size because of the way he was sitting, little swirls of dark hairs covering them. It was like loving your own thighs, he was thinking.

The bedroom door opened, and Simon stood in the doorway, mouth agape, mercifully mistaking the situation for postcoital. "I'm so—" he said in a stammer.

"Sorry." Malcolm finished the phrase for him. The door closed. Malcolm looked at Curry, who looked not stricken—but maybe struck.

"I'm not happy right now," he said. He sat up. "Clothes," he said. "I feel particularly naked.

"You know…" he continued, pulling up his trousers. They were nice ones, not shiny black slacks made of moleskin or something like that. "I didn't want to come tonight—to this party, I mean."

"I see," Malcolm said, finding his shirt and shaking it out before putting it on. There was a knock on the door.

"My coat," they heard Simon bleat.

"Come in," Malcolm said, zipping his pants. The door opened slowly. The marching-band music had stopped—how long ago? He wondered whether the party had ended. Simon stepped between the two half-dressed men, glancing quickly at both of them with the intensity of someone with a photographic memory.

Once Simon had left them, the men finished buttoning and tucking in silence. Malcolm was unable to restrain himself from picking a speck of white from Curry's shoulder. He turned around and found his coat on the bed with the pile of others. He checked to make sure it wasn't his that had gotten spattered.

"Are you leaving now?" Curry asked.

Malcolm made a sad smile. "I am."

"I'll wait then," Curry said.

Malcolm asked, "Why?"

Curry paused, his mouth open enough to show the tip of his tongue. Malcolm felt his own eyes narrow. "People will think we're leaving together," he heard Curry say.

"We're not," Malcolm said. "But what would be wrong with that anyway?"

"Well, nothing, really," Curry replied. "It would just be inaccurate, that's all."

Malcolm sat on the edge of the bed. "So you're really a virgin?"

Curry turned to look at himself in the mirror, adjusting his turtleneck. Malcolm couldn't wear turtlenecks, unable to find any that would accommodate the girth of his neck.

"In a manner of speaking," he sighed.

"Ostensibly," Malcolm said, noticing for the first time the gold band around Curry's finger. He reached for another speck of white on the man's shoulder.

"Do I have dandruff?" Curry asked.

"Lint," Malcolm replied. He watched as Curry admired his reflection in Letitia's mirror.

"Which is worse?"

"Depends," Malcolm answered. "Dandruff, I guess."

"No, I mean being a real virgin or a virtual virgin."

123

"Are you saying you're not really a virgin?"

"Well," Curry drawled. "You know what I mean, don't you?"

"But you're really married."

"Well, yes," Curry said, glancing down.

There was a knock at the door. Simon poked his head in, looking so much like a turtle that Malcolm had to laugh. Simon stuck his arm through the doorway, holding a coat. "Not mine—do you mind if I come in?"

Malcolm got away from the enigmatic Tom Curry and his wedding-ring problems and thought himself a better man for his restraint. "I can't be a home wrecker," he told Letitia, who had called inquiring just what he and Curry had been up to in her closet the night of her party.

"Was it some teenage kissing game? Five minutes in the closet?" she asked. "How did it go otherwise?" Malcolm conjured an image of her, phone pinned between her head and shoulder, chucking her bare foot under the furry chin of her Lhasa apso, Baron von Richter, better known as Bear.

"Otherwise?" he said, exhaling. "Otherwise, he was incredible." He imagined Curry's uncovered prick. "Absolutely incredible."

"Not him," she said, annoyed. "My party, darling, the soiree."

Malcolm straightened his back. "I have two words for you, or maybe it's three, Miss Blaze: hors d'oeuvres."

The next phone call was from someone he'd met at another party a month ago, the wrestler who had trained on the DuPont compound until it had become too freaky. He was a young one, fresh from an Iowa high school with a graduating class of 29. His name was Cal, and he wondered whether Malcolm had plans for the evening.

"It just so happens," Malcolm said, rifling through the pages of *Wallpaper* as though it were his engagement calendar, "That I have a few hours free."

What he liked best about Cal was his spontaneity, these impromptu hook-ups, and that Cal was just shy of five foot six and had a killer leg-lock. Malcolm quickly changed the sheets, but left them mussed, took a shower, towel-dried his hair and did a few sit-ups, shooting not so much for fitness as for that lightly man-scented thing that seemed so popular these days.

There was no pretense with Cal. He came for two things: beer and ass. He drove through the door with a hard-on, the fly of his jeans half-open, and with his broad chest he pushed Malcolm into the kitchen, pinning him against the counter by the refrigerator, getting a bottle of Red Star for himself. "I have wine in the bedroom," Malcolm said.

Cal eyed him suspiciously. "No candles, right?"

"None," Malcolm said. "I swear."

"This has got to be quick," Cal said. "I have an awards banquet to go to tonight."

"Dressed like that?"

"Is that all you fags think about—clothes?"

Malcolm undid the fastenings of Cal's jeans.

"I hope you realize you just opened up a fresh can of whup-ass," Cal said, his grin all toothy like a perfect row of pearly white corn.

Cal believed that foreplay was for girls and fags. He let Malcolm suck on his hard joint just enough to wet it good, and he spat a gob on Malcolm's pucker. Malcolm—on his knees, chest to the mattress, his butt up and almost ready—closed his eyes. The initial stab was always the worst, but Cal had a cock that was perfectly suited for fucking—narrow-headed, flaring out at the base, giving him some formidable girth, and a set of rocks that swung furiously once they got going, banging Malcolm's balls hard, making them ache.

"You *are* going to take your shirt off, right?" Malcolm asked. He wanted, eventually, to be able to see Cal's chest, his huge areolae, the wispy corn silk that grew in the dip between his pecs, and the little tattoo of Casper the Friendly Ghost on his right hip.

Cal sighed, taking a deep dip into Malcolm's slick gash, and Malcolm gasped, not wanting to but unable to help himself, and thinking for some strange reason of Tom Curry, maybe because of the tickling fuzz on Cal's thighs that reminded Malcolm of the hairy man at Letitia's.

"I fucking missed this ride," Cal said, plunging, going up on his toes to get in deeper, wrapping his big arms around Malcolm's waist, his wrists trapping Malcolm's sweaty cock.

"Tell me you love Cal's dick," Cal whispered.

"I love it," Malcolm said compliantly.

"Say it."

"I did."

"No, like I did."

"I love Cal's dick?"

Cal stopped fucking, though firmly planted. "You're asking?"

"No," Malcolm panted, wanting to feel the rough ride of Cal's prick against his prostate where it had been lodged for the last five or so minutes. Its absence was driving him crazy. "I love Cal's dick," he shouted. "I fucking love Cal's motherfucking cock!"

"Oh, yeah, recognize the Cal-man's cock, baby. Recognize it." He made his thrusts short and quick, and Malcolm quickly realized that the ride was coming to an end. It was like being on a roller coaster—for all its brevity, it was a hell of a ride.

"Aw, shit now," Cal bellowed, and Malcolm lifted his torso, his back pressed against Cal's, whose sliding cock buttering up Malcolm's insides. Malcolm loved the buttons of Cal's tits against his shoulder blades, and he pulled out terrific amounts of come from his own hot, weary piece. Another change of sheets was in order.

Cal grabbed his beer and drank it down, pulling himself out of Malcolm's stink hole. "Dude," he said, "I'll be in town next week. See you then?"

"What do you think?" Malcolm said, his thighs all aflutter, sensing the imminent drip of his asshole.

He ran into Curry in the lobby of the Strand Theatre. *The wife's in the bathroom,* Malcolm figured, and wanted to make a quick exit. But no, he learned after Curry spotted him and waved him over. Curry'd left her home.

"She's not much for visual stimulation," Curry explained, and Malcolm nodded. "Which movie are you seeing?"

Malcolm bit his lip, a little embarrassed. *"You've Got Mail,"* he said, adding: "I'm a sucker for Meg Ryan. You?"

"She's the blond, right? She's all right, I guess."

"No, I mean which movie."

Curry looked up at the listings. "I hadn't really thought about it. *Armageddon,* I guess." He shrugged his shoulders. He was wearing a fuzzy sweater that gave him a football player's proportions. "I just wanted to get out of the apartment."

Malcolm looked over the listings himself, coming across a foreign film and getting an idea.

"You know," he said; "I heard this *Dead Dog Day* is awesome. Want to see that one?"

"Who's in it?" Curry asked.

"It's Asian—probably Jackie Chan."

"Who's she?"

What an angel, Malcolm thought, stepping up to the counter. "Two for *Dog,*" he said.

As he'd expected, the theatre was nearly empty save for an elderly couple sitting in the third row, sharing popcorn and talking loudly.

The two men sat in the back. Malcolm was eager for the lights to dim, having decided there was no dishonor in wrecking a marriage that was already earmarked for the divorce courts. He was beginning to consider himself a sort of divorce counselor and prepared himself to go down with the lights.

Tom Curry sat quietly, his big hands flat on the wide wales of his corduroys. He stared at the blank screen.

"You know," he started, turning to Malcolm, his gaze not eye level, but downward. "I spent a lot of time this week thinking about that party."

"You did?"

"A lot," Curry said, dragging his stare up the front of Malcolm's torso.

The film started. Up on the screen a mangy yellow dog licked himself in the middle of a dusty unpaved street until a battalion of small boys—"Are they Vietnamese?" Curry whispered, and Malcolm shrugged—pelted the rough-looking thing with rocks. Subtitles announced the film's title and the names of its actors. Malcolm settled in, slackening his body into his seat and sprawling outward until his massive thigh pushed roughly against Curry's.

"They look Vietnamese," Curry said, his leg rocking against Malcolm's ever so slightly and a little bit nervously. "Jackie Chan's not Vietnamese, is she?"

The film, as far as Malcolm could tell, was about the preparations this small village was making to celebrate a holiday—Dead Dog Day.

"What's the big pot for?" Malcolm asked. A huge cast-iron kettle, the likes of which one usually saw in cartoons about cannibals, simmered in the center of the village, the fire under it ministered to by the old women, squatting and cackling and poking the fire with sticks.

"I'm not sure," Curry said.

Malcolm increased his leg pressure, and Curry responded in kind so that they seemed both to be jockeying for more room with neither making any headway. Suddenly, Malcolm reached over and into Curry's crotch, taking a handful of his package and squeezing.

"I'm sorry," he said lightly. "I thought we had popcorn."

"I thought you might have forgotten where you were and wanted the remote control."

"It *is* bad, isn't it?"

Curry nodded.

"Well," Malcolm confessed, "I was thinking that the film would become something like background to another sort of activity."

"Like what?"

Malcolm smiled. "Like if those two up front turned around they'd only see one of us."

Curry puzzled a moment. Malcolm saw it on the man's face, and then it cleared, giving way to amusement. Curry began to fiddle with Malcolm's fly, the sudden attention causing Malcolm to harden, his dick doubling up and threatening to burst from its cramped quarters. One after another, Curry managed to unbutton Malcolm's fly. The project required much finagling, as the holes were smallish and the fit rather tight. It might have taken 20 minutes, but finally Curry managed to open Malcolm's jeans single-handedly, all the while trying to make the other hand look casual on the back of the seat beside him.

"I just want you to know," he said, glancing up at the screen, "that my experience at this point is perhaps not as extensive as what you might be accustomed to. Though I did come close to blowing another altar boy when I was 16." He drew back the waistband of Malcolm's briefs, baring the high-tension buzz of Malcolm's cock.

Malcolm watched the dark head tip forward and felt steamy breath in his crotch, Curry's tongue darting at first, then slowing to a long fat swab. He handled Malcolm's prick delicately, like caviar on toast points. Curry kissed the wet cock head, making it wetter, smearing his lips with Malcolm's salty balm. His lips parted, toothy gates lifting, and Malcolm entered the hot foyer of Tom Curry, his tongue flat as a welcome mat, the gape dripping with an astonishing amount of saliva. Malcolm wondered whether the back door would be so soft and wet. He wondered whether he would be allowed to make a delivery.

Curry's fingers walked up abdomen steps, hard rubber plates of muscle, up to the fat, flat nipples hanging from the undersides of Malcolm's pecs. A fine spray of hair covered Malcolm's belly, tapering at his sternum. His shirt, tight black rayon, rolled up his torso like a pair of nylons.

Curry's oral fixation amply compensated for his lack of experience. He explored Malcolm's cock from tip to base, every millimeter of skin, sucking on the piece like it was candy. He favored the head, tonguing and teething the rim of it and hitting that funny gut-sucking spot near the split that triggered a steadier stream of precome. Curry slurped loudly and suddenly froze. Up on the screen, a little boy was feeding a puppy in a bamboo cage. "You're safe now, little one," the subtitles read. The elderly couple was engrossed in the film and completely oblivious to the shenanigans behind them. Curry's slip of the tongue went unnoticed.

Curry jiggled his nutty handful and turned away from his labors a moment for some feedback. "Super job," Malcolm intoned, feeling slippery and kind and close. "Back to work," he said quickly, replacing Curry's mouthful. Curry wedged his way between Malcolm's formidable thighs again, rubbing them briskly as if to warm them—as if they weren't quite hot enough already. Malcolm tensed them and they turned to stone and Curry moaned, taking his mouth from Malcolm's hair-trigger piece to tell him about a dream he'd had:

"And you had your legs locked around my waist and you were squeezing the hell out of me. I couldn't breathe and it hurt like hell, but I had a hard-on like you wouldn't believe, and I woke up just as I was popping."

"Nice, nice, yeah, but could you, you know—" Malcolm whined.

Curry gripped the steely prick and Malcolm's juices ran like candle wax. They both regarded the swollen head, flat capped and blunt. Curry licked his lips and bowed his head. This was the home stretch.

Malcolm's orgasm seemed to originate mid thigh—the hairs there stood and waved. His balls tightened, shrinking up into him, and the bands of muscle above his groin quivered. He whispered, "Look out."

Curry's uvula received the first shot. It caught him unaware, despite the warning. He choked, falling backward. "Sweet Jesus!" he said, watching in amazement the fountain of come that leaped from the split end of Malcolm's cock—no less than eight ropy wads of semen.

"Switch," Malcolm said, unsure of what to do with the big mess he'd made of himself but otherwise determined to show Curry a good time. He scraped himself off and flicked the excess—and what excess—off his hands. Curry looked up from his haunches, shrugging.

"What?" Malcolm said, trying to get down on his own knees for a little reciprocation.

"No need," Curry said, plucking the front of his pants.

"Seriously?"

Curry shrugged again. "It doesn't happen like this at home, I'll tell you that much."

Malcolm lifted his eyebrows.

"I'm not kidding—I usually have to fake and hope the little precome I have suffices."

"Any kids?" Malcolm asked.

"What do *you* think?" Curry asked. "Are you dissatisfied?"

"Not really," Malcolm answered. "Just a little incomplete."

"I hear you," Curry said.

Malcolm grabbed Curry, who had stood, a little uncomfortably, getting ready to return to his seat and watch the rest of the film. Malcolm turned him around and undid the man's belt and threw down his trousers. "You might experience a little more *delay* this time around," Malcolm said, spinning Curry around and taking the man's come-sodden dick between his lips. It was soft, but big, a hefty droop, sweet and musty smelling. It buckled, filling Malcolm's mouth, and he felt the brush of pubes under his nose and the soft skin of Curry's balls against his chin. The cock pulsed to monumental proportion.

He tickled his fingers into the fuzzy split of Curry's ass, feeling the end of his spine and, lower, the wrinkled kiss of Curry's butthole. He stopped trying to swallow the man's dick down whole and asked, "Ever?" as he pressed a finger into the little volcano.

"I don't think so," Curry whispered.

"You don't *think*?"

"Well," Curry said. "I'm not sure I'm following you."

Malcolm pushed his finger a little deeper. "Ever get it up here?" he asked.

Curry dropped his ass a little, sucking up a little more of Malcolm's digit.

"Not that I know of," he said, "Although I was almost fucked by my first roommate in college."

"Hmm."

"Does that count?"

"Did he stick it in?"

Curry shrugged. "He was this big hockey player, nose like a cliff, fists all scabbed. He actually scared the shit out of me. But his dick was so—not that I cared or anything, but—*small*."

"But did he penetrate you with this little thing?"

Curry made a thinking face, slowly shaking his head. "We were doing shots of tequila." He pressed his fingertips to his eyelids. "Does it really matter?"

"That I'm the first?" Malcolm asked. "Not really. Not at all, really."

"Do you want to?" Curry asked.

"Fuck you—yeah."

Curry looked up at the screen. He looked like someone waiting for a bus. He leaned against the back of the seat in front of him. "I imagine it hurts the first time."

"But this might be the second—you can't remember."

"It *does* make a difference to you."

Malcolm shook his head. "No, no, no—I'm trying to convince you to go for it, for Christ's sake. Just go for it."

Curry looked down at Malcolm's flagpole, thought a moment, then turned around and sat down.

"Jesus," Malcolm muttered.

"My sentiments exactly," Curry gasped. "I guess I wasn't ready." Pulling out hurt him even more, but they were able then

132

to slick up Malcolm's cock with spit, and Curry, a firm believer in the virtue of getting back on the horse that threw him, sat down again, and Malcolm's wet prick slid into him with very little resistance.

Malcolm put his hands on top of Curry's thighs, and Curry kept his hands on the back of the seat in front of him, and they worked together silently, like some sort of human engine, fuel-injected, piston-popping. Sweat ran down Curry's back, into the furry ravine of his ass, over Malcolm's honey-dipped cock.

"Is it hot in here?" Curry asked.

"It's just you," Malcolm breathed, reaching under Curry's shirt and finding two pearls to twist and turn. He grabbed handfuls of pecs, gripping them mercilessly.

"Oh, God," Curry whispered.

The movie, unfortunately, had come to an end. "Jesus, that was fast," Curry muttered, pushing his fanny onto Malcolm's prong with a little more urgency. "If they don't stay for the credits, we're screwed."

"You most certainly are," Malcolm said, standing up, his cock slamming Curry's insides. He bent his dick-recipient over the seat-back and fucked him with tight rabbit-like humps that caused Curry to hold his breath and fist himself in a strangling manner, hosing out a spray of freshly manufactured come. Malcolm felt his eyes cross, and he fell over Curry's broad back, his cock pulsing, emitting a nut-clenching load up Curry's ass.

"Jesus," Malcolm sputtered, sitting down shakily while Curry flicked his own spew from his fist.

"Yeah," Curry agreed.

"Are you hungry?"

"For what?" Curry asked, turning around. The couple up front were getting up, satisfied with what they'd seen.

"Remarkable," Malcolm heard one of them say.

Yes, quite, he thought to himself.

GOING QUEER

Clay Newton decided to go queer, I guess, the second time he was in my parents' hot tub. It was the smoothest transition from hetero to homo that I'd ever been a party to—not that I've been invited to many of those parties. One day he was shelling out a couple of hundred bucks to pay for the Kleiven girl's abortion—yeah, it really was his—and the next he was sitting in the hot tub with me. Well, not sitting, exactly: he was munching tacos, and he had his foot between my legs, trying to work his big toe up my ass, and wondered out loud how my little chin beard would feel against his newly razored balls. This from a boy as pussy-dedicated, to my knowledge anyway, as Rocco Sifredi, and with a dick to match—not that I'd seen it before then. Even this night in the hot tub, our second, we were both wearing shorts—until we weren't, that is—and Clay's jams were tight enough across the crotch to disclose the thick wad there, a covered terrain with which I was all too familiar.

I didn't know him for shit, to tell you the truth—I mean, not in the classic sense. I was watching my parents' new condo as they travel-trailered across the USA. I was between jobs, between apartments, between boyfriends. Clay lived next door with his parents, just out of college with a bullshit degree in business. He was as ambitious as I was that summer. The only straining I did was over some Internet porn. I'd thought about trying to hook up online, but it seemed like too much trouble. Besides, there was Clay next door.

Late one afternoon I was jacking off to some Internet pics of guys in Speedos when I heard the dribble of a basketball next door and the vibrating rattle of the backboard taking another shot. I traded the porn for a few stolen moments at the front window, watching Clay Newton work up a sweat in his driveway, shirt discarded, shorts sagging to reveal the waistband (and then some) of his Structure briefs.

It wasn't just that he was built, that his shoulders were nearly three feet from deltoid to deltoid, that his pecs were tipped with wide brown nipples which were in turn surrounded by rings of dark hairs. It wasn't just that his fine rippled gut dipped down, separating his bared hipbones. Not just that his calves were as thick as Sunday hams. And it wasn't just that his green eyes, overshadowed by the sweep of dark bangs, glanced my way as I pulled on my spit-soaked hard-on. No: It was the thick bobble in his shorts; the jumping, banging baggage there that he fumbled with again and again, constantly poking, pulling, tugging, scratching, readjusting. I ruined my mother's curtains over and over, watching him miss easy lay-ups, dribbling back to the end of the drive with one hand, the other dug deep into the bunched crotch of his shorts.

One day the ball glanced off the backboard and came bouncing into my parents' yard. I hadn't really noticed, trying hard to avoid another mess on my mother's sheers, cuffing my dick closer and closer to a glutinous end, having watched my neighbor huff and sweat and grope himself for half an hour. I opened my eyes for one more inspirational glance, ready to put down another basketball fan's load, when I noticed his driveway was empty. Just then, Clay stood with his ball, catching me window-side and dick-handed. I dropped to my knees, not knowing what else to do, quickly trying to figure what he might or might not have seen from his vantage point, given the height of the window sill and his own line of sight. He had seen everything— at least a quick glance, I decided, come dripping dejectedly out of my sorry cock.

"My ball," I heard him say through the window. I tried to nod solemnly. He was smiling as I let the sheers fall closed, and I crawled out of sight behind the sofa, wounded with mortification.

There were boys who mowed the lawns—I didn't have to do anything except make sure I sent out the checks for the house-hold bills on time, which were all written, dated and stamped for me—a piece of cake. These lawn boys, they look younger than 18, but the one that did my parents' yard, who eyed me up as I sprawled on a hammock—spread-legged and spilling out of my shorts, no less—swore he was 21, and he went for his driver's license to prove it. I'd already given him a beer and a shot—a clear shot of my crotch, and he found something else to fumble for in his pocket, namely a hefty semi. A fountain of hair rose up from his ripstop shorts, which were hip-slung and uncovered the top half of his boxers, his shirt hanging like an off-centered tail from his back pocket. He hadn't told me his name yet.

He eyed the house suspiciously, as though I had some hidden surveillance center or a surprise birthday party secreted inside. He emptied the beer with a couple of loud swigs. I watched his lips come off the bottle. He burped softly and lifted the brim of his palm-greased baseball hat. His eyes were Hershey brown, and the stubble on the side of his head was translucent.

"You want another?" I asked, and he looked at the house then turned, glancing over his shoulder. The idle mower sat in the middle of clipped green. He was done for the day—he knew it. I knew it. He handed me the empty, nodding.

His cock hung like a tree branch from his groin, wood-stiff, drippy. He studied my mother's Lladró collection, my father's hand-carved duck decoys, and the collection of pictures of me from kindergarten through high school, through 13 different hairstyles.

"Black eye," he says, looking at sixth grade. So far, he'd been monosyllabic, and I hadn't minded much, enjoying a man of few words and a dick like a billy club. He'd asked which way to the toilet when we first entered the house, and came back with his dick hard and poking out of his fly. He didn't offer an explanation and I didn't ask for one. He looked down at his thick, bobbing pole, and I sat down hard on my father's recliner.

"You like it?" he asked. What wasn't to like? I tried shrugging.

"It's big, right?" he asked, and I gave him my best "sort of" nod.

"Damn straight," he said, and he slapped it around, sending droplets of pre-jizz flying. I imagined my mother coming home and walking around the living room and quizzing my father: "Where in heaven's name did all this *semen* come from, Walter?"

"You think so?" I asked, and he smirked. His glance dropped to the front of my shorts.

"Is that big?" he said, and I shrugged again.

"Size is relative," I told him, and he snorted.

"Well, meet my motherfuckin' cousin," he said, stepping forward. I sat up, leaning toward him, wanting to get closer. Pink and thick and heavy-headed, he swayed in front of me, and the want I felt for him made me dizzy. I made a grab for him, getting the warm tube of it in my grip, and I pulled him to me, pulling out crystalline pearls that appeared fully formed in the slot of his piss hole.

He worked his face into an almost comically stoic expression. His shaft was harder than any other part of him—bones aren't as hard—and he covered his chest with folded arms. I made his grass-greened shorts fall to the floor, admiring the inventive plaid of his boxers. I heard him breathe through his nose, short bursts that usually signal something strenuous—resolve or something, I was thinking, picturing a diver on the board, about to attempt a triple whatever, so I was not expecting the huge gush that sprayed my face and the arm of the recliner.

"Christ," I said.

"Sorry, bud," he replied. "There's more, though," he added, and he took my hand off his cock and started jerking himself off. He stared hard at the tented front of my shorts, wet with white dots that weren't mine. His balls banged against his fist, and his cock made a slapping noise against his palm.

"Let me see it," he grimaced, the words tight and lip-bound. I hauled out my cock, a stubby blunt thing with a head reminiscent of a mushroom cap. His lower lip shined; the pink tip of his tongue flickered just inside. He slapped his cock around again like a wad of pizza dough. He stepped out of the shackles of his fallen shorts and climbed aboard the USS *Recliner* with me, straddling my middle. His cock lay between my tits appreciatively, enjoying the cleavage I'd built with bench presses and inclined-fly presses. He left a buttery trail there, grabbing himself again.

I wanted him to lean back so that he might feel the press of my dick against the cleavage of his ass cheeks. I wiggled a finger behind his balls, and he moaned and let me wiggle my way inside him. He steadied himself with one hand by my head, and I stared into the mossy cave of his underarm, smelling him. His asshole was tight and as daunting as a New York bouncer; he let me in a little at a time, joint by joint, until I could press on the inner doorbell, the hardened knob of his prostate, gaining full access, total entry.

"Aww, Stuart," I heard him say.

"Hmmm?" I asked. "What's that? Stuart?"

The boy blushed down to his chest. Red spread across his cheeks like wine on a tablecloth.

"Me," he said sheepishly. "I'm Stuart."

I smiled and pushed into him. His eyes closed and he put his face close to mine. I could smell his quickening breaths. He whispered "Stuart" again, humping my finger. My cock filled his ass crack, riding along his tailbone. His slippery prick rutted my belly. His bush was black, his dick was ruddy, his prickly scalp rasped my cheek.

I opened him up and played my dick against his fingered hole, testing. He bumped his puckered lips against the fat head, making noises that sounded welcoming. I got inside a little at a time, making him gasp and squeeze his eyes shut. He took what he could as he could, working his hole slowly down the length of my shaft until he was satisfied with his intake, although he howled when I took my first tentative thrust, which was as gentle as I could manage. "You ain't the first," he said, because maybe I was looking a little cocky.

"The second, though," I told him, "and the first had a tiny prick."

His mouth opened. "You're a palm reader."

His ass was furnace-hot and had an exceptionally firm grip, a real he-man handshake. *We might not have to do anything more than this,* I thought, holding the boy who had curled up against my chest, his lips at my neck, his fingers in my ear. I felt every rippling shudder his insides made, playing my dick like a slide trombone.

I held him by the ass, keeping him far enough away to allow for some thrust. I eased out and then back in, then out again, and he was perfectly still, his tongue darting out of his mouth and onto my throat.

"Is this OK?" I asked, and he nodded. He played with my tit and I heard him say he liked it fine. I went into him a little more insistently.

"Yeah," he said, tilting his head back. His eyes were still closed. I fucked him harder and he said, "Yeah," with each thrust, and I made each one more forceful, and deeper, and I tried to make him say no, to say stop, but he kept on saying, "Yeah," and then I couldn't stop myself. I slammed into him, making loud grunts that grew louder the closer I got to coming.

"Not yet," he whispered. "Not yet, not yet." And he started getting himself off with short, tight-fisted strokes, trying to catch up with me. I opened my mouth and he stuck his fingers there and I squirted off into him, and I looked down to see his cock gush, come flying out of him in thick white ribbons between us, draping my chin, my chest, my gut.

"And then he licked me clean," I told Clay.

"Get the fuck out," Clay said loudly. "His own splooge? That's fucking sick!"

I stared, incredulous. *Could it be that he's never eaten his own jizz? Impossible,* I thought. I wasn't having it.

"Fuck you, Newton—you've eaten your own, and you know it."

He looked at me, shock all over his face.

"That is fucking gross," he said simply. "It's like picking your nose and eating it."

I shrugged my shoulders. "Yeah? So?"

He shifted in the tub, reconfiguring his long legs. His toes popped out of the water to my left. He draped his arms along the fiberglass edge behind him. He changed the subject.

"So you're a basketball fan, too?" he said, his grin arrogant, all chin.

I settled into the water, letting it rush across my lips. "I like to watch," I said after a moment of silence.

"You sure do," he said, shifting his body a bit, his huge calf bumping me. "Don't mind watching myself. I wouldn't mind watching you and your lawn jockey doing a little one-on-one."

"Wouldn't you?" I said. I propped myself over his feet, pressing my wrist against his ankle. He toed my forearm. "And just what do you hope to gain from such spectacle, Mr. Newton?"

"Well, Mr. Flanagan," he said, smiling goofily, "a little insight, a little insight."

"Take off your shorts, Clay, and I'll give you some insight."

I watched him finish off another taco, getting shredded lettuce in the frothing water. "All in good time, Wade," he said, his mouth still full.

Not long after that night, there was a knock on my door. I figured it was Clay and was surprised to find the grass cutter, Stuart, on my doorstep.

"I think I left my lawn mower here, sir," he said, obviously liquored up and giggly. He had his hands shoved into the pockets of his oversize jeans. His shirt was too big, too, and did not reveal any of the sweet contours I had explored the week before.

"You left something, but it wasn't a lawn mower," I told him, and a lopsided grin spread across his face. I opened the screen door and he stumbled through, falling against me, and I could smell the whiskey and cigarette smoke of his evening out. Catching him, I felt the muscles of his arms, the tightness of him. He bumped my chest with his forehead, butting me, and I held on to him, closing the door.

His shirt fell to the floor—he was more nimble-fingered than I would have expected. His wife beater glowed against his tanned skin.

"Gotta beer?" he said, swaying. He played with himself through the front of his jeans.

"Later," I said.

I stripped him down to his hard-on in the middle of my parents' living room. His cock was beautiful, jutting from a thick chestnut bush. I went to my knees before him and started to suck him. He grabbed my head roughly—lustfully, I was thinking, but more to steady himself, and before I took a drop of precome he asked if he could "sit this one out." He fell onto the couch, his head back. His dick stood thick and tall. He lifted his head, squinting at me.

"Well?" he said. "Get going."

I got between his legs, my hands on his smooth thighs, and put my mouth on the fat pink head of his crotch monument. I licked into the split and tasted the first seepage, working up a good amount by squeezing his shaft like a near-empty tooth-paste tube.

"Aw, Stuart," he said. I agreed. "Shtuarr," I gulped.

He used his hips to derrick my mouth with his fatty. I choked on him, holding on to his waist, after positioning his bare feet on my thighs. He played with my hair and said sweet things I couldn't hear. I had him at the back of my throat and kept him there, holding him still, trying to swallow his fat head.

"Well, Jee-zus!" he whispered as he leaned forward to watch. When I pulled myself off him, my spit hung between us like a thick rope, and he slapped the side of my face lightly and said, "Boy, you got that right!"

I got myself out of my shorts, stood up, and gave him my dick to contemplate for a while. He sucked me roughly and without any finesse, holding my shaft like a ballpark frank. It felt great nonetheless, and I put my hands on my hips and enjoyed the boy's handiwork. He gobbled and snorted and huffed all over my crotch until, just when I thought he was getting REALLY good, he leaned back and said, "Well, let's get to some fucking!"

He pulled me onto the couch with him and turned me over, getting me butt-up across his lap. He licked a finger and poked it between my ass cheeks. He found my hole easily—and he found my hole easy: I was only too happy to be the recipient of his big fat cock. I squirmed and put up a good fight, all the while working my dick across his muscular thighs. He got hold of me and maneuvered me into a sitting position, squatting over his oozing pole. I sat on him, his cock filling me like none before, and I gasped like a virgin, and he laughed behind me.

"I hear that all the time," he said, all proud of himself. At that point, I was glad to be facing away from him, not wanting my grimace to give him any satisfaction. I slipped down his shaft slowly, careful now not to show any signs of discomfort. When I felt his curlies on my stretched-out ass lips, I took a deep and well-deserved breath. *Motherfucker, he's a wide one,* I was thinking. He reached around me on both sides and played with my tits and put his mouth on my back, licking between my shoulder blades. He pumped his big prick up into me, invading my innards. *My spleen!* I thought, or whatever you call that thing he was poking and hurting. I managed to pivot myself on the staff of his cock so that I was facing him, letting him chew on my nipples and more or less controlling what he did and didn't hit up inside me.

"Aww, Stuart," he said, looking me in the eye. His tongue played between his lips. He slapped my ass cheeks and brought me down on him hard, and my dick bounced off his muscled gut, and he spat on it, on us, and made a slick slide for me. I was slipping between the two of us, and he slapped my ass again and fucked me hard.

"You're big, you're fucking big," I said, putting my face near his, wanting to kiss him. He looked away.

"Someone's watching," he said, his face stony and still.

"Probably my fucking neighbor," I said. "He's cool."

"Yeah? Cool," Stuart said and continued to slide up into me, although he became a little more showy, getting me facedown on the couch, our asses to the window, fucking me with broad ball-slapping thrusts. One hand behind his back, he pumped me hard, and smacked my behind again and again. I squeezed down hard on his prick, my own about to burst, and he sucked in his breath.

"Man!" he spit and yanked himself out of me, leaving my hole gaping. I felt him shoot all over my back. I scrambled then, getting on my knees, not wanting to get any more come on my mother's sofa. I turned fast and tossed off a nut all over Stuart's face, just able to make out the shadowy figure behind the sheers: Clay Newton hanging courtside, watching the whole dirty scene.

"Man," he said, dipping low in the hot tub. "You two were fucking hot, that's all I got to say."

His feet bubbled between my spread legs and his dick buoyed. It was charming, all pink and fat and sturdy-looking— an excellent piece, and quite a bit larger than I'd given him credit for. He found my soft spot with his big toe, and I swallowed some tub water. He laughed at my spitting, and I heard him say over the roar of water that he was seriously considering switching teams.

"For a little while," he said. "You know, experimental and everything. Hey! I shaved my nuts, did you notice?" He lifted his torso up out of the water, and I leaned close to inspect, my balls draping his feet.

He grabbed a taco from the bag behind his head. "You hungry?" he asked.

I couldn't answer—my mouth was already full.

ONE OF THE BOYS

Mr. Arden sat in the bleachers. I knew him pretty well because he was a neighbor and I'd gone to school with his son, the one they called Sandy because of the color of his hair. The rest of us, his school friends, called him Pete, his regular name. There was something else about him, though, not just his hair, that made him sandy—to me at least—and that was the way he slipped through my fingers right when I thought I had him. He was in Arizona now, engaged or something, and I was working a concession stand for this Triple-A baseball team, handing out beer and dogs, swatting flies, pretending to be interested in the girls going by. The girls did indeed go by, and Rick Devert—better known as The Pervert—stared them all down, looking right at their tits, following their asses, licking his lips and touching himself through his jeans shorts. Missy, our boss, would flick him with a rag or toss a cup of water down his back when he got out of control. She was barely able to keep him from drooling.

"They're fucking *girls*," she would say. "Children, you fucking pervert."

"I know, I know," he'd say, getting his hands under his apron and pretending to whack off, anything to piss Missy off. But putting money in the cash register wrong pissed Missy off. It just didn't take much.

I could see part of Steve Arden from my place at the stand, see the funny tan lines on his ankles from his little golf socks, his bare heels coming out of his deck shoes. I could have walked out from the booth and reached up and tickled his feet if I'd wanted

144

to. He might have been 45, but I think he was closer to 40. I remembered his last birthday, hanging out on the edges of a backyard party with Pete, a little stoned from half a joint and plenty buzzed from a shared six-pack, a week away from graduation and loving it. When it was dark, the parents put on the "Saturday Night Fever" soundtrack, and Pete and I hung out for a while, watching our parents dance by the pool.

Pete's eyes hung a long time on Mrs. Don Vito, who was at the party alone because her husband hadn't come home from work one night a month ago. She was doing some dance in between Mr. Arden and Mr. Hogan.

"She's got nice tits," Pete said quietly.

I said, "Yeah," but I was really more interested in the bug-zapping lamp that crackled and flickered by the garage. "Did you see that?" I said, nudging him.

We were in discarded lawn chairs, tiki torches burning behind our heads, throwing our shadows and competing with the light from the pool and the Arden's back deck. Pete leaned over and put a finger between his toes, hair falling into his eyes. I watched him.

I was hoping that Mr. Arden would come by the stand for a beer or something because I want to ask him about Pete—like how he's doing and when he's coming back.

Devert sucked beer through a straw stuck in a soda cup, giving Missy the eye, and put singles into the cash drawer upside-down while blowing her kisses. "Fuck you, Devert," she said smiling quietly, not wanting the customers to hear.

The Mudhens were losing yet another game. We called them the Dudhens. They were a bunch of cocky assholes who played lousy ball and acted like fucking studs the way they cruised around, chatting up the local girls and getting laid because they'd met Sammy Sosa. The local girls were pretty gullible, especially the ones that hung around the ballpark.

There was one ball player who gave me a good vibe—Billy

Dale, the first baseman. I liked the way he looked in his uniform. Seeing him suited up made me wish for some reason to be in the locker room with this bunch of sorry fucks. I'd have been willing to hang out with these sad sacks at the end of another woefully lost game, the whole mess of them dejected and getting ready for a shower, just so I could catch a glimpse of Billy Dale, naked and sweaty, soap and towel in hand. I imagined his jockstrap a musky, wet memory on the floor tangled up in his cleats.

Dale had furry forearms, sinewy, leg-thick. I turned into a little girl when I saw him walking across the field, adjusting and readjusting his cap, his ass switching tightly, setting off little hot alarms in my brain, and I'd get all faggy, my dick swelling and worrying me. Just not cool.

Devert drove me home because my car had been stolen. He was talking about sex all the way, and I was glad I only lived a few blocks from the ballpark. I was thinking I just should have walked, and then I looked over at Devert's hand resting on the crotch of his shorts.

"And then there was this girl at the shore," he was saying, his fingers doing a little dance on his fly, hypnotizing me. I got that little head-spinning rush I'd been getting lately, kind of like getting dizzy, but really it was about getting horny. I felt my cock squirm in my pants, wrestling with itself in the damp pouch of my briefs.

"Love sucking pussy," I heard him say. He held himself in a pinch, the head of his dick clearly the size of a golf ball. I stared. He pulled over in front of my apartment. "You have a PlayStation, don't you?"

I nodded slowly, barely comprehending.

"My parents took mine away when I got arrested," he said. "Can I come up? Do you have any beer?"

I had a studio in Centre Parke. Everybody knew about it because *Dateline NBC* had filmed a drug bust here last year and the dealer jumped from the roof of my four-story building and

146

managed to escape on a broken foot. I didn't even know he was a dealer—he was pretty cool, always said, "Hey, how you doing, brother?" He was kind of good-looking, even—a little skinny, though, looking kind of like Matthew Broderick on a slightly bad day.

Devert flopped on the couch and immersed himself in Duke Nukem, and I sat off to the side watching him, lowering my standards. I started finding him attractive, more attractive with each beer I chugged.

"Aw, fuck, that bitch at the shore tore me up," he said, grabbing himself. "Left her fucking teeth marks."

I saw this as an opportunity. I'd actually been thinking of Billy Dale strutting by me before the game started, getting his ritual soft pretzel at the next stand. He took it back to the dugout, and it sat beside him, laced over with mustard, uneaten. I was thinking how nice it must be, being Billy Dale's good luck charm, even if you're just a pretzel.

"Whatever," I said, an edge of challenge in my voice. "You're so full of shit, Devert. I swear to God, you might as well talk over a toilet, the shit you say."

"Yeah?" he said. "Well, fuck you. I ain't lying." And he yanked down his zipper and dug into his pants and pulled out his prick. "Now tell me you don't fucking see teeth marks."

I looked down at the enormous wad, awestruck, speechless. It was fat and long and spilled out of his grip. Tumbling below the base of his fist was a pale set of balls. I leaned forward, inspecting, and noticed Devert's hand closing, inflating the prick, and pulling it away from its nut sac.

"It's—" I said.

"Bigger than you'd imagined," he finished for me. I nodded. "It's not hard yet, though," he said, smiling.

"I ain't into no gay shit," he added.

"Whatever," I said.

"Are you?"

I made a face that clearly said, *No way*, but I was staring at his

147

crotch in a way that could only be described as gay. I wanted to feel the soft snaky thing stiffen on my tongue, ready even to sniff the rank underside of his balls and lick his asshole, if that's what was required of me.

"Do you know what the chicks say when they see this?" he asked me. I shook my head.

"Nothing, dude. They're speechless."

I was thinking again of Billy Dale's pretzel, the way he squirted the mustard over it. I was hard, poking up in my jeans, very uncool.

"Like you," he said. "Speechless. Why don't you say something?"

I shrugged.

"You can suck me off, or whatever," he said, simply. "I don't do anything else, though." He was still holding on to the game controls: Duke stood still.

I nodded, swallowing.

The cock inched upward, stiffening. It fattened and lengthened obscenely. Rick Devert had a porn dick, much to my amazement. He looked down at it, indulgent and hopeful. I looked down, too, unable to process the dimensions. I was looking at a little Devert—a stick version of the man himself.

He stood up and undid what was holding up his pants and I sat there, shaking my head. His prick fell at an odd angle, engorged, twitching and stiff, a new addition to Devert, another limb. He whacked it lovingly, pleased with his possession. I knew I was pleased. He blushed and shook his head and made his pecker wag shyly. I touched the pink helmet, a crystal dot emerging from the piss slit already.

"Dude," he said, and I leaned toward him, ready to taste the Devert stick. He flinched when I touched him with my tongue. He tasted like butter, better than butter, more like margarine, and I leaned back to tell him so, but he told me to shut up.

"I tell all my bitches that," he added, apologizing.

I went back to work. I gripped him, but my fingertips didn't

148

come close to touching my palm—he must have been five inches in diameter. I fisted his pole by the base, where he was thickest, and he settled his ass into my sofa, picking up the joystick again. It pleased me to think I'd be able to give him the kind of attention that would make Devert stop thinking about girls—for a little while, at least.

I was thinking about my own first time, for some reason. It was with Paul—beautiful Paul—the guy I met up on Skyline Drive. We'd walked down a path, swatting flies, nervous as shit. He'd worn Calvin Klein jeans and a nice shirt and said he worked in town, at the court house, and I'd thought maybe I'd see him again, like maybe I'd see Billy Dale up there looking to get off. About as likely. Never saw him again. I was thinking that was how it would be with Devert, how it would be so cool if I never saw him again after this. I was thinking of how it was going to be in our stand, standing next to him cruising minors and selling hot dogs. It seemed unbearable sometimes, but staring down a 10-incher was a different proposition altogether. I put the fucker in the back of my throat. Devert.

He touched my head, which was totally uncool, because he was fucking up my gel—I was going to have to reactivate the shit. He did something stupid that made the television come on, and suddenly we were watching *The Real World*. The dyke from Hawaii was passed out and topless, ready for the ambulance— and I was totally freaking out because she looked like my very best friend from high school, who'd gone through the same fucking thing.

But I kept sucking. I sucked Devert like he was the last man on Earth. I slurped him down like a raw clam, all 10 inches of him. Thankfully, his formidable tool wasn't as difficult to manage as I'd originally thought it would be.

"Sweet," Devert murmured, almost tenderly.

"Don't," I said when I could, because it was a little too easy, the way he was slipping to the back of my throat. It was fucked up, really, the ease with which I took him in. I swallowed him to the base, my nose tickled by his stinky pubes, and he giggled, feeling tickled himself.

"Dude," he laughed, and I tried to laugh, too, with a mouth full of prick. He rolled out of me, a pretty sight.

"You're a little too fucking good at this, bro," he said. I had my hands on his knees, moving them back and forth. His dick stuck up, dripping, and he made it twitch. He was killing monsters— the game had just resumed—and his gaze kept going from the TV to me and back again, the game pad resting on my head. "You done already? Your jaw aching?" He smirked at me, spreading his legs wide. I caught a whiff of french-fry grease and drool between us.

"You started it," he said. "Now finish."

I went back to him, getting the sticky knob into my mouth, using my hand to stroke the thick shaft. He stiffened again and dropped the game controls to play with his titties, his breath hastening now, the muscles of his thighs going to stone under my elbows.

"More hand," he said, his voice not his own anymore. "More fucking hand." And I backed off to tickle the slick slit of his dickhead and I whacked the shit out of the slippery stalk, pounding my fist into his crotch.

"There you go," he started saying with each quickening breath. His head rolled back and forth, and I pulled harder until he sat up straight, prick rigid and pulsing. Then he sent up fireworks of white, wet sparks. I capped him and swallowed what I could, but there was so much of it, all this warm, gushy pudding. I swallowed and swallowed, and there was still some of him dripping out of my mouth.

He stood up fast, panting, getting away from me.

"That was freaky," he said. "Fucked up." He pulled his pants up, putting his wet monster away. He looked around, as though he was missing something. "I gotta go. Cool?"

"Cool," I said.

He patted his pockets, smoothed down the lumpy front

between them, pulled at the bottom of his shirt to cover as much as he could.

I thought maybe things would be fucked up at the hot dog stand with Devert, but everything was exactly the same, as though that night had slipped into some time warp and had never really happened. He was the same old Devert, grabbing himself for the girlies and talking about this bitch and that one, nudging me when one of his favorites walked by, saying, "That one makes me wet, bro."

"Business as usual" was something else he said to me, most-ly when Missy was taking a cigarette break and we were alone and there wasn't anything to do but kick back. Then Devert would put his foot up on one of the kegs, and I would stare at his greasy apron front—like it was a map and I was lost. That's when he'd say it, "Business as usual"—a warning to keep things cool. Things were very cool.

I saw Mr. Arden often enough to wonder about him. I won-dered why he was coming to the games by himself, and then I thought, well, maybe he missed Pete. I know I did.

I needed to find a real job, but liked sleeping late and bor-rowing the money from the folks when rent was due. "Better than going to college," I reminded them. Cheaper, anyway. My old man was quick to agree, and my ma would slap him with the newspaper she was reading, and he'd ask, "What'd I do?"

Sometimes I read the papers myself, looking for work, trying to fit myself into some position that didn't require too much education. But I didn't think I could handle that kind of daily grind, and my dad said, "Maybe bartending's something you ought to consider—hear them boys make some pretty good money for themselves, good-looking ones like yourself."

There was a beer deck at the ball field—that seemed like a good place to start—and one of the guys there looked like he could whack a ball pretty good himself. He had a big smile that dazzled me—you can see why I didn't feel like leaving the

Mudhens' stomping grounds—so I looked into making a move. I was turning 21 in two weeks. In my opinion, I was perfect for the job.

Pete, Pete, Pete, I was thinking one night, a little high, a little lonely, lying on the couch listlessly playing Road Rash on the Play Station, the game control firm against my crotch, steering my motorcycle again and again into pedestrians. I was starting training as a bartender the next day, working with the guy with the amazing smile; it was almost like he was embarrassed about something, or knew something I didn't. Either way, J.B.—that was his name—was short but packed, and I liked the way he looked me up and down and said I'd do OK. I was glad to be leaving Devert and Missy, too. Devert was getting a little weirder every day, trying to make sure, I guess, that I knew that what had happened between us was a total fluke and unrepeatable. Not that I minded much, but still, it would have been nice to have another stab at his proud, fat porker. How often do you come across 10 stiff inches?

Anyway, it seemed like everything was going my way, but I was feeling low at the moment, having called the number Pete's dad gave me at the last game. He wasn't there, and the answering machine picked up, and I left a lame, stuttering message about getting his number, and I saw Sedona on the Weather Channel, and then I felt completely stupid—like I watch The Weather Channel!—so I added quickly that I hoped he was doing well and all that, and I hung up.

The phone rang, and I cheered up fast, psyched as hell to talk to my bud.

"Hey," I said, trying to sound all fucked-up, and I heard this surprised voice on the other end say, "Kevin?"

"Mr. Arden," I said, snapping out of it and sitting up straight.

"I'm sorry. At first it didn't sound like you," he said.

"Oh," I said, "I was just fuck—I mean fooling around." I was screwing up big-time.

Thankfully, he moved things along. "I was calling to—oh, by the way, did you speak with Sandy yet?"

"Uh, not yet. I did just leave a message on his answering machine, though."

"Oh, great, then. Hey, the missus has got it into her head that we need a flagstone patio at the end of the lawn. I was wondering if you were free this weekend to give me a hand. Of course, I'll pay for your services," he added quickly, which made me smile. I liked thinking about servicing Steve Arden. He was thick and solid and kept himself in shape with five-mile runs and workouts in the gym.

The Mudhens were away that weekend, so I said sure, I'd be happy to give him a hand.

"Thanks a lot, Kevin. Come by early Saturday morning—around eight, OK?"

"Eight's fine," I said, and we hung up.

J.B. was teaching me how to serve beer from a tap. "You got to tip the cup until the foam hits the nozzle, then you straighten the cup and slowly drop it down until the head's at the lip, see what I mean?" I watched his hand, veins all over the back of it, his wedding ring glowing dully, a reminder to me that sometimes a smile was just a smile. He held the cup up for me to see his handiwork, and I nodded admiringly. What the fuck else was I going to do? His wrists made my dick twitch—that's all I knew at that moment.

"So that's about it," J.B. said, giving me another one of those grins, white teeth shining between his plump, sexy lips, which I wanted to kiss. "What do you think?" he asked me.

"About what?" I said, realizing I'd been caught fantasizing. I was sure I was found out—like it was printed out across my forehead or something—and I heard him snort, watched him shake his head.

"Oh, I don't know—about the fucking job, what do you think?" He crossed his arms over his chest like an umpire waiting out a rain delay, and I scratched an itch and looked out over the left-field seats.

"I think I'm going to like it fine," I said and left it at that.

Saturday morning, I got myself out of bed and rode my bike over to Mr. Arden's house. He met me at the door in his pajama bottoms, holding a cup of coffee. His chest was hazed over with a fine spray of brown hairs, soft and wispy looking, swirling like pencil marks all over him and he had a set of tits that rode high and wide atop his rib cage. He pushed open the screen door, and I pretended not to notice his flat gut, pretended not to see the knock his dick was doing as he stepped back to let me in. "How you doing, bud?" he asked.

"Fine and dandy, Mr. Arden," I said, walking to the kitchen.

"You drink coffee?" I heard him ask behind me, and I told him I'd been known to drink a cup or two, which kind of made him laugh, and I turned back to smile and caught his eyes on my ass.

"Well," he said. His face lit up when he realized I'd caught him. The corners of his eyes wrinkled when he smiled and said, "Well, let's have a cup before we start then."

Mrs. Arden was gone and wasn't coming back soon, late afternoon at the soonest. We had our cups of coffee, sitting at the kitchen table, talking like a couple of guys about the Mudhens and their shitty season.

"I don't know what's wrong with Blanchard," Mr. Arden said, taking a sip from his cup.

"Dude, I know—it's like he went cross-eyed or something. Can't catch anything anymore."

"He says it's the new lights," Arden said, nodding.

"Whatever," I said, finishing my coffee and wondering when the work was going to start. It was going on 9:30, and Arden was looking like he was ready to go back to bed, sitting there in his pajama pants and bare feet, gazing sleepily at his mug. He tapped his wedding ring against the rim and looked up at me.

"You have breakfast?" he asked, as if I actually kept eggs in the fridge and cereal in my cupboard. I said, "Nah," anyway, though I wasn't hungry, but Arden said, "Come one, let me make you some eggs," then he reached out and flipping my hair around with his fingers, like I was a little kid or something, and I ducked my head, not wanting to let him see me smile.

He stood up and went over to one of the counters. "More coffee?" he asked. I looked over at him standing there, seeing the long press his cock made against his pajama bottoms. He asked again. He didn't look to me like anyone's dad, but it was still hard not to connect him with Pete, his Sandy. I remembered the summer when I'd gone with the Ardens to the shore and seen Pete and his father wrestling in the breaking water, the muscles across Pete's back shining, Arden's arms doubling from exertion, their shouts and grunts coming to me over the waves. Arden's shorts had slipped down as he twisted out of Pete's grasp, the tops of his ass cheeks as pale as the breakers themselves. Later that night, when I was alone on the couch downstairs, I took away their clothes and their family name and made them lovers and jacked off to the two of them grappling for one another in the sun.

After eggs and toast and more coffee, Arden was still half-dressed. It was nearly eleven. I could see the stack of flagstone from where I was sitting. Arden looked up at the clock over the sink. "I told him around nine, and I guess he's taking me literally. Maybe he thought I meant nine P.M."

"Who?" I asked, my arm over the back of the chair. I didn't have to go anywhere anymore, so I was content to sit and watch the lap dance Arden's dick was doing as he walked around his kitchen cleaning up. I wasn't so sure I could stand up anyway without betraying myself. I'd been nursing a swollen prick for almost an hour and had sprung a major leak that was becoming embarrassingly apparent. I was thinking of actually spilling some orange juice on my crotch—accidentally—for cover.

"J.B. Dylan. From the Fieldhouse—you know him, right?"

"Yeah, we work together now," I said. "Or we will next week-end, anyway. I left the hot dog stand."

Mr. Arden's face changed somehow—his brows got close, and his smile went tight, and then there was a knock on the door. J.B. was yelling, "Come on, Arden, get your fat, lazy ass out of bed and let's lay that fucking patio and you better have some fuck-ing beer or you're just plain fucked."

"Well, look who's here," J.B. said, coming into the kitchen and pulling at the crotch of his sweatpants. I tried to nod casually.

"Kevin's a friend of Sandy's," Arden explained. "A friend of the family's," he added. "His parents live up the street."

J.B. glanced at Arden with lifted eyebrows. "OK, OK," he said with mock gentleness. "I mean, whatever," he added, holding up his hands. "So where's the beer?"

It was hot outside, once we finally made it out of the house. Arden changed into shorts and a T-shirt, once again looking to me like Pete's father, but do-able, nonetheless. J.B. had me digging up the turf before Arden had a chance to mark out where he wanted the patio to lay.

"Better to make it free-form, Steve," J.B. said, standing in the shade of the arborvitae that lined the yard. I stepped on the shovel, feeling the grass break, the sod give.

"Yeah, but Liz wanted it over to the left more," Arden said, looking worried. I stopped shoveling.

"So move to the left, Kevin," J.B. said, taking a swig of beer.

I cleared most of the grass away myself, working up a stinking sweat, while Arden and J.B. argued about the placement of the stones. Empty bottles gathered at the edge of our project site, thrown here and there, an easy case gone by noon. I went into the house to piss and grab another round. In Arden's bathroom, I searched the medicine cabinet, looking for anything to cover my stench. I washed my pits at the sink with a hand towel and tried to use the petrified stick of Brut deodorant I found.

I looked at my reflection, liking what the shoveling had done to my shoulders. I made a muscle and sniffed my pit. It wasn't so bad, really, I was thinking, touching the front of my shorts, pushing on my doughy shaft. I had a bone in a second, and it was all I could do to keep from dropping my shorts and jacking off. And then I heard the screen door slam and J.B. whistling, as his footsteps came my way. The loud bang on the door made me jump, and I had to find my voice to answer.

"Yeah?" I said weakly.

"I'm making a beer run—you wanna come with?"

In a few minutes I was sitting in J.B.'s Bronco, watching him while he drove, one hand on the wheel, the other along the back of the seat, his hairy-backed hand close to my shoulder. He lifted himself and farted, looking at me and winking, and I worked up a belch, and we both laughed, although I couldn't say why. I looked at the pine tree air freshener, twirled it with my finger, and glanced at J.B.'s crotch, his sweats concealing very little, as easy to read as a topographical map.

"Dude," he said, catching me.

"Sir," I said.

He smiled at that. "You calling me 'sir'?" His dark eyes crinkled. "So anyway," he said, "I've got to ask you something. It's kind of personal."

"Go for it," I answered.

He looked at me and then at the road. He signaled to turn into the liquor store parking lot, stopping the truck with a jolt and a squeal. He shut off the engine and opened the door. "Do you suck dick?" he said, squeezing his eyes shut. He opened them fast. "Don't answer now." And he was gone, his ass twitching into the store for a couple more cases.

The ride back was tense and quiet. J.B. didn't ask again, didn't say anything at all, just hummed with the radio and kept both hands on the steering wheel. A block away from Arden's, he pulled over abruptly.

"Look at me," he said, and I looked at his face. He was look-ing down at himself. I looked, too. His dick was fully at attention, standing up with a fierce turn to the left. "It's just that I haven't been able to stop thinking about you since you started at the Fieldhouse," he said. He laughed. "I'm wasted, man. It's not even one o'clock and I'm fucked up." He turned toward me then, his eyes all over me, and then he touched my shoulder with a finger.

"Dude," I said. "I am completely into this and everything, but my folks live across the street." I pointed at the little blue Cape Cod. "And that's my father mowing the lawn."

J.B. put the truck in gear. I waved at Dad.

Arden was huffing as he hauled flagstone around, trying to find an appealing arrangement, and J.B. was mauling me in the garage, pawing up under my shirt, nipping me, rubbing his crotch against my thigh. I liked looking over the top of his black-haired head. He licked my belly, tonguing into my navel, giving me the chills. He looked up at me, mouth sliding up my side and into my armpit.

"Dude," I said, and he groaned and grabbed my hand and put it on his boner. It was as hard as a log and soaking the front of his sweats. He swabbed my pit hairs and grabbed my ass cheeks.

"I'm going to tear this up," he said, plucking a stray hair from his tongue.

He got rid of his sweats, freeing up his cock. It dripped and pulsed in my hand. I went to my knees, making J.B. moan again, and licked the leaking tip, a salty bubble that went sour on my tongue. I took his whole buddy into my mouth, showing off and making a pig of myself, snorting into his flossy bush, feeling the tip playing the rings of my constricting throat. He held my head and used me for a while, shoving himself all the way in and then dragging it out, dick-slapping me and calling me a cunt, pushing my face into his balls. I sucked hard on his nuts and tried to tongue my way back to his pussy, but he tightened his thighs and kept me away.

"Oh, no, you don't, you nasty trick," he said, pulling my hair and getting me back on his prick, slamming his hips into my face.

He let me put my hands on his ass, laughing at me when I wriggled my fingers into the tight clamp of his crack. "I'll be doing the driving," I heard him say, laughing again.

The garage smelled of old cut grass and gasoline. J.B. leaned back against Arden's workbench. We could hear him swearing outside, and I looked up from what I was doing, and J.B. shook his head.

"You don't have to worry about old Steve-o," he said. "He's got a nut for Billy Dale—been doing him all season. That's why he's so off his game, I think."

I choked.

"Easy, baby," he said gently, his hand nice on my chin, cupping it. "You gonna let me fuck you?" he asked, nodding my head for me. "Come on," he said, taking my hand and lifting me up from my crouch.

He turned me around and got down on his own knees. "Fucking boy-butt," I heard him say right before he split my cheeks with his nose and twirled his tongue all around my asshole. I felt myself melt, my pucker going slack for him. He kissed me down there, his lips on mine, his tongue going rigid and cutting into me. He put a strong hand on my back, getting me to bend over, and I felt myself opening up to him. He worked a finger into my hole, fucking it around and loosening up my insides. He went for two, then three, working up thick hawkers of spit in the back of his throat and tossing them out against my butt. He slapped my cheeks and jiggled his fingers up into me, hitting my little buzzing spot.

I looked back at him over my shoulder. He lifted my shirt and licked up my back. He pressed his prick into the hot ditch of my ass, looking to get in, coming close but missing the mark until I finally helped him in.

"Shit," he said, suddenly hitting my heat. He licked between my shoulder blades and worked himself into me a little at a time, slowly rocking from side to side until I felt his hips and he got as far as he was going. He felt a foot long, lingering there, pressing his body against mine, getting me into a gentle full nelson and bringing my torso up against his own. His hands roamed my chest, going in through the armholes of my T-shirt, finding my nipples and twisting them, teasing them with his thumbs, chewing on the back of my neck.

He started fucking me hard, keeping my arms up over my head, kissing behind my ears and whispering to me, telling me how much he loved my ass, how hot it was, how hard he was going to plow it. I was just taking it all in—what he said, his sliding prick—and having the time of my life. My own cock was hopping around, eager for some touch, throbbing with every thrust of J.B.'s pole. His crotch fur tickled my ass as he went deep, letting go of my arms, and finally took hold of my bud, jacking me off like a real pal. I felt his tits against my shoulder blades, wide-spaced, hard as pebbles. His chest was packed and smooth, sweaty now and heating up. I wiggled my fanny for him, wanting to make him laugh again, but now he was all business.

He stepped back and unplugged himself. Then he made me turn around again, facing him this time.

"Put your arms around my neck," he told me. "Then jump up and put your legs around my waist."

I gave him a look. "Come on," I said.

"Seriously," he insisted. I did what he asked me to do, and he slid right up into me, deeper this time. He held on to me by my ass and bounced me off of his hips like a baby boy. My dick rasping against his stomach drove me crazy. He looked me in the eyes until I had to look away. He bent his head toward mine and kissed me hard, fucking the breath out of me. I closed my eyes and felt bright hot flashes go off in my brain, and I felt my dick tremor, about to shoot. J.B. slammed into me, holding me tightly, crushing my dick between us, and I creamed against our bellies, groaning up a storm, making him smile and dick me to the moon.

"Oh, you sweet boy," he said haltingly, his lips near my ear. He held his breath and squeezed shut his eyes and unloaded inside my buttery ass.

Arden stood in the doorway. "Anytime now, boys," he said.

"Hey, leave a tender moment alone," J.B. said, wiping his dick off on his balled up sweats. My legs wobbled as I looked for my shorts.

"Come on, I want to get this damn thing laid," Arden said.

"Don't we all, my friend," J.B. said, pinching my ass.

Every Inch of the World

Cary says his roommate—a lacrosse player named Brigham—left him, although they weren't really together, not that way, anyway. They shared a dorm room in Blake Hall and not even for very long. Granted, Brigham had asked Cary to be his roommate when they met orientation weekend. That was because they'd shared a room then, too, and Cary hadn't snored, and Brigham hadn't known anyone else—all the other lacrosse players had gone to the first orientation in July.

What had Brigham been doing in July? Working at Ace Hardware, racking hammers and sorting boxes of screws, almost wishing he were heading back to high school in the fall. They'd liked the same kinds of music, though, he and Cary—Dave Matthews, the Chemical Brothers, Stone Temple Pilots—and neither one of them smoked. It hadn't seemed like a bad idea back then, in the middle of August. He could've left it up to the lottery that paired up everyone else. But why tempt fate? He might have ended up with that guy in the wheelchair or the fag with the eyeliner and the black-and-red hair.

"The name alone should have done it for you, man," his lacrosse buddies said. "Like that fucking chick with the pig's blood and John Travolta."

"Was I even born when that movie came out," Brigham said in his defense. "What the fuck do I know? Besides, he spells it different. C-a-r-y."

"Add an S, dude," one of his buddies said solemly, "and you've got scary."

Brigham got all his clothes at Abercrombie and Fitch, at the Lehigh Valley Mall. He'd spent nearly $600 the week before school started and not told his mother. That was his book money. Tuition and everything else was paid for with money from his father's accident. He packed up plaid shirts, long-sleeved Henleys, carpenter's jeans, cut-off khakis. He looked like the blown-up photos that hung in the store; he looked like a model—Cary had said so, anyway.

"You should model for Fitch," he said. Brigham would look at himself in the mirror at the gym where he worked out every day, sipping Creatine and grape juice, going into the locker room to quickly elbow out of his shirt. If he managed to find himself alone, he would stare at his pecs and his abs and ignore his calves. His hair was straight and perfect, his teeth were white and perfect. He had beautiful skin.

Cary didn't do much more than go to classes, do his home-work, and watch television. He liked old movies, black-and-white ones. Just the look of them bored Brigham, who liked *The Simpsons* and MTV. That was about it. He also liked computer games, especially strategy games: Warcraft, Lords of the Realm, Myst. He liked music. He liked working out.

Cary sat on his bed in his boxers, his legs crossed, shin over knee. He had long toes, and so did Brigham, who didn't care for his own feet, but didn't mind them so much, seeing Cary's. Brigham was putting things into a bag, clothes for the gym: a - T-shirt from high school, its sleeves cut off and holes meshing the back, warm-up pants, socks, briefs, and a towel, because he was going to shower there.

"Where you going?" Cary asked. He glanced at the bag on the bed. "Never mind."

"You ought to come sometime," Brigham said.

"Yeah, right," Cary snorted. He was drinking tea he'd made in the microwave. Brigham picked at a scab on his knuckle, staring blankly at the television. The black and white looked dull, out of focus. He thought everyone was so phony, the way they talked, the way they laughed. He picked up his bag.

"See ya," he said.

"Later," Cary returned, not looking away from the little screen.

Brigham liked to study in the library. It was quieter than the dorm, where quiet time was blatantly ignored, Puff Daddy and Primus a dull rumble in the walls of the room. And Cary was always around. It wasn't that he was noisy; Brigham was just used to a certain amount of solitude. He had grown up as an only child in a quiet house. His mother used to plead for his silence, suffering headaches that blinded her, she said—headaches that had begun to plague her after the accident. She needed quiet. He knew how to be quiet, and liked being alone. He went to the library for it, sitting on hard chairs with stacks of books and studying.

There were messages for him when he'd get back to the room. "Your mom called," Cary would tell him, waiting for him to pick up the phone.

"Cool," Brigham would answer, throwing his bag on his bed.

He liked maps. He liked the way they looked, the way they made sense. You are *here*. You want to be *there*. Simple as that. He liked knowing what was around him: the names of towns, parks, and lakes. He went to the library and pulled down atlases no one had touched since 1978, when countries had different names from the ones they have now. That was another thing he liked about maps—the names could change, but it all stayed the same.

He wanted to learn every inch of the world. It was a mission, a goal, not unlike wanting to read a dictionary from front to back. It made him feel lofty, admirable, eccentric.

There was a note from Cary: "Your mom called again. I think she was crying. She wants you to call her back. I went down to Dean's."

He liked the gym at six o'clock because it was pretty much his. Everyone else was at dinner or studying or drinking or doing bong hits. He could watch himself in the mirror without feeling too self-conscious. There was one other guy there, older, not a student like Brigham, though he could have been one of those non-traditional ones. Maybe he was a professor. They nodded at one another, both intent on the weights.

They showered together afterward, having finished their workouts at the same time. Brigham glanced over at the man, who soaped himself up unhurriedly, his chest wide and high, a small crest of hair growing in the crevice between his pecs. He was thick all over. Brigham watched the floor, dragging a washcloth between his legs, thinking.

The man cleared his throat and spat. Brigham turned to the spray of water, clearing the soap from his face. He'd brought his razor in with him to do some maintenance on his chest, a quick trim, but couldn't with the man there with him. The man reached for his soap and lathered himself up again. He turned his left foot out and slid the bar over his tensed thigh. Brigham looked down at the steel drain cover, which was stamped with a W for Wade. He knew this from his job at the hardware store. He looked over at the man's feet, trimmed toe nails, little tufts of hair at each knuckle. The man rinsed himself, turning his back, and began to wash his hair a second time. He turned around again. Brigham saw the man's dick rising up from suds that washed over him. He looked away, looked back, aware of his own burgeoning cock, its twitching ascent, the nasty dryness he tasted, the sudden thickness he felt in his throat.

There was no sound save for the water raining on the tile. The man used his soap around his crotch, building lather, working the bar under his balls. He had stopped looking at Brigham, interested in something else now, the way the dim light cast weakened shadows, maybe. He was not interested in Brigham touching himself, how he held himself in his hand, his cock engorged. He stroked his soapy dick, watching the man do the same, staring into the corner of the shower. He watched the way the man's butt cheeks tensed, the way his spine straightened, before the sudden

165

ropy toss that flew from his prick-end. Brigham felt his own shuddering end, come spilling out of his fist, a warm white flow that clotted on the tile, swirling slowly toward the drain only to stay there, clinging and obstinate.

He went home for the weekend. His mother insisted. "Thanksgiving is in three weeks," he complained; "I'll be home then."

"I want you here now," she whined over the phone.

It went the way he'd expected it to go. She hid in her room, and he hid in his. They got together for meals, and she asked him perfunctory questions about school: how his classes were, what his roommate was like.

"I talk to him more than I do you," she said. "Are you ever there?"

"I study a lot," he told her. "In the library."

"Then you'll have good grades," she said slowly, as if coming to some realization.

"Yeah," he answered.

She looked at his shirt. It had cost him $60. She would have died if she ever found out he'd spent that much on a shirt. "That color looks nice on you," she said.

The plan was that they'd see his father on Sunday, and then the two of them would have dinner at Wallace's, where they'd always had dinners on Sundays after visiting his father.

"You're so far away at school," she said. She hadn't wanted him to go, had begged him to stay. He'd almost given in.

At night he'd studied the map of the campus they'd sent, peering at it under the small study lamp at his desk in his little bedroom, the radio on low, his mother trying to sleep. *Here,* he thought. I'll go to classes *here.* I'll eat *here.*

He couldn't make it to Sunday dinner, though. "I've got to go," he told her Saturday night.

"You can't leave," she said, her blue face moonish. "You *can't* go. It's *dark.*" She didn't like him driving at night and used to hide the keys to the car when he was younger, when he'd first gotten his license.

"I'm going," he told her. His bag was packed and by the door. He stood in her doorway. The room was lit by the television. Next to her bed—his old bed, actually—was a card table set up with a coffeemaker, boxes of crackers, a broken clock, magazines, some rotten bananas, a telephone with caller I.D. The room smelled a lot like the nursing home his father was in.

"That car's in my name," she screamed after him, not getting out of bed, not having the energy. She yelled his name, saying she'd call the police, but he knew she wouldn't—she wouldn't dare. He closed the door quietly behind him.

He unlocked the door of his dorm room. It wasn't yet midnight, and he was expecting to find Cary home with the television on, not unlike his mother really. As he opened the door the light behind him swept into the room. Cary's bed was empty. He was sleeping in Brigham's bed.

"What are you doing?" Brigham asked, turning on the light. Cary bolted upright, his face wrinkled from the press of the pillow. He didn't say anything, though, offered no explanation. He put his feet on the floor and uncovered himself—he was naked and hard—and walked across the room to his own bed. *So big,* Brigham thought, seeing the stiff bob of Cary's cock—*Huge.* Brigham's hand was still gripping the doorknob. Cary settled into his own sheets, drifting back into sleep. Brigham couldn't get the image of Cary's cock out of his mind.

It's ruined, Brigham realized. Everything was ruined. Something bad had happened, although he could not say what that badness was, not just then. But it had something to do with Cary's old movies and his mother trading her queen-size bed for his old twin. It had something to do with the man in the shower and the wrinkled skin of his own fingertips that day.

He put down his bag and turned around. He left the room, closing the door, aware that he was leaving home the second time that day. He'd go back later, the next day, when Cary was at the student union where he worked at the information desk, and clear out his things. He'd move in with the other lacrosse players and steer clear of all fine lines. He would become unambiguous, get good grades. He would prepare for the future. And he would never touch a man with an open hand without thinking of Cary and his long toes.

Knowing that would've made Cary the happiest boy in Blake Hall.

JASON

It had been a long time, and Jason was closer than he wanted to be, so he let go, putting his hands behind his head, getting lubricant in his hair. He wasn't sure why he'd put this off for so long. True, he'd had other things on his mind—the move, not least among them. But he also loved the challenge of abstinence, which was why he'd started smoking (so that he could quit a year later) and why he often thought about going to AA meetings, even though he didn't have a drinking problem per se.

He had the CD cover of Tom Jones's latest effort propped on the nightstand beside him. Tom Jones was a guilty pleasure, reminding him of nights he'd stayed up with his mother to watch Jones's TV show when he was very young. Young, but aware enough to take note of the Welsh sausage Jones took no effort to hide, stuck inside light-colored trousers chosen expressly, Jason decided, for what they would not conceal. The memory of those unbuttoned white ruffled shirts and those skintight slacks was enough to cause some serious seepage in Jason's taut joint. Women would throw their panties at him at his concerts; Jason was content to throw a yard of ropy jizz at the jewel case of the CD.

"I do not need another tequila," Jason told Micah in the hallway to the kitchen at the party for Jason's leave-taking. It was a "Get Outta Town" party.

"I need one, then," Micah said. "And you too, Stevo," he said as Steve Schlenck lurched up.

169

"Not Stevo," Jason said, feeling protective of his soon-to-be ex–office mate.

"Why not?" Steve asked.

"You're already fucked up," Jason told him.

"So?" Steve replied. He threw his arm around Jason, putting his beery face close to his human leaning post. "I love you, man," he said, his chin coming to rest on Jason's shoulder. "If I was a fag—" he said, then stopped, catching himself. He tried again: "If I was *gay*, I mean," he said slowly, his face full of effort, "I'd want you to fuck me."

"What the fuck," Micah laughed. Jason smiled.

"That's real sweet of you, Stevo," Jason replied gamely, "and if I was 'a fag—I mean, gay,' I'd want you to fuck me, too."

"What did you guys do without us?" Micah said.

"It's gonna suck here without you—no pun intended," Steve said, ignoring Micah, and shifted from Jason's shoulder to the wall behind him, the move looking only half intentional. He looked at Jason as if he were his next drink. There were about a half a dozen guys in the kitchen talking about T-bonds and breast implants and the first time they'd seen their parents having sex.

"Like there'd be a second time," Joel Russell said.

"I kind of liked it," Dave Blaize said. He was blond and on the thick side, looking to Jason as though he'd played football at some point in his life. He picked a potato chip out of a bowl and looked it over before he ate it. He had a faint dust of gold hairs on his arms. "I got some good pointers from my old man." He looked at his audience blearily. "Doesn't anybody buy dip any more? Where's the fucking dip?"

"I got a real good pointer from the old man," Micah said, grabbing his crotch uncharacteristically.

"What was it?" Steve said, perking up.

Jason left them for another beer. "You need another tequila," Micah called after him. Jason waved a dismissive hand behind his head.

He had his head in the refrigerator, trying to pick a beer from the forest of bottles—it was a distributor's dream: beers from all over the world. He picked a Belgian white he'd brought himself, trying to ignore the moldy cheese and blackened vegetables rotting away in plastic bags. This was Steve's house, a suburban bachelor's pad. Whenever he was here, Jason always had the feeling that Steve's parents were going to come up from the basement—from the "rumpus room," as Steve called it. There was paneling and shag carpeting and plenty of Herculon in plaid earth tones. "Wow," Dave B. had said when he walked in the front door tonight, his first time at Schlenk's. "Uh, hi, Mr. Brady. Is Marcia ready to go to the prom?"

Jason looked at Blaize now, the new guy in the firm. He was sitting on the counter, the bowl of dipless chips wedged between his legs. He wore shorts and a baggy rugby shirt. It was the first time Jason had seen Dave's bared legs, and he was impressed with how they looked. His calves were like little hams, and his thighs filled the hems of his shorts, each leg tanned brown, save for where anklets had covered skin, his bare feet stuck inside little boat shoes. Such tiny feet, Jason marveled. Dave was a golfer, always practicing his swing, playing "air golf" when he wasn't actually using his putter, hitting a ball into an overturned coffee cup when he should have been writing copy. "Helps me think," he said once, looking sheepish and boyish, when Jason caught him one time. So which was more apt, Jason wondered—sheepish or boyish?

Somebody put on the Doors and turned up the volume. "L.A. Woman" blared through the house. Not the first time that night, Jason thought, *I don't want to leave.* But it was "*O and D,*" as Micah liked to put it: Over and Done. Jason would be officially unemployed as of next week.

The doorbell rang, and somebody shouted, "Gland's here!" Jason's heart started to flutter.

"I still don't understand what you intend to do," Jason heard, and he turned to see Dave B. standing quite close, in his hands the bowl of chips.

Jason looked over Dave's shoulder. "Is Gland really here?"

"Gland is with the du Ponts, golfing," Dave said in a monotone, repeating a well-worn office joke.

"And you're wearing madras," Jason said, glancing down at Dave's plaid shorts.

"So?" he said, looking down as well. "Oh, yeah—stripes and plaids—a fashion no-no."

Jason half-smiled. "I just didn't picture you having anything like that in your closet."

"They were in my drawers," Dave said, deftly handling Jason's double entendre. "And you'd be amazed at what you'd find in there, too."

"Would I?" Jason asked.

"Peg leg," Dave said quickly, putting his back again the wall to Jason's left, sliding to a crouch and then sitting on the floor. "So you're really going to chuck it all away for a cabin in the woods and a paint-by-numbers set or two?" Dave said,

"Faux finishes," Jason said, hating the phrase already. "Wall treatments" seemed equally faggy. But painting sounded so professional and difficult—not to mention artistic—and therefore monetarily unrewarding.

"I see," Dave answered. His eyes were already glazed. He looked up at Jason. "You heard about Micah and Dick, right?"

Jason nodded. It was pure conjecture, so far as he was concerned, but he did like to imagine what those two might be doing together. He had long felt isolated as the only queer in the whole building.

"I just can't imagine Dick taking the plunge," Dave said. "So to speak."

"I can," Jason said, looking at the light fixture over their heads.

"That doesn't surprise me."

Jason looked down at Dave's thighs, which had doubled in size in their crouched state. *Here was a man who could squat,* Jason thought.

"You're so much more imaginative, I mean," Dave added.

"Uh, yeah," Jason said.

"I'm sorry," Dave said after a moment of awkward silence. "It's just that this stuff—I mean, first you, then Micah and Dick—" His hand shot out helplessly. "I don't know—it's just different. Or something."

"Or something?"

"You know what I mean—where's that generosity you're supposed to be famous for? Help me out here."

"It's more fun watching you flounder," Jason replied.

"Ah. The inevitable fish reference," Dave said, slapping his forehead. "So tell me, is Micah shooting the move on poor defenseless Schlenk?"

"You're a real dick," Jason said, grinning.

"I guess I am, aren't I?"

"Most definitely."

Dave smiled then, showing a row of perfectly beautiful teeth, and Jason found himself suddenly, swiftly, enamored of David Blaize.

"You golf, don't you?" Dave called out to him at his desk the next day. Jason was up to his armpits trying to pass every client he was working with over to his replacement, a smallish Asian woman with exceptionally loud jewelry. "A sssmooth transsssition," the Gland had lisped, "iss your sssole mission."

Jason snorted. "Golf? Are you serious?"

"Do you want to learn, then? It's hugely fun, you know."

"Hugely? Yeah, well, I've always heard it was a good walk spoiled," Jason replied.

"Twain's a cynic," Dave said.

"Shania?" Jason countered. "I thought she was a singer. Does she golf, too? Celine Dion loves to golf. I read it in *In Style*."

"You're saying no, then."

"Not at all. Where? When? Should I buy some funny shoes?"

"This isn't a lark," Dave said seriously. "This is devotion."

"I'll need serious shoes, then, I guess," Jason answered.

They met at the golf course. "I'll meet you at the front desk," Dave had said, making the event seem almost clandestine, a no-tell motel rendezvous. It was anything but, what with all the retirees clipping around in their cleats.

"Reminds me of tap-dancing lessons I took in first grade," Jason said quietly. Or the last drag show he'd had the misfortune to attend.

Dave looked mortified. "You tap-danced?"

"Yeah, it was just like *River Dance*," Jason answered with a small amount of indignation.

"Wow," Dave said, nodding.

"But different," Jason added.

"Oh, yeah, I'm sure," Dave said, continuing to nod.

Jason tried not to look too long at Dave's mouth, and he tried not to look at his eyes, either, which made him feel shifty. He looked at the lobby of the country club and wondered how big an ass he'd make of himself.

"Not bad, not bad," Dave said after Jason finally made a shot that landed on the fairway. "You've got some purchase." He squinted at the little ball some 200 yards away. "It doglegs to the right, you know," he added, stepping up to his teed ball.

"I love that—'dogleg'—that is so cool," Jason said. "It's so visual."

Dave looked at him, his club stuck in back-swing position. "You're a fucking riot—you know that, don't you?"

Jason smirked, but beamed within. *I don't know a goddamn thing right now,* he said to himself.

Golf was arduous, Jason decided. There was a lot of trudging about, looking for balls, missing easy putts, and riding around in an impossibly slow golf cart. Jason didn't even want to consider the water hazards at this point. He hadn't felt so tortured since the last time he tried bowling. For the last time he slid his club into the bag strapped down to the back of the cart. *Not for me, I'm afraid,* he said to himself.

But there was the sight of Dave's ankles in his little short socks. Jason wondered whether they had a name. Maybe something like "socklets?" Whatever they were called, they radiated an aura of sex for Jason, who willed himself to look instead at the clod of dirt—the *divot*—that he'd lifted with his nine-iron. *Please,* he prayed, let there be something like showering after this murky, hellish event. Only the sight of Dave Blaize naked and wet could make up for this fiasco.

It wasn't the sport that was hellish so much as his inability to make things happen with club and ball. It hadn't seemed so difficult at the outset, when Dave described the game to him— it had, in fact, sounded like an interesting game. The actuality of it, however, was a series of humiliations. Dave tallied their scores, doing a slow scratch with his little pencil that unnerved Jason. He'd never realized how competitive he was.

"Oh, my," he heard Dave murmur.

"What?" Jason asked, leaning over and trying to decode the score card. "High isn't good, is it?"

Dave bunched his lips together and squinted at the card. He finally shook his head. "Not really," he said.

"So you're saying you won."

"No," Dave said. "I'm saying you *lost,* pal, and big time. I *never* saw a man so defeated."

"Fuck you," Jason said, giving Dave's shoulder a push.

"Crushed, killed, *annihilated,*" Dave bellowed.

"Enough, asshole," Jason sneered.

"Toasted."

"Whatever."

"So, you know what happens when you lose, right?" Dave said, grinning like a madman. He pulled his shoulders back and stuck out his chest.

"I don't want to know," Jason replied, ignoring the presence of pecs.

"You don't know?" Blaize said, his grin broadening.

Jason looked down, shaking his head. "I don't," he said, trying

175

to soften the peevish edge that had crept into his voice while he wasn't paying attention. He hitched up his shirtsleeves.

"You have arms like Madonna," Dave said.

"That's not good, either, is it?" Jason asked, his tongue tasting bitter.

Dave shrugged his shoulders. "Maybe yes, maybe no."

An evil silence hung between them, lasting about a minute and a half.

"I mean, I don't know why I said Madonna," Dave said finally. "I meant a man, like a man's arms, like you've got these muscles that show and everything. It's just that I saw her last night on MTV, and, Christ, her arms. And then there's your arms and every- thing—I mean, I could have said—Christ, I don't know, some guy, some guy's arms. You're toned and everything. You're fucking *buff,* for Christ's sake,. You're an honest-to-God he-man hottie. Shit." He rubbed his eyes, looking disturbed. "Look, I thought we'd go to the clubhouse and figure out what we're going to do next—I don't know why I had such a hard time trying to get that out."

"Me, neither," Jason said, but he liked it.

They sat at the bar with stingers. "I don't like the sound of this," Jason said when Dave ordered the drinks for them.

"No, really, you'll like them," he said. "Or you'll get used to them. What are you reading these days?"

Jason blinked. "Well, the Starr Report, actually," he said.

"I never took you for tabloid," Dave said. "Good reading?"

"Salacious enough. How about you?"

Dave shook his head, looking at his drink. "I don't know how," he said. "I used to, but I forgot, I think. I like to watch television."

They were silent for a moment. Jason picked up his drink and held it—he didn't like the smell of it, but it didn't taste so bad. It was something he felt he could get used to. He stopped himself from contemplating anything about Dave. He wouldn't ever be as lucky as Micah was with Dick. Just then, Dave said to him, "It's an acquired taste."

"So I'm told," Jason answered.

"The drink, I mean," Dave said, stifling a grin.

"Indeed," Jason said.

Dave gave in and smiled. "You're the only person I know who says 'indeed'," he said.

"That's not good, is it?"

"It's not bad. In fact, I think it's very cool. You say 'Good day,' too."

"I picked that up in college. There was this girl that always said it, and it was so plainly affected but sounded so cool. So I affected it myself." He shrugged. "I don't sound too Crocodile Dundee, do I" he asked.

Dave shook his head. "Nah. He says it differently—'Good 'ay.' Something like that." He took a deep breath and held it. "Kind of sucks I'm just getting to know you right when you're leaving," he said.

"Yeah," Jason said, feeling a little flutter down around his belly. It was an unfamiliar sensation. *It's a crush,* he realized instantly—*I have a crush on him.* He felt the corners of his mouth turn up, and he covered it.

"Are you laughing at me?" Dave asked.

"Not exactly," Jason said, finally allowing a little laughter to bubble up from the fluttering spot in his belly. "At myself, actually." He shook his head. "Tell me about your girlfriend," he said.

"Why?" Dave asked.

"I just don't know anything about her," Jason said. "I met her at the Christmas party last year and she seemed cool, but you don't really talk about her."

"We date," he said. "I wouldn't call her a girlfriend. I don't think she would call me her boyfriend, either, to tell you the truth. A little too limiting, if you know what I mean."

"Limiting?" Jason asked.

"You know what I mean," Dave said, looking at him significantly, then glancing away.

"I don't," Jason said.

"Come on," Dave said, holding his hands open in front of his chest, a gesture that conveyed something else that Jason was unable to decipher. He stared at Jason, lifting his eyebrows and nodding. "You know," he said.

"I know," Jason repeated. He shook his head. "OK, I'm sorry. I don't."

Dave leaned forward. "She likes girls *and* guys—she's bisexual."

"And I'm supposed to know that?" Jason said. "Do you think we have some sort of secret handshake or something? Some identifying mark only we can see?"

"Well, she sure picked you out fast," he said.

"I'm not exactly Tom Jones," Jason said.

"Is he?"

"No, he's the straightest man I can think of, other than my dad, but if I said my dad's name, you wouldn't know who the fuck I was talking about, now would you? Let's get another. Do you want another?"

Dave looked at his glass—it held three small ice cubes. He looked at his watch. And then he looked at Jason as though Jason had proposed they slip into something a little more comfortable. Like socklets.

Sitting beside Dave at the bar, Jason found it hard to keep his gaze from lingering on the tan lines on Dave's thighs. Dave's shorts tightly hugged his crotch, quite clearly revealing the lay of the land in that region. His package was equally divided along each leg—balls to the right and dick to the left, both portions on the hefty side. Jason looked up into Dave's stare, cool and green as a drag on a menthol cigarette, and just as breathtaking.

"Yeah," Dave began after Jason asked him about his not-girl-friend. "She brought one of her friends home once, but it was a little weird for the both of us, really. I mean, it was cool and every-thing, but we didn't talk to each other for three days afterwards. It was like we both had done something stupid, like we'd shaved the cats or something."

"People *shave* cats?"

"I said it was a *stupid* thing," he replied. Then he asked abruptly, "Am I just paranoid, or have you been staring at my crotch?"

"Man, are you paranoid!" Jason said dramatically. "I was just looking at the interesting trim they picked for the stools. Elevate yourself, Dave, get your mind out of the gutter. Who do you think I am—Micah?"

"You're not seeing anyone, or am I wrong here?" Dave asked.

"You are not wrong," Jason said. "I'm congenitally single, I guess."

"Could be worse," Dave said.

"I could be missing a limb," Jason nodded.

"Does it bother you?"

"Not at first, but as time goes on," Jason replied.

"I catch your drift."

It was quiet then, the perfect time for a pause. Their drinks were empty again, and the clubhouse bar was all but empty. The bartender stood at the end of the bar, smoking and watching *Oprah*. Dave drummed his fingers on his thighs. Jason looked down.

"That trim really is nice, though," he said.

How did they end up at Dave's apartment? Through no little maneuvering on Jason's part, he'd be the first to admit. Four rounds of stingers helped matters, too.

"This place is so cool," Jason said. Dave lived above a garage, in a loft-like space that looked more like a movie set than someone's home. "And you're not even in the art department," he added.

"What's that supposed to mean?"

"I was expecting something a little less—"

"Tasteful?" Dave inserted.

"Something like that."

"Beer signs, a basketball hoop, Budweiser cans."

"Well," Jason said, "Now that you mention it."

Dave looked around his apartment. "None of it's mine—it's all her doing."

"Those lamps make me wet," Jason said.

"You really are gay, aren't you?" Dave said. "I mean, up to now I had my doubts, but after hearing that—"

"The lamp thing clinches it for you?" Jason asked. Dave nodded.

Jason sighed. "Yeah, it's true. One hundred percent gay." He looked over at Dave. "And you?

"Me?" Dave snorted.

"You."

Dave pushed his mouth around with his hand and seemed, in Jason's inexpert opinion, to be hedging.

"Or are you a fence-sitter?" Jason asked, cutting him some slack.

"A what?"

"You know, sitting on the fence, able to fall over on either side at any given moment."

Dave laughed. "No way. Not me," he said. He walked over to the wall of windows that looked out into late-afternoon light. "But let's just say, for argument's sake..."

Jason's hopes rose.

"That I'm 150% straight," Dave finished, and Jason took a step over the heap of hope at his feet.

"Anything to drink around here?" he asked.

"There isn't," Dave said. "Well, there's something in the fridge, but I don't think you can drink it anymore."

There was one thing Jason did not love, and that was this kind of a challenge, one in which he had no hope of winning. This was starting to feel a lot like golf to him. He was willing at this point to cut his losses and call it a night. But there was one thing that Dave Blaize seemed to love, and that was competition. He also seemed not to want their evening to draw to a close.

"There's a bar down the street that serves decent food," Dave said. "And they've got a killer jukebox and a dartboard. You throw?"

"Only fits," Jason said. Dave hitched up the sleeve of his shirt, baring one of his biceps. It was marked with something Jason recognized as Greek.

"You were in a fraternity?" he asked.

"Briefly, until I came to my senses," Dave replied, touching the inked letters.

"I love fraternities, the idea of them. They're so—"

"Fraternal?" Dave offered.

"Oh, yeah," Jason said, grinning.

"They're not," Dave said.

"You know, you're busting all sorts of balloons for me tonight," Jason said before he realized what he was saying.

"I am?" Dave smiled.

"Never mind," Jason said.

"Like how?" Dave persisted.

"Like never mind."

"Like what kind of balloons?"

"Like forget it."

"You like me, don't you?" he said.

Jason looked at him, forcing a hearty laugh. "God, you are so—"

"Right?" Dave ventured.

"Right?" Jason said. "No, you're vain, you're stuck on yourself, you're—"

"I'm right," Dave said simply. He pulled his car keys out of his pocket. "Come on," he said. "Let's go."

"Why don't we go to one of your bars," Dave suggested.

Jason looked at him, thinking, *He's playing me*. He said, "One of *my* bars? I don't have any bars, Dave."

"You know what I mean. Cut the shit. Take me to your bar."

"Why?" Jason asked, crossing his arms across his chest, playing stubborn.

Dave gripped the steering wheel with both hands. He looked out through the windshield. It was dark, but only just, the sun having gone down about 20 minutes earlier. The sky still held some light, the horizon blood red, and Dave watched it going dark for moment.

"None of your beeswax," Dave said cryptically.

G-Bar was dark and fairly deserted. It was too early for any real action. The bar itself was populated with the diehards, mostly older men with set bedtimes and serious drinking problems. Jason ordered two beers and brought them over to the table where Dave sat, looking disappointed. "You were expecting go-go boys at nine?" Jason asked.

"Hey, look, fuck you—I hadn't the slightest idea—"

"But you were curious," Jason said.

Dave looked at the bar, eyeing the line-up of geezers and queens. "I was," he admitted. Then he turned and held Jason in an open gaze. "I am," he said.

CLIFF

Cliff sat at his desk, his hand inside the unzipped fly of his khakis. It was Friday and after business hours; he assumed the office was deserted. Everyone was on the way to the shore, to Point Pleasant and Cape May. Cliff was sticking around for the weekend. He had some stuff to do around the house—the lawn, for instance, hadn't been mowed in nearly a month. He'd been spending nearly every weekend down in Delaware at his friend's condo, getting sunburned if not laid. After figuring out what he'd spent in the last month on beer and gas alone, he thought it best to turn down Breck's standing offer this time around.

"You sure?" Breck had whined on the phone earlier in the week. He was as single and horned up as Cliff and was hooking up even less, and he'd started to count on Cliff's company. All of his condo mates had found their summer flings, and he had the place pretty much to himself every weekend. Gerry, he thought, after Cliff made his excuses, or maybe Todd. They were acceptable company, though inferior to Cliff, who was in Breck's opinion a righteous hottie.

What had Cliff digging into his shorts—breaking company policy, he was certain—was a Web site he'd read about in a smutty magazine. It was probably unwise to be checking it out at the workplace, but it was Friday, and he had a pretty good friend in Char, the MIS specialist who could work wonders with the network. Once, when he'd tried to open a highly inappropriate attachment sent to him by an ex, the system froze up and the

183

mainframe went down. Once she'd figured everything out and fixed the problem, Char let Cliff know she'd "saved his ass." She never told him what the attachment was, except to say that he was lucky he still had a job.

"I'll tell you this much," she'd teased over a light lunch in the cafe down stairs. "It continues to bring me pleasure."

The site he'd brought up on the screen was called Blink.com, a voyeuristic endeavor based on the premise that most of life's treasures are missed in a blink of the eye. The site comprised pictures of candid split-second images, largely involving men's crotches. The photographer was obviously a size-queen with a fascination for trouser-bound girth. Cliff himself was not averse to crotch watching. Logging on to Blink.com, he found a kindred spirit who shared his enthusiasm for impressive manly terrain.

There were other galleries, but none appealed to Cliff as strongly. He did not care for the stagy "hidden urinal cameras," regardless of the ingenuity of the camera work. Nor did he find Locker-room Lothario as interesting as Crotch Watch. He was brick-hard, stroking himself, clicking each icon and bringing up another delectable dangle.

"You must be trying to impress someone," he heard a voice say behind him. He nearly jumped out of his skin when he saw his supervisor, Vin D'Angelo, standing in the doorway. "Would that someone be me? I am impressed, let me tell you. Hard at work at six o'clock on a Friday. Oh, I am impressed, indeed."

Cliff stole his hand from his pants and deftly minimized the screen he was viewing. "I was just getting ready to take off," he sputtered. "Just checking some late E-mails." He brought up the office E-mail screen and at the top of his in-box saw a message from Vin written a few hours ago.

"So," Vin said, "You up to one or not?"

Clicking to open the message, he found an invitation for a drink downstairs at Giggy's. Cliff's eyes darted from the message to Vin's face. "Absolutely, absolutely," he said. A social call from Vin was out of character and a little ominous. Vin was new to the company, nice enough, but very by-the-book. A little too "corporate" for Cliff's tastes. He was also good-looking—very good-looking, Cliff realized.

Vin left him to "finish up." He said, "I'll meet you at the elevator in 10, OK?" Cliff shut down his computer and zipped up his fly.

He sat next to Vin at the bar at Giggy's. For a Friday, the place was deserted. It was usually stuffed with happy-hour fanatics, all loosened ties and shoulder-slung jackets, secretaries slurping apple martinis and flirting with project managers and stockbrokers. Everyone was at the shore, he decided, and he found himself wishing he were there, too.

While Vin rambled on about the Drexler account and production numbers and forecasting, Cliff was thinking about sipping a margarita at the Blue Moon and cruising this season's finest, all sun-browned and worked-out. Visions of tattooed boy toys in wife beaters danced through his mind. He tried to picture Vin in a wife beater. Vin was short and sturdily built, his dark hair short and thinning. He might've been a wrestler in college, Cliff speculated, and probably a scrappy little right guard, as well. His image of Vin in a tank top morphed into Tony Soprano, complete with saggy-ass boxers—not unattractive but not very Rehoboth.

"You want another?" Vin asked Cliff. They were drinking beer, and Cliff wasn't going to have another, but Vin ordered two more before he had a chance to decline. Besides, when the boss tells you to have another, you have another. He glanced around the bar. There was a good-looking guy sitting a few spots to Vin's right. He was wearing a tight white T-shirt and jeans; brown hair curled appealingly down his neck.

"You're not married," Vin said.

Cliff reached out for his beer. There was a shot glass filled with something amber. *Vin, Vin, Vin,* he was thinking, *what has gotten into you today?* "No," he replied. "Single for life."

He watched Vin's eyebrows lift. "A confirmed bachelor? You're smarter than I thought, Cliff." He picked up his shot and held it toward Cliff. "Here's to bachelors," he said.

Cliff lifted his glass and sniffed the contents. "What's this?" he asked.

"Your downfall," Vin said easily, tipping his glass back sharply. He made a face and shivered and looked at Cliff again. "Come on, don't be a pussy."

Cliff swallowed the stuff. It wasn't at all bad—butterscotchy and smooth. He licked his lips.

"You like?" Vin said.

Cliff nodded. "I like," he said.

Ties and tongues loosened. Vin propped himself on the bar with his elbows and began to describe for Cliff in intimate detail what he called his latest casualty—his marriage.

"It's me, Cliff—it's all me. I do it. I know I do. I suck at being a husband. I am the absolute worst." Vin shook his head. There was another round, another set of empty shot glasses. Cliff could look easily over Vin's dropped head at the handsome man at the end of the bar. By this time, the man was looking back at Cliff. Which indicated nothing, Cliff realized. Men at the gym were always returning his glances, probably simply wondering what Cliff was looking at, more often than not. Cliff loved a vain man. There wasn't anything better than a good-looking guy who knew he was good-looking. A well-tended ego required little stroking, Cliff had found.

"Personally," he heard Vin say sadly, "I don't think I was ever meant to get married. I'm not sure why I did it to begin with." He was looking at Cliff with a forlorn expression, leaning toward him while precariously perched on his stool. He looked long into Cliff's eyes, and Cliff looked at the man over Vin's shoulder. The man smiled at Cliff, and Cliff smiled back. Vin smiled feebly at Cliff. Things were getting tricky. The evening had presented Cliff with difficult choices.

"Oh, Jesus, look at the time," Vin said, consulting his watch. "Man, I've got to get my ass home. Marilyn will poke my eyes out if I'm late."

Cliff smirked. "You'll find out one day," Vin warned, missing his mark widely. "Oh, yeah: the confirmed bachelor. Well, I guess you get the last laugh then. We're going out with the in-laws tonight."

"I'm not laughing, Mr. D'Angelo," Cliff said with mock sincerity.

"Fuck yourself, Mr. Dillard." He clipped Cliff on the shoulder lightly. "This was cool," he said. "See you on Monday."

Cliff laughed and nodded. "Monday it is, Mr. D'Angelo—bright and early."

When Vin was gone, Cliff turned to the other object of attention, but the stool was empty and the man was no where to be seen. Not wanting his quarry to slip away, Cliff hopped off his stool and headed for the john. He found it empty and stood at the mirror, reading his disappointment there like yesterday's horoscope.

He went back to his office to get his cell phone and check his voice mail. He needed to try to sober up—it was a long drive to Manayunk, though traffic wouldn't be so bad this late. He checked his watch as he got off the elevator and headed down the hall toward his office. He heard singing coming from the other end of the hall, loud and kind of sweet, a man doing a little crooning. Probably the cleaning guy, Cliff figured, unlocking his door.

His cellular was on his desk. He checked it for messages, and then he used the office phone to check his messages at home. There were two from Breck, who was whining over his absence and begging him to come down next weekend. *Fucking Breck,* Cliff thought, hanging up the phone and checking his pockets for keys, taking a last look around at things. *This could be anyone's office,* he was thinking, looking at the anonymous and innocuous art he'd hung on the wall, the generic cleanliness of his

187

desk. He shrugged. "Good night, Innocuous. Have a nice week-end," he said.

"You too," a voice came from behind him. Cliff jumped, his shoulders seeming to pick his feet off the floor. "Only, my name's Alex."

"Jesus, you scared the shit out of me," Cliff said, recognizing the good-looking man from the bar.

"Sorry, didn't mean to," the man said. He had a Walkman on, and a faint buzzing emanated from the earphones around his neck. "I didn't realize both of you worked up here. I thought that sort of stuff was against company policy anyway. Not that that means anything to anyone, I guess."

"What sort of stuff?" Cliff asked, shaking his head. "Company policy? I'm not following you."

"Look, I'm just the janitorial supervisor," Alex said, looking down at Cliff's shoes then up to Cliff's eyes. "But I know when I see inappropriate fraternization. D'Angelo was working hard to bust a nut with you."

Cliff stared at Alex for a half a second, wondering, *Is this guy for real?* Then he let out a short sharp laugh that echoed down the dark hall. "I'm sorry, uh, Alex, but I've got to be going. It's been nice chatting. Have a great weekend." He stepped past Alex's formidable shoulders. He thought for a second that he recognized the song he heard coming from the earphones, something by David Gray he couldn't get away from. It reminded him of his ex, Kevin.

"He writes your name on a pad he keeps in his desk," Alex said. "Just your first name, but he puts hearts around it."

Cliff stopped mid stride, the idea ridiculously improbable but luscious nonetheless. He imagined Vin bent over his desk, penning "Cliff" with calligraphic skill, a flourish of hearts and flowers encircling the name, his tongue in the corner of his mouth, the concerted effort of his affection.

"Me, I'm just an outside contractor," Alex said, "if you catch my drift."

Cliff blinked.

"There isn't anything in company policy about fraternizing with an outside contractor, not even one engaged by your august employer. Now, do you catch my drift."

This is where he unzips his workman's overalls, Cliff thought, only he wasn't wearing overalls, just that bright white T-shirt and those tight faded jeans. He leaned against the door's frame, folding his arms across his chest. His face wore a smug half-smile that was not completely unattractive. He was waiting. Cliff had his briefcase in one hand and his jacket in the other, looking, he thought, like the model of corporate ridiculousness. His tie askew, his head buzzing, his cell phone sadly quiet, he baldly assessed this janitorial supervisor. He was impressed by the rise of his pecs pushing up from his crossed arms, and the way the front of his jeans rolled over the impressive mound. *How does he get normal Levi's to do that?* Cliff was wondering when his phone rang. He looked at Alex. Alex shrugged.

It was Vin. "I can't believe it," he said. "I didn't really think you'd be there, but I, well..." He paused, clearing his throat. Cliff watched Alex put his hands in his pockets.

"Can I tell you something?" Vin asked, his voice wavering and broken by static. "You there?"

"Yeah, I'm here," Cliff said. He turned toward his desk, trying to concentrate on the conversation and not the hard-on he was getting as Alex peeled off his white T-shirt.

Can We Still Be Friends?

They were waiting for Shawn, always waiting for Shawn. Travis sat in the backseat with Bobby, playing with the hairs on his knees and whistling tunelessly, making Bobby whistle, too, just as badly.

Mike said, "Dude, this guy's like a fucking chick. If I miss this movie, I will be wickedly pissed." They were going to see the new movie with Jewel in it.

"She's got to be able to act, man—she sure as fuck can't sing," Bobby had said. The original plan was to get something to eat first, but Shawn was taking too long, and now they were all sitting in Mike's car, watching Shawn's door, waiting for him to come bounding out.

"About fucking time, asshole," Mike said, getting the car started and in gear before Shawn actually had a chance to sit down.

"Jesus Christ, take it easy," Shawn said. "It's fucking Jewel, man—JEWEL."

"Tits, man" Mike said. "Derek saw it yesterday and told me she shows both of them."

"Yahoo," Travis said. "Two tits."

"Can't hardly wait," Bobby added.

Mike turned around. "Shut up, homosexuals."

"Stop undressing us with your eyes," Travis said loudly.

"Yeah," Bobby chimed in. "You're not our daddy."

He leaned over the front seat and looked Shawn over. "I thought you'd look a little better for all the time it took you."

Shawn slammed his hands on the dash. "I had to fucking take a shower, all right?"

190

"But I kind of liked that manly scent you had going on," Travis said, leaning over the seat with Bobby. "What is that, CK One? Does your sister know you're wearing her signature scent?"

"I have to see Jewel's tits tonight," Mike said, more to himself than to anyone else. He stared hard through the windshield, and Travis studied Mike's right sideburn, the way it grew halfway down his jawline. Mike caught him staring in the rearview mirror but kept his mouth shut. Bobby's shoulder was hard against Travis's, and it seemed to him that they were like a couple of kids taking a road trip with their bitching parents.

Shawn kept looking down at himself and pulling the rearview his way to check things out, mumbling, "I look cool, I look cool."

Mike was the biggest of all of them, and he was always throwing his weight around, launching near-miss punches at Bobby and Travis, and getting Shawn, because he was the next biggest, in nasty-looking headlocks that turned Shawn's face red and made him very quiet. Mike was a huge WWF fan, idolizing Stone Cold Steve Austin, fantasizing about Chyna. He would tug on his crotch through the whole show, alone in his room, waiting for the Holly cousins, the two buff blonds who looked more like brothers. He liked their shit, was what he told himself, the way they fucked around and threw chairs and kicked ass and did these amazing flying leaps on one another. It wasn't their broad bare chests, or the tight Lycra they wore, or that they almost looked like brothers that made Mike's dick itch so—no fucking way. It was Chyna and her monster tits, man (but not her monster arms and legs—and definitely not that she looked like a guy when her back was turned).

He was stretched out on his bed, still dressed, warm-ups, Hilfiger tank, the newest Adidas, the whole room reeking of pot smoke and Tommy Boy cologne, listening to Missy Elliott and watching *Friday Nitro* with the sound down. *These guys are so lame,* he thought, moving his dick around in his pants, Structure boxer-briefs tight in the crotch, his boner rolling easily, like a piece of dough.

can we still be friends?

The movie had sucked. *Jewel's tits probably would have been the best part,* he thought. And he'd missed them—and really missed them now as he felt a sudden wetness seep through his pants. Before the movie had started, he'd spied a boy in a yellow Nautica jacket sitting three rows up—wicked sideburns, bleach-tipped hair gelled forward, and a killer mouth, his pouty lips all over some chick,. The boy turned around once and caught Mike staring, but played it off, smiled even, before turning around again right before the lights went down. Mike had the scene studied and committed to memory while he was waiting for the movie to start, listening to Bobby and Travis complain about the butter in the popcorn and watching Shawn stare down at his own pecs, probably wishing he'd done another set on the bench.

Mike lifted his ass off the bed and pushed his pants down, leaving his shorts on, rolling his dick across the hard flat surface of his belly, boxer-briefs going wet. His hand slipped under his shirt, fingers dragging through the hair spread across his chest, swirling around his left nipple. He'd gotten up to piss during the movie—that's how bad it was. When he stepped up to the urinal, he heard one of Jewel's songs playing on the sound system. As he was pulling out his dick, the door opened behind him. He didn't turn around because he thought that was the surest sign of being queer.

He stared at the tile in front of him, his dick gripped firmly, catching sight of a yellow jacket—Mr. Nautica—heading for a stall. The boy nodded because Mike did turn when he realized who had joined him.

"You went to Hempfield, right?" the boy asked, and Mike turned again, not pissing yet, unable to. He leaned closer to the urinal because he felt himself boning, which totally freaked him out. He was staring at the guy with his mouth open, unable to come up with an answer.

"Um, yeah," he said finally. "You?"

"I transferred there your senior year, I think."

Mike nodded, checking out the guy's shoes, Polo Sport flip-flops; his toes looked pretty with their trimmed nails. He remembered the time he was on the thruway heading for a Phish concert and stopped at a roadside pisser. A kid with Birks and dirty feet flashed him an awesome piece of uncut hose, peeling back the skin, looking at Mike as he'd stiffened up like set concrete, just like now. The bone in his hand raged, and Mr. Nautica rested a finger on the door to the stall but didn't go in. He had a questioning look on his face, his gaze dropping again. "You're Mike Kelly, right?"

Again, Mike nodded. His cock was like a brick in his hand. He leaned closer into the urinal until he felt its coldness against the slippery end of his prick. He stifled a gasp.

"Jason Caldwell," Nautica said. "You live in Reading now?"

"Yeah, yeah," Mike said, trying to maintain a little cool. He set his shoulders back and shook his stick like he was done and tried to fold it back into his warm-ups, tucking in his wife beater to cover the stiff lump down there. "You?" he asked.

"I'm still in Lititz. I work in Lancaster for the paper."

"Cool," Mike said.

"Movie sucks," Jason said, leaning against the metal doorway. "You look horny."

"What was that?" Mike asked. He couldn't be sure of what he'd heard.

"I said you look horny," Jason replied casually.

He was too flustered to be angry, too shocked to speak. He put his hands in his pockets, feeling the massive ache under the fingers and thinking, *Holy fuck!*

The door opened—it was Travis. "Dude," he said to Mike, laughing. "You missed the tits." He looked at Jason. "Hey, I remember you," he said, wagging his finger.

Mike sneaked off then, glancing at Jason's crotch and Travis's butt, and wishing he had the balls to make something happen.

"See you," he heard Jason say as he was leaving, stepping out into the hot-buttered air of the lobby and still needing to piss.

Mike rolled over now, squirming out of his underwear, looking over his shoulder and above his dresser into the mirror that tilted down, allowing him to see himself. He liked seeing his own ass, the dark split, his balls hanging heavy, knocking between his hairy thighs. He grabbed a pillow from the head of the bed and pulled it under him, dipping into it, looking for a smooth groove to hump. He reached behind and went between his ass cheeks, into all that hair, pushing a finger into himself. He dropped his head, cheek against the mattress, imagining that Jason dude finger-fucking him. He licked the bedspread, his cock fluttering against the smooth pillowcase, heart knocking hard in his chest, finger wedging deeper into his butthole.

"Fuck," he whispered, squeezing his eyes shut, creaming into his pillow, his finger going deep one last time. He heard his old man walking down the hall, farting.

Bobby was doing what he liked best: lying on his back with Shawn's bony ankles on either side of his head while waiting for Shawn's ass to drop down onto his watering mouth. Shawn steadied himself with his fingers on Bobby's chest and leaned over to take the red tip of Bobby's cock into his mouth.

"What's up with that?" Bobby asked into the crevice of Shawn's creamy ass. Shawn had made it clear when they first started fucking around that he wasn't a cocksucker.

"Just want to bust a nut, you know," he'd said, grabbing the front of his jeans. The first time had been during the long ride home after a night out at the Vault. Shawn had been all pissed because he hadn't hooked up.

"Shut the fuck up, would you?" Bobby had said, trying to drive, fucked up on kamikazes.

"No, *you* shut the fuck up. You don't understand. I'm backing up seriously. I got to *drain,* man—you know what I'm saying?"

"So drain," Bobby said.

"Get the fuck out of here," Shawn had said, cuffing Bobby's shoulder. They rode in silence for maybe a mile before Shawn turned to him and said, "Seriously, man? I'm in pain here. Feel this fucker." He took one of Bobby's hands off the steering wheel and placed it on his crotch. Bobby found out what all the girls' whispering was about.

"Damn," he said.

"Right?" Shawn said nodding. "So, do you mind if I—"

"Dude," Bobby said, pulling the car off the road sharply. "I'll even give you a fucking hand."

Bobby blew at hairs around Shawn's pucker now, his squat not quite complete, his brown eye a kiss away. Shawn was still going at Bobby's knob, stopping from time to time to pick hairs off his tongue, battering the spongy rim and giving Bobby the willies.

"Do not make me come yet," he warned Shawn, trying to sound stern, like he would kick some ass or something. Shawn held him by the fat base, jiggling balls up and down over his own butthole, making Bobby giggle.

"Dude, seriously," Bobby said, the toughness gone. He stuck his tongue into the plush heat of Bobby's underside, stabbing the point into the hole as far as his smashed ass-kissing lips would allow. He felt Shawn let out a long sigh. Shawn took a quick nip at Bobby's sac and replaced his mouth with his spit-drenched hand as covered Bobby's face with his ass.

"I just don't get why *you* like it so much," he said, riding Bobby's slithering tongue. "Make it hard like a finger," he said, taking a hand off his own dick to tug at his beefy pink nips.

Bobby's nose was clamped shut by Shawn's clinched butt cheeks. He chowed hungrily, as always—never sure whether this was going to be his last meal. He gnawed the puckered ridges, snorted into the dark ditch, fucked his tongue in and out of Shawn's tight pinch. He held Shawn's ass firmly, moving his hands up his thighs, his fucking monster quads, dipping beneath them to catch Shawn's pendulum balls beating time against his Adam's apple.

Bobby tugged on Shawn's dripping log, which bobbed up and down heavily. He caught the cock head in his fist and felt Shawn shudder and drop his ass even more heavily. He banged on

Shawn's cock, making his whole body buck and writhe. Sweat ran off Shawn's back, down the ravine of his butt and onto Bobby's face. Bobby stiffened his legs, feeling his own cock twitch and spray an early warning. Shawn fell across Bobby's belly, trying to get to it before the flood, and Bobby slapped Shawn's prick against his chest, unloading him with a yell. His own satisfied grunts were lost in Shawn's loosened ass.

Travis sat on his couch, unfolding the dampish piece of paper. He could barely make out the inky numbers Jason Caldwell scribbled. He looked at the 717 area code and thought about his long-distance bill.

"What the fuck is wrong with me?" he said out loud, laughing at himself, seeing his reflection in the mirrored wall across from him.

That wall was the main reason he'd rented the apartment. He liked sitting here with his buds, watching the television over in the corner and sneaking peaks into the open legs of their shorts, never seeing much, but enough. The upper region of Mike's inner thigh was like porn to Travis, who was always following Mike into rest rooms at bars and movie theaters, like he'd done tonight. Why? It was like that stupid Cub Scout song about the bear going over the mountain—the one his father used to make him sing: "To see what he could see."

He dialed Mike's number.

"Dude," Mike breathed into the phone, giggling a little, making Travis uncross his legs for comfort's sake.

"Where'd you get the shit?"

"Usual," Mike said, his voice going scratchy. He stretched and yawned, Travis guessed. "What's up?" Mike asked.

Travis paused, looking between his legs, the tented front of his shorts. He found his voice. "Nothing. Just wondering what everybody's doing tomorrow. You up for some tubing? All that rain last week raised the river big-time. Probably brought back a lot of the white water."

"Sounds cool," Mike drawled, his voice suddenly too intimate, too much in Travis's ear, like a warm puff of air, almost moist.

"OK, then," Travis said, impossibly hard, power-poled, spotting. He got off the phone, handling himself through his shorts, grabbing hold of his thick shaft and pulling hard on it. He was unable to think of anything but the hairy insides of Mike's thighs, so close to his crotch. He imagined the thick sweaty meat sticking to the skin there, Mike's balls loose and rolling. It was almost tragic, the way he wanted Mike Kelly.

Travis stood up, admiring his profile, the stocky jut of his prick. He stripped off his shorts, down to white BVDs, the tightest whities no match for the ardent elbowing his dick made against the pouch. He licked his thumb and swirled it against each nipple, popping them up, causing his crotch to swell even more.

"Fuck," he said, looking at himself: short brown hair, bluish eyes, smooth chest, shoulders needing some work in his own opinion, but good enough, really. He was put together nicely, he had to admit, admiring the thin ribbon of hair that trailed down the center split of his abs and under the cover of his briefs. He squatted, making his quads thicken, his calves tensing, splitting. He brought his buddy out, pink-headed and honey-tipped. Tucking the BVD waistband under his balls, he stroked himself. The phone rang.

"I knew you wouldn't call," he heard on the other end. The voice was only slightly familiar.

"Um, yeah," Travis said, uncertain.

"Bud, it's Jason? You remembered me, remember? I gave you my phone number in the movie theater shitter?"

"Dude," Travis laughed, still holding himself. "It's not even tomorrow yet, man. You didn't fucking give me a chance."

"I'm giving you one now," Jason replied, making Travis smile at himself in the mirror. *This dude is funny,* he thought.

"So how well do you know Mike Kelly?" Travis asked carefully. He thought about how it felt as though he'd broken something up when he walked into the toilet, looking for Mike. Jason and Mike had the funniest looks on their faces.

"Me? I don't know him well at all." Jason said. "I just remember him from school is all. He was like the nicest guy. My sister thought he was hot—used to have his pictures from the school newspaper all over her room. Blown-up color Xeroxes, man. Cost a fortune."

"Yeah," Travis said, "Mike's cool." Travis liked the dark hairs on Mike's ass that peeked out whenever Mike bent over to tie his sneakers. Travis had never seen Mike without his shirt. *Lucky for me,* Travis thought, afraid of the embarrassment he'd endure, sure he'd pop a boner at the sight of Mike's naked torso.

"You there?" he heard Jason ask.

"I am," Travis said.

"So what's up?"

"You tell me?" Travis asked.

"Well, I don't know—you're kind of a hard read."

"Like Shakespeare?"

Jason laughed. "I was thinking more along the lines of that Rand chick."

"Dude, do not try to impress me with Ayn Rand."

Jason paused. Travis listened to the music of his breathing, feeling that same tug he felt when Mike went meaningfully silent. "I'm not trying to impress you," he said finally.

"I hear you," Travis said, instantly understanding the implication.

"So when am I going to see you?"

Travis's turn to pause. His fingers played the long stretch of his cock, hard still and leaking onto the ugly carpeting.

"Whenever—you tell me," he answered. That was Travis's answer to everything at this moment—let someone else decide.

"Tomorrow?"

Travis reeled. "Dude," he said. "Plans."

"Yeah, right," Jason snorted. "Cold, man, cold."

"Totally serious, dude. We're going tubing on the Delaware, up in the Poconos, me and Mike and a couple of other buds. How's about after?"

"Kelly again. Dude, are you in love with him or what? You can tell me."

Travis wondered: *Can I?* And then: *Am I?*

"What the fuck ever, dude," he said. He teased the soft, sensitive skin just under his piss hole, chucking it with his forefinger. He could come in a split second; his whole prick was buzzing with all of this new shit.

He needed a name for what he felt for Mike, for this stranger phoning him up and calling him on his shit and offering entry into a world Travis had tried to ignore for what felt like most of his life. *Don't fuck with me,* he thought now, tensing his stomach, the muscles of his thighs, his whole back. When he was younger—not that long ago, really—he used to jerk himself off, lying on his back, butt against the wall, his legs up, heels leaving marks on the eggshell-white plaster as he dropped shot after copious shot of warm, viscous come into his open mouth. Remembering this tightened his balls.

He had to get off the phone, but it was too late. The come blasted out of him all over the carpet—like it was shooting out of an unattended hose. He shuddered and sighed, the phone tight between his shoulder and ear.

"What?" Jason asked. "What's going on over there?"

Travis shook with a postejaculate convulsion. It was the first time he'd been with a man, he realized. *Totally fucked up.*

"Nothing," he muttered. "Just tired. Let's get together late tomorrow. I got to crash."

"Yeah, yeah," Jason said. "Me, too. Later."

"Right," Travis said, hanging up.

Mike wore a T-shirt that tore at Travis's heart: Abercrombie and Fitch, cream-colored with green ribbing at the neck and sleeves, accentuating the girth at all three places. Wetness crept up from underneath, but the fabric refused to go sheer like most tees do.

199

Even so, Travis watched it closely. Mike floated by Travis, kicking water at him, his feet in Adidas sandals that he'd lose by the end of the run. Bobby tried to tip Shawn over, climbing onto the top of his tube and jumping over onto Shawn's, hollering like a banshee. He landed on Shawn's bare stomach and sneaked a lick of his armpit.

"Not cool," Shawn hissed quietly. "You're fucked up, man."

"You fucked me up," Bobby whispered back. "It's all your fault, hot boy."

Travis watched the transaction, not quite deciphering it. He was the only queer in the group, as far as he knew. There wasn't room for anyone else in the club he found himself in. He could never have imagined Shawn and Bobby—the things they did together. He moved closer to Mike, who was spinning. Travis's forearm brushed the edge of Mike's shin. Mike's eyes were closed; he was smiling up into the sun. They'd killed a couple of six-packs before getting on the bus, inner tubes strapped to the top.

"There should be music," Mike said. He opened his eyes and looked at Travis. "Wouldn't it be excellent to listen to Dave Matthews right now."

Travis looked at Mike, sprawled on the black rubber donut, his knees and shins shining, feet and elbows dipping into the dark water. He reached out and put his hand on Travis's tube and they floated like this, connected. Travis thought about what Jason had asked him the night before: *Are you in love with him or what?*

What the fuck ever, Travis thought.

Bobby and Shawn floated ahead downstream. "Dude," Bobby said. "I gotta piss."

"So piss," Shawn said. He pulled the brim of his hat down, shading his eyes, squinting at Bobby. He wondered where his buzz had gone. He leaned his head back; his hair, blond and touching the nape of his neck, dipped into the river. He drifted, eyes closed, sun burning images on his lids.

Shawn listened to the voices of the other tubers, the ones he didn't know, laughing girls and guys. He tipped his face toward Bobby. "I've got to get to the gym. My shit's melting."

He looked down at his pecs, two creamy stacks of muscle, hairs making halos around his dark nipples, areolae almost as wide as the bottom of a beer bottle. He lifted one of his feet from the water, old suede Vans soaked and dripping. His thigh tensed and divided. He slipped a hand into the drippy waistband of his shorts and squeezed his stuff. Bobby stared, shaking his head.

"You're one sketchy bastard," Bobby said, the water carrying his voice between them. They moved toward each other.

Mike watched them, seeing Shawn snag Bobby's tube with his foot, the two of them floating down the Delaware connected, just as he was connected to Travis.

He turned to Travis and held his friend in his gaze for a moment. "Dude," his said finally, quietly, when he had Travis's undivided attention. "My dad rented *Braveheart*. You want to come over tonight? Just you and me?"

Travis's heart stopped just for an instant, and he answered Mike with a broad, beaming smile.

TREES

There are boys in the trees. Justin can see them from his bedroom window. White T-shirts glow in the moonlight. They are climbing, climbing and talking. He can hear them, though he can't make out what they are saying. The breeze that carries their voices is cool on his belly, coming in through the half-opened window.

It is Sunday now, but still hours before church. There is a broad-shouldered man in his bed, snoring. Justin has just had a dream about a dog locked in his bathroom. The dog needed to be let out. It could have been any kind of dog. It is the man's snoring that wakes Justin—that's the noise the dog was making in the bathroom in his dream. It is low and growling, this snoring.

The snoring stops when the man rearranges himself, heaving over onto his other side, hiding his shoulder under the covers, mumbling. Justin watches the boys, their foolish enterprise, and wonders what would make a boy climb a tree at one in the morning.

In church, he sits on the hard pew. The boys climb through his mind and make nonsense of Father Timmons's sermon. The broad-shouldered man is there, too, in Justin's mind still nameless. The man left before daylight, getting up with the cows. He has a wife and a farm, Justin recalls, but not the man's name.

Beside Justin sit the McIntyres: Troy and Emily and their boy, Ethan. Ethan looks behind his parents at Justin. His eyes are sky-colored, April-colored, and his lashes are dark and heavy—girl's lashes, really—and the softest thing about the boy. It is a quick, meaningless glance, and Justin goes back to wondering about the man last night and what he called himself and then it comes to him: Harley or Harlan, something like that, some H name. Close enough, he thinks, looking again at the McIntyre boy, who returns his gaze.

He does not see Harley or Harlan for almost two weeks, and when he shows up next on Justin's doorstep he's carrying tomatoes and corn.

"You can throw them away if you want," he says, coming inside with his bushel basket. "I'll take that basket back with me, though." He is wearing farmer's jeans and a straw hat, Justin notes with a little dismay. More like a Halloween costume than clothes for hard work. They are, in fact, spotlessly clean, stiffly blue and new. But his hat is darkened with sweat and frayed around the brim. *A scarecrow's hat,* Justin thinks, though the man is big and wide, not stick-like and angular, certainly not hay-filled or innocuous. He walks around inspecting the rooms decorated with Justin's odd furniture, a strange yard-sale selection that might not, Justin thinks now, be so very odd in these parts.

There are the paintings, though, and they are certainly odd here: huge black-washed profiles of men with the big blooms of palm trees behind them, the skeleton of an umbrella, a study of whirling helicopter wings. He sees the man—Harley? Harlan?—examine them, moving up close to one and then another. There are bits of text written across the silhouettes: "He flirts with disbelief"; "I have lost my will to charm"; "It is because I said so."

The man squints, touches his chin. Justin watches his back. He thinks, *We could sit on the porch until it is dark. I have some bourbon.* It sounds like a good idea, a pleasant suggestion. He knows that regardless of how they pass the time they will end up in Justin's bed. He wants to make the journey there easy and pleasant.

"I didn't paint them, so you don't have to say anything flattering about them," Justin says. The man smiles.

"My name is Harley," the man says. "I can tell you don't remember. No shame in that. Some people aren't very good with names." He turns around, putting his hands inside the bib of his overalls, holding them at his stomach as if in a muff. His hat is tipped back, revealing a tangle of straw-colored hair and eyes that refuse to pick a single hue.

"Would you like some bourbon? Out on the porch?" Justin asks, feeling like a '50s hostess—Donna Reed, gracious and girly.

"If that's what you want, Justin," Harley says simply.

When the sun sets, they put down their empty glasses and stand slowly, stretching like old men. Or, rather, like men not used to sitting so quietly so long. Harley follows Justin into the house, the walls gone red like the sky, and up the stairs, each step creaking.

"This is not a sneak-around house," Justin says and immediately regrets it.

"I understand," Harley says behind him. At the top of the stairs he stops Justin, his hand on his shoulder, turning him around. Standing one step down, they are eye to eye, and Harley closes in to kiss Justin. His lips are firm and ringed roughly with a day's worth of stubble. Justin's tongue is dulled with bourbon; he wants to brush his teeth. He thinks he can make a nice salad with the corn and tomato that Harley's brought.

In bed, they do not jockey for position. There is no wrestling for an upper hand. Justin lets Harley do whatever he wants, lying prone and mobile, readily on his knees or spread-legged.

Tonight, Harley wants his ass eaten. He hovers over Justin's face, dropping his great white cleft, smothering Justin, who makes do with a short tongue and an appetite for Harley's little brown blink. He works on it, the shrubby knoll around it, challenged but not confounded by the hard hairs there. He bites the heavy, tensed ass cheeks. He sucks hard on the drawn sphincter, poking it with his blunt tongue until it slowly unfurls, as if a drawstring has loosened.

Harley kneels, his calves tightly against Justin's ears. Justin listens to the ocean-roar of his own body, heart beating blood through his veins as Harley plays with his cock, pinching its tender end, coaxing the dick into erection. His balls rest on Justin's chin, a formidable and heavy dangle, razor-smooth, skin soft but thick, like calfskin or some other buttery leather.

Harley fingers into Justin's foreskin, into the slick sleeve, edging Justin's cock head with a callus. Gooseflesh crawls across Justin's belly. He tips his head back for air, but it is on his lips—Harley's scent—smeared across the lower half of his face. He smacks his lips, tasting him, as Harley makes a fist around Justin's long cock.

Justin makes his body a languid arch and Harley lifts himself, pivoting, and drags his balls over Justin's mouth and comes to rest on the bridge of his nose, pressing his cock against Justin's lips. In the near darkness, Justin makes out the pale fuzz of Harley's ass, blurring his outline. His crack is shadowed. He puts his finger there and Harley moans.

They do not fuck because Harley has said he does not think it is "appropriate." Justin can't fathom what that means. He aches to get inside the man. He knows Harley would love a good ass plowing. Instead, they do everything else that leads to fucking. Justin worms a digit into the tightened knot of Harley's asshole; he licks the firmed flesh of his shaft; he breathes in Harley's shitty fragrance. His own cock swells.

Harley fists Justin's aching shaft, pulling the tight cowl down, causing Justin to dribble with precome. Harley pauses after each tug to lick the pink head. He drives Justin crazy with steady jerks, flicking at the steady flow that heralds one of Justin's explosive ejaculations.

Justin's legs stiffen. He forgets about the fingers he has wedged in Harley's ass and gives himself up to the shudder deep in his belly. The orgasm wells up and out, through Justin's balls and along the length of his cock. Harley lets the come splash over him, his eyelashes and nose, his sunburned cheeks. Justin's groin is on fire. He twists under Harley's continued manipulations. His gush is warm and copious; Harley's face drips with it. Justin hears him laugh.

"Where does it all come from?" Harley wants to know, repositioning himself. Justin is learning that Harley likes to jerk off with his mouth on Justin's, wrestling Justin's feet with his own, toeing the tendons and long arches. His jerking-off arm is tense, its biceps taut and pale, glowing in the feeble light seeping in from the hallway. Harley's tongue is rambunctious: it swirls and darts and slides. Their teeth collide, and Harley grunts, his breath catching, and he rolls onto Justin, fucking his fist. He comes between their pressed bellies, heaving clenched sighs.

When he's done, he rolls away from Justin. He sits up and swings his legs over the side of the bed as if he's about to leave, to beat a hasty retreat back to his farmhouse and farmwife and their three little girls, their eyes just like daddy's. Justin touches the man's back and traces the length of Harley's spine with his finger.

In church, Justin sits beside the McIntyre boy, keeping his fingertips close to his nose to smell the perfume Harley has left on them. Even the most attentive washing won't banish the scent right away.

Ethan McIntyre is wearing a suit this Sunday. It is dark blue. His tie is badly knotted. He has informed Justin that his parents are in Emmaus, taking his grandmother to her church because it is the anniversary of his grandfather's death.

Ethan yawns and sits up straight, shifting his shoulders every couple of minutes. Justin watches him looking at the backs of heads, his eyelashes catching the colored light of the sun coming through the stained-glass windows. The light is milky, the window a configuration of opaque white and green glass.

Justin watches as Ethan's eyes droop and his chin drops. Ethan tries to rouse himself, shaking of sleep. He looks at his watch and then at Justin.

"You were up late last night," Justin whispers conspiratorially. The boy nods.

"What were you doing?" he asks, leaning close to Ethan, stealing whiffs of his soap and his hair. He is expecting something typical involving beer cans and girls. The boy only smiles.

Joining the murmur of the congregation, they chant together, "It is right to give Him thanks and praise." And then, "Lord, I am not worthy to receive you, but only say the word so I shall be healed."

The boy looks less boyish without the company of his parents. Justin puts him at 17, maybe even 18, though, last week, sitting next to his mother, he seemed younger. Perhaps it was the sheer size of his parents—the McIntyres are both over six feet. Their son is almost puny by comparison. As they stand for a hymn, Justin notes that he and Ethan are about the same height.

They part in the parking lot. "So long, Mr. Duffy."

"See you next Sunday, McIntyre," Justin says, watching the boy lope off, shrugging out of his suit coat and wrestling with the obstinate tie.

He wonders why he called the boy by his family name, avoiding familiarity but evoking at the same time the adolescent intimacy of locker-room talk. He walks slowly to his car, tilting his head up to catch the sun, and he notices to his right a woman corralling three bonneted girls and herding them toward a black minivan.

"Warm for September, isn't it?" he hears behind him. It is Harley, in a blue suit like Ethan's but without a tie. The sun catches the silver in his ashy-blond hair. "Don't look so surprised. I'm not quite a heathen."

"Not yet, anyway" he adds, unsmiling. Justin turns with him to watch as Harley's wife struggles with one of their daughters, who is straining against her mother's grasp toward a small bed of marigolds.

"Carly," Harley's wife says with rebuke in her voice. "You stop this right now."

"I just thought I'd come by church to see what I've been missing," Harley says as he turns back to Justin.

Justin feels conspicuous. He finds his keys in his pocket, trying to come up with something to say, to shake off the surprise and the odd sense of guilt that have welled up in him like a bit of nausea.

"Didn't figure I'd be missing you," Harley says as he punches Justin in the arm playfully and walks over to his wife, calling out to the girl named Carly, who pats the golden flowers carefully, as if they were a litter of puppies.

"I do not love you," Justin tells Harley because he is drunk. They are in bed, sweating. Through the bedroom window come the voices of the boys in the trees.

"That's a good thing," Harley says, sounding amused. A boy shouts; another answers with a high-pitched laugh. They are good boys, decent ones, who like to climb trees late at night. Justin has stopped trying to figure this out. He has come to like hearing their arboreal romp, because it happens on Saturday, and Harley is with him nearly every Saturday.

"What do you tell her?" Justin wants to know.

Harley is quiet, breathing deeply. Then he says, his voice low and very deep, "She never asks."

"I can't ever love you," Justin says after a while. The boys have quieted down, but he can still hear the shaking leaves and the branches groaning under their weight. "I just thought I'd let you know," he says, finishing his thought.

"Any particular reason?" Harley asks. He plays with the hairs that have spread across the center of Justin's chest over the past few weeks. Justin has left off that bit of preening since they've been together.

"None in particular," Justin says. He stops watching the ceiling fan's circuit and relishes Harley's rough cheek against his temple. He falls asleep and doesn't stir when Harley leaves. When he wakes just before dawn, he immediately misses Harley's warmth and bulk and the sound of his deep, steady breath.

"Do you think it's bad?" Justin asks the next Saturday, only slightly less drunk. "Do you think it's bad that she doesn't ask?"

"Doesn't ask me what?" Harley wonders. The sun hangs low on the horizon. Across the street there's a cornfield losing its green, waving dryly in the early-autumn breeze. Harley's pickup is in the driveway behind Justin's unwashed car. *We could hold hands,* Justin thinks. He isn't sure what Harley would make of the gesture.

"About me," Justin says.

"That's because she doesn't know about you."

"She looks at me at church," Justin says, studying Harley's hand on the arm of his chair.

"She looks at everyone at church. She comes home and tells me about who she sees."

"But not me."

Harley looks at Justin. He smiles.

"Not you," he says.

"It's not a bad thing," Harley says later, because Justin has grown quiet. He squints into the distance and his face catches a low shadow cast by the wisteria that creeps along the eaves of the porch.

"It doesn't matter," Justin says.

"Doesn't it?" Harley asks, catching Justin's hand and squeezing it.

"Not much, anyway," Justin says, waiting for Harley to let go of his hand, but Harley holds it and squeezes it again. Justin wonders to himself whether it's some coded message that he is failing to decipher.

Later, upstairs, their fingers interlace as Harley pushes himself into Justin's warm insides. "I'm not sure I like this," Harley says, as Justin moans gratefully.

"You seem to," Justin tells him, because he does: Harley is hard and panting, a good fuck. Justin squeezes him with his thighs. "You like it," he tells Harley.

"Maybe on your knees," Harley says, and they try it that way. It's different, easier, better, for both of them because their eyes don't meet.

Harley fills Justin's ass, holding him by the waist. When he pulls out, Justin fights the urge to hold him inside, not wanting him to leave the hungry hole. He hasn't been fucked in a long time, and he hadn't missed it until now.

Justin comes up off his hands, pressing his back against Harley's hairy torso. He holds on to the head of the bed, and Harley wraps his hands around Justin's thighs and pounds him with long hard strokes, pumping Justin's ass, licking his back and whispering. "It's good, right? You like this?"

Justin can only nod, unable to speak. He follows Harley's trajectory, feeling pried open, pulled apart. He can't get enough of Harley inside of him. He slaps back with his ass, impaling himself until he's close enough to come, and then he stops.

"You worry me," Harley says, laughing. He withdraws his cock. It glistens between them, oozing syrup—his own and the juices of Justin's ass.

"Lie down," Justin tells him, and Harley stretches out on the bed. His cock hovers over his belly, charged and stiff. It is arched and red from tip to base, and his balls are covered over with hair the color of straw. Justin takes the cock in his hand and throws a leg over Harley's midsection, planting the dick head in his hole. He rides Harley like this, teasing his nipples, bright flat things that refuse to harden. He fucks himself hard enough to hurt, and Harley watches, head lifted, his stomach tensing into panels of muscle.

Justin thumbs the dimple of Harley's navel, the little knot inside, and Harley squeezes his eyes shut and fucks himself up into Justin's hole, hoisting Justin skyward with each thrust. Harley's jaw clenches and his toes stretch and he buries his load deep. Justin comes, too. As their breathing softens, they hear the boys frolicking in the trees.

Justin says later, "There's this boy at church."

"There are lots of boys at church," Harley says quietly. He has his arm under Justin's neck.

"Aren't there," Justin says.

After a spell of silence Harley turns. "You got something to say? About this boy?"

Justin blinks at the ceiling. They're in the darkest dark; they could be anywhere. Outside, the cornstalks rub and rustle. He thinks of Ethan, his thighs in gray flannel, of the soapy wholesomeness of him. Nothing: There's nothing to say.

"Oh, no," Justin says. "Nothing at all."

SCOTTIE

We put Darren on top because he didn't mind sleeping so close to the ceiling. Me, I wouldn't have been able to close my eyes. Plus, rolling over would've been a real problem because of the cast. I was knocking it into everything—furniture, doorjambs, innocent bystanders.

The table folded down and became a bed. Covered with its cushions, it slept two closely. That's where Paulie and I were sleeping. We each had a sleeping bag, but it was too warm for them. Paulie found some blankets in a cupboard and made a palette. I stepped out of the little camper, clipping my elbow on the way out. Darren was poking at the fire with a stick, listening to the radio. He looked up at me, his face lit by the flames, framed darkly with his shoulder-length hair.

His shirt was unbuttoned. I could see the shadow between his pecs, the patch of hair that grew there, narrowing as it went down, making a thin brown line that rolled over the muscles of his stomach and made a sharp drop into his jeans, which hung low. I could just make out the edges of his hipbones and the dark fringe of his pubes.

He'd been looking at me lately but not saying anything, as though he knew something about me, and I wondered what it was he thought he knew. Maybe he'd seen me go into the bathroom at the mall and come back for an hour. Or maybe Joe Panotti let something slip about me—he didn't care anymore what people thought about him now that he lived in New York City and was practically married to a *guy*. I think he loved the looks he got from the old high school buds that used to call him the "Pussy King." All of his buds, that is, except me.

I wasn't gay like Joe, one of the gay guys I worked with, who called everyone "girlfriend" and scrambled to wait on every good-looking guy who came in the restaurant. No, I was going to settle down and get married eventually, just like any normal guy would. This was the way I looked at it: I had this taste for dick that would pass when I met the right girl. I was still young enough for it to be a phase, as far as I was concerned.

But the way Darren looked at me got me all undone in about two seconds flat. I was going to say something—I just didn't know what—when Paulie stepped out of the camper. Paulie was like my little brother. He was most definitely my best friend. He walked across the sand to where Darren and I silently faced off, the campfire sparking between us.

I could just hear the waves breaking a few hundred yards away. We hadn't actually seen the lake yet, having come in so late. We were lucky, really, to have made it to the campground at all. Darren had gotten us lost outside of Watertown, and all of a sudden we were heading south again and passing signs for Syracuse, where we'd come from. That's when things got a little tense, and Darren and I exchanged some shit, and Paulie, sitting between us in the little pickup cab, told us to cool it.

Darren had stopped fast, skidding into the gravel on the side of the road. The little Scotsman camper we were towing nearly came up alongside us.

"If you know the way, why the fuck don't you drive?" Darren had growled at me. He got out and stood in the headlights, pulling out his dick to take a leak. I watched the arc glistening in the halogen spot. Paulie stayed where he'd gotten thrown—right up against me. He was always doing stuff like that—putting his arm around me, playing with my hair, leaning into me when we walked together. I guess some guys might have taken it to mean something, but coming from Paulie it was more innocent. I liked that about him.

I think, though, that his ease with me had something to do with the frustration I felt around other guys. I wanted to touch them the way Paulie touched me—casually, intimately—and that just didn't happen. It tied me in fucking knots sometimes, and I'd have to take a trip to the mall and sit in a bathroom stall to sort things out, waiting until someone would try the door and find it unlocked and not mind the stall was occupied.

That's when the touching became easy, my hands doing their own thing, and I could relax for a while, my pants undone, my dick getting worked over, and I'd touch the guy's head, finger his hair the way Paulie sometimes fingered mine. Those weren't the highest moments of my life, but I did feel some sort of release— and not just the obvious kind. I would feel free for a while.

But it was a fleeting feeling, and then I usually felt like shit. I'd swear that it was the last fucking time, that I was going to shape up and act like a man. Then I'd call whatever girl I was seeing at the time—because I was always seeing some girl—and I'd ball her brains out. But the things I would think about while I was fucking her had nothing to do with the woman underneath me. *It's a phase,* I kept telling myself, *just a phase.*

Paulie said we ought to check out the lake. Darren didn't move from the low folding chair he was sitting in. *Fuck him.* I picked at the frayed edge of my cast.

"Who's coming?" Paulie asked. He looked at me. I nodded. "Darren?"

Darren shook his head, staring into the fire.

Paulie shrugged, but I was thinking, *What a fucking baby.* We were going to get the silent treatment because he fucked up and got us lost. He was going to punish us all week. I shook my head, tired of the asshole. It was going to be a long week.

We passed the dying fires of campers who'd gone to bed. There was a moon in the sky, just a bit of it shining through some gliding clouds. Paulie said something about it being late. We passed a trailer that was lit up, a couple inside playing cards, and

I wondered if Paulie was still seeing that girl from Marcellus, the one with the braces and the mosquito-bite tits.

Paulie had been here before, so he knew the way, but the road was rocky and rutted and the moon slid behind a heavy bank of clouds. Paulie led the way and he kept swinging his hand back and hitting mine, screwing around or just making sure I was keeping up. I stubbed my toes a couple of times and cursed the fucking sandals I was wearing. Finally, the road went soft and sandy, and the waves sounded as though they were almost on top of us. I saw the lake then—Lake Ontario. It was black, and the breakers shimmered when the moon reappeared. Paulie's hand swung back and caught me hard in the nuts.

"Christ," I gasped.

"What'd I do?" he asked.

I tried to fight the urge to crumble to my knees but I went down anyway. Paulie's hands went to my shoulders.

"Are you all right?" he asked, his head bowing down towards mine.

I nodded feebly. It seemed for a couple of minutes that the only way to be rid of the agony would be to have my balls removed, pulled free from my guts. Then they dislodged themselves from wherever corner they'd been knocked into. Some of the pain subsided, but I still felt like a freshly snipped castrato.

I stayed on my knees a while longer, and Paulie delivered a litany of remorse, but I was finally able to straighten up and walk around a bit. "No big deal," I said, trying not to squeak. "I never liked kids enough to have any of my own anyway."

We walked over the sand, which still held the heat from the day's sun. The water was warm, too, washing up over my feet. My groin ached dully, and I wondered if you could actually bruise your balls. Paulie put his hand on my shoulder.

"I'll tell you," he said, talking up close so he could be heard through the noise of the wind and the waves. "If Darren's going to be an asshole all week, he can leave now."

I agreed but kept my mouth shut. Besides, Paulie's lips moving so closely to my ear caused my dick to flutter. I was wearing shorts that were thin and baggy, and the wind went up my legs, fingering around my crotch like a horny old man. I went bony then, my dick twitching up and doing a little dance. I was glad for the dark and hoped my hard-on would go away before we got back to the campfire and Darren's moody eyes.

"Where's the toilet around here," I asked. Suddenly, I felt I needed a little time to myself.

"We'll walk back that way," Paulie said, facing the water.

"The waves are bigger than I expected," I said.

"How are your nuts?" he asked.

A tongue bath wouldn't hurt, I thought right away, giving myself reason for a stupid grin. "They're doing OK," I told him.

"We're going to have a great time," he said, pinching the long muscle at the top of my shoulder in a sort of Spock grip. I pulled away.

I saw the lights of the bathroom up ahead on the left. "There you go," Paulie said, but he followed me in.

The place stunk and buzzed with mosquitoes. There were showers at one end, and Paulie stepped up to a long trough that passed for a urinal, and I got myself into a stall, even though I didn't have to shit. I took the one by the wall—the one in the middle was occupied. I looked down and listened to the steady stream of Paulie's piss. I could see my neighbor's foot. It was bare and tanned, his toes lifting off the concrete, the tendons along the top in sharp relief. The foot tapped soundlessly, making me wonder. In a mall, the foot would be shod—I'd be looking down at a loafer, say, or a Nike, but the tapping was usually some sort of sexual Morse code. Or not. I'd been wrong before.

"I'll meet you outside," I heard Paulie call out, and I mumbled, "Yeah," back, feeling caught and guilty. I thought about Paulie getting undressed in that little trailer and sliding under the blankets with me, and I got a fatty all over again. The foot tapped some more, toes pulled up, tanned and sandy—a young foot. I moved mine, pivoting on the heel, bringing the toe of my sandal closer to the invisible line on the floor that separated our stalls. I saw a hand slide down the ankle to scratch at an itch. My cock was too hard to ignore. I started dry-jacking myself, listening to the papery noise of skin on skin, imagining what the man beside me looked like and if he could hear me. I wanted him to be young, my age, and I wanted him to have a chest covered with short dark hairs—like his ankle—and I wanted him to stick his big fat cock down my throat.

I listened for bathroom noises from my neighbor—telltale grunting or the rip of toilet paper or a trickle of piss—but there was nothing. Finally, I heard him sigh. And then I heard the sound that spit makes when it's used to jerk off.

There were no holes to peer through, no way to judge what this person looked like save for his foot, which I deemed beautiful. The toes were long and there were sprigs of hair on each. I'd never thought much about feet, but seeing this one made me want to have it in my mouth, toes curling on my tongue.

His foot moved closer to that invisible boundary. I squeezed my prick, and juice leaked out. I cleared my throat. I watched his toes flex and heard them crack. He sighed again, deeply, and my knees began to shake. I heard Paulie whistling outside—I was taking too long, he'd get suspicious. I moved my foot closer to my neighbor's, wiggling my toes, waving like a baby. And then he put his foot on mine.

I started dribbling, unable to control myself. Come bubbled up and out of my prick, running down my hand, falling on the toilet seat. I shuddered, holding my breath, trying to clean up with toilet paper. The man's foot still rested on mine. I felt the first drops before I realized he'd come across our feet.

I practically ran out of rest room, barely able to compose myself. My cock tented the front of my shorts, and I was thinking there was no way Paulie wouldn't notice the big wet spot. My cock felt gigantic, the way it bobbed and swayed, and I tried to push it down, but it wasn't going anywhere yet.

"Jesus!" Paulie said, laughing.

I said, "What?" trying to sound innocent, and Paulie laughed some more, and my wrist started aching the way it had been doing lately, and we walked back to camp.

I dreamed about the episode in the toilet that night—that I went there to piss when everyone was sleeping, and all the lights were off. I felt around for a light switch and touched something that felt very much like a hard cock. *Well, it couldn't be anything else,* I thought, touching it carefully and fingering the loose sac of nuts that dangled beneath the firm rod. It was as hard as a log, jutting out at an angle from the wall, hanging like a trophy. *Not real,* I thought, although it certainly felt lifelike. In my dream I decided, since I was alone, that it would be all right to suck the thing a little. *Need one of these at home,* I was thinking, touching my lips to the fat helmet.

It was sticky with juices, and its end felt like the real thing, a cushion that gave way to a hard bluntness. I got it into my mouth. It was hot as a bonfire and quivered with a life of its own. I started blowing it, getting all the way down to the base. A soft fuzz of pubes tickled my lips.

I took hold of the balls and held them gently, letting them roll on my palm. With other hand, I gripped the shaft, pleased with the way it felt in my hand. I must have tugged too hard, because there was a sudden flood of light. I blinked in the white glare and made out a crowd of guys, all of them laughing. There was Darren in the back of the room, a huge grin on his lips.

"See what I mean?" he said laughing, "I told you he was a cocksucker."

I woke at dawn. Paulie snored softly beside me, hugging the wall, keeping to his side of the bed. I listened for Darren in the back, pressed up against the ceiling in the bunk. My wrist itched and my balls still ached from Paulie's accidental blow the night before. Of course, my cock was bone-hard again.

Paulie mumbled something in his sleep. I put my wrist cast between my legs, giving myself something hard to hump against. I held my breath. I closed my eyes and pictured one of my favorite fantasies—the hot guy who played for the Orioles—and rubbed my dick against my cast.

Darren moaned, and I stopped dead still. There was a thud. "Shit," he said, looking around the corner, rubbing his head. "Fucking bed," he said. "Paulie's sleeping here tonight."

He threw his legs over the side of the bunk, letting them dangle. They were long and covered with hair. He threw back the covers, and I saw the hard poke of his cock sticking up out of his boxers. It was tall and leaned to the left, its head shaped a little like the end of a baseball bat, blunt and flanged.

"Where's the toilet?" he asked.

"Up the road," I said. "Not far."

"What time is it?" Paulie said, rolling over, not opening his eyes. Darren looked at his watch but didn't say anything. He noticed his bared dick and gave me a look as though it was somehow my doing. He eased himself down to the floor, covered himself up and angled toward the door. He stood there, not a foot away from me. His back was wide and brown, and he had dark hairs growing in a spade at the small of his back. Paulie pulled on the blankets. Darren held his hair back, twisting it into a ponytail. I always thought he'd look cool with a brush cut like Paulie's and mine.

"Where is it?" he asked me.

"The toilet?" I said. "It's, um—Paulie, where's the toilet?"

"Might as well be in a fucking tent," Darren said.

Paulie lifted his head. "It's just up the road, asshole. There are signs all over the place. Even you should be able to make it there."

Darren smirked, looking down at us.

"You two look cute together," he said as he stepped out of the camper. "Ever think about coming out? Moving to Hawaii? Getting hitched?"

"He's an asshole," Paulie said to me when Darren was gone. I sat up, looking for my shorts, feeling the need for some cover. Paulie stretched across the mattress, stealing the extra room I'd given up. His arm, tanned and copper-haired, lay across my pillow.

"He's got issues," I said, looking at his arm, wanting to put a finger it where I could see a vein pulsing.

"You sound like that Danny guy," Paulie said.

"Danny said that about Darren the first time he met him—that he's got issues." Danny was someone else I worked with, a really cool gay guy.

"What the fuck does that mean?" Paulie said, lifting his head. "That's bullshit anyway—Darren fucks more chicks than the both of us put together."

Just like Joe Panotti, I wanted to say. Fucking Joey and his sweet little prick. There was no end to that guy's libido, which I'd tried my best to satisfy the summer right after we graduated, before Joe left to go to NYU. We'd dicked just about every single day: Joe dropping his pants in the car for a quick knob job during my "smoke break" at the restaurant. Sometimes he took me into the mall and pimped me out in the men's room, joining in when`ever he found someone to his liking.

"Whatever," I said to Paulie, trying to shake off the horny walk down memory lane I was taking.

"You're hanging out with Danny too much," Paul said. "He's rubbing off."

"I work with him, for Christ's sake," I said. Danny was the gayest gay guy I knew. What I liked about him was that he didn't have the faintest idea what I was all about. He'd flirt like crazy with me, then throw his hands up and shake his head. "I'm wasting my time with you, Chris, just wasting my time." He was always telling me all guys were bi; they just didn't know it. "Ask Freud, honey—he knew the score. Probably got his salad tossed all the time."

On the beach that day, I looked for my toilet buddy, and I thought I'd found him about 20 times. Every time I thought I'd nailed him, some other guy walked by with hot-looking feet, long and hairy-knuckled toes. I stayed on my stomach most of the time.

"Your back's getting burned," Paulie warned.

"I know," I said, staying put.

"I'm hungry," Darren said after a while, glowering, like it was our faults. I looked at his feet. His toes were stubbed, blunt-ended things. They didn't seem to have anything to do with the rest of him. They dug into the sand, like they were fat, pale slugs.

There was a concession stand at the other end of the beach, close to the toilets, which were set back from the water. It was funny to see where everything was in the light of day—how close things were when they'd seemed so far apart the night before. I wasn't moving from my blanket at that point, so I threw my wallet at Darren and told him I wanted a couple of hot dogs and something to drink.

"I'll go with you," Paulie said.

I closed my eyes, the sun crisping my back. I could hear the waves and the sound of the music that Paulie had brought along. I felt myself being pulled out and away. Paulie put his foot on my stomach. The wind blew across my shoulders. Darren whispered in Paulie's ear. I could see the white flash of his teeth. He asked Paulie to shave his head. "It's lemonade," I heard someone say. I opened my eyes.

"Dinner time, Sleeping Beauty," Darren sang.

I went back to the toilet that night, hoping to relive the experience of the night before, but the place was empty. I sat in the stall for nearly an hour, waiting, getting hard, going soft, waiting some more. Someone came in and took a quick shit. I could see by his yellowed toenails that he was not the guy from last night. And someone came to brush his teeth. I squashed a mosquito that landed on my thigh, and I waited until I was too bored to wait any longer.

I got up and flushed the unused toilet and went to wash my hands. I looked into the mirror and wondered when I would shave again, when a man walked in wearing soccer shorts and Adidas sandals, a towel over his shoulder. He nodded, glanced down at my feet, and I looked at his. My heart started pounding. It was my guy—I was sure of it. He went over to the showers, throwing his towel over a bench. He slipped off his sandals and pushed himself out of his shorts. I stood at the sink dumbly, staring, hands drip-drying. He stretched his arms up over his head—his rib cage hollowed. He scratched his head. He was ignoring me, acting as though he was by himself. He stepped behind the partition that provided some privacy, and I heard him turn on the water. It made a ringing splash on the concrete floor.

I'm not sure what I was thinking. I'm not sure I could identify any thought process at all. I went over to the bench and started undressing, standing in front of him, watching him, his wet skin, the water that ran over him, off him. I had no towel, no showering supplies. I turned on the shower directly across from him and stepped under a shock of cold that took my breath away and made me hop away like Saint Vitus.

"It takes a while to warm up," the man said.

"Christ," I said, hugging myself. I stuck my foot into the falling ice-cold water. "How long is a while?"

"This one's hot," he said, his back to me. His ass was high and tight, his crack a thin line. He reached back and soaped himself. "I'm almost finished," he added.

"It's getting warmer," I said, going under the spray. I had to turn away from him because my cock was hoisting itself up, pulsing with blood.

"Pressure's good, at least," I heard him say, and I looked at him over my shoulder, ready to agree. His dick was lathered. He was facing me. He handled himself casually, sliding the tube of his palm up and down his shaft. He looked at me with green eyes, brown shoulders, flat stomach feathered with dark hair. Soap suds gathered in his pubes, dripped from his balls, ran down his long thighs. He leaned back in the water. I liked the way his toes curled against the concrete.

The door pushed open and we both about-faced, making poor attempts to hide what was dangerously apparent. I listened to the intruder taking a piss. My cock deflated and I turned and looked over at my shower-mate. His ass cheeks shined. He looked over his shoulder at me, winking. The scene was a little too public for me, and I gathered my stuff together and wiped as much water off me as I could and left.

I went back to the little camper in an agitated state. My dick flopped around in my shorts like a salmon in spring. The guys were playing cards and passing a bottle of Jack between them.

"You're going to have to catch up," Darren said, shirtless, handing me the bottle.

"Did you swim?" Paulie asked.

"Yeah," I said. I took a swig and put the bottle on the table, looking at Paulie's shitty hand. I got a bottle of beer from the cooler and took it outside. I needed fresh air and something to look at besides Darren's bare torso.

It wasn't long before he joined me. "Help me put Paulie up in the bunk," he said.

I looked up at him. "Are you sure that's a good idea?"

"I'm not sleeping up there again," he said, "And you sure as hell can't."

I looked back at the fire. "He'll be all right," Darren said. "Come on, just help me get him up."

Paulie wasn't as drunk as all that. He probably could've gotten into the bunk by himself. He acted helpless and stupid, though, and let Darren and me pull him out of his clothes. Stripped to his briefs, he was smooth, compactly muscled, a little wrestler. I spied his soft prick, the way it lay cradled in the pouch of his underwear.

"Get up there," Darren said.

"I'm trying," Paulie whined. Darren put his hand on the white cotton of Paulie's ass, pushing him upward. Paulie tumbled into the bunk, his left arm and leg hanging over the edge.

I went to where Darren and I were going to sleep and started clearing the table. Darren stood behind me, taking off his shorts. He was naked underneath—I saw the bright white strip of untanned skin, the dark brown beard that surrounded his long prick. "You sleeping like that?" I asked.

"I never wear anything," he said.

Did last night, I thought, but let it go. The thought of climbing into bed with him bare-assed like that wasn't bothering me too much. Or maybe it *would* bother me too much. I stripped down to the ratty old boxers I had on and got under the covers, hugging the wall.

"Fucking Paulie," Darren said, turning off the light. Paulie sucked up a snore and started coughing, mumbling something about an airplane. Darren slid into the makeshift bed with me, his feet brushing against my legs tantalizingly. He settled himself, nowhere near me, and I listened to his breathing. It stayed shallow and nasal, and I wondered what he was thinking.

"You ever hear from Joe Panotti?" he asked out of the blue.

I swallowed hard.

He accepted my silence. I thought I could hear him smiling, lying there beside me, flat on his back. He had to keep his long legs bent to fit the short bed.

"He was a horny motherfucker," Darren went on. "I remember when we went up to Cross Lake for Senior Weekend and he and I shared a tent. Fucker was all over me as soon as he thought I was asleep. His hand crawled into my boxers like a fucking spider. He started jerking me off once he got me hard. It was fucking insane. I mean, there we were with half the fucking baseball team. Some of them were still up drinking around the fire, you know? And besides, everyone fucking knew that Panotti had just gotten his dick sucked by Titties Janson."

I lay there in disbelief, my eyes crossing in the dark, my dick throbbing, trapped between my thighs. I didn't dare move, not wanting to betray myself or to give him any reason to quit his narrative. He shifted, bringing his arms up over his head.

"And then he put his head under my sleeping bag and started blowing me." He kind of giggled. "It was my first blow job, man, I am not ashamed to admit it. I've had a few since—chicks only—but not like that one. Joey could suck the dimples off a golf ball, man."

Tell me about it, I was thinking, remembering a couple of blow jobs when he'd seemed intent on taking my dick off.

Darren rolled over me like a wave. I felt his skin all over my body—hot, a little sweaty. His mouth found mine surprised, and I tasted his tongue for the first time, never having imagined his flavor. He pumped his hips, digging his hard-on into my boxers. His hands found mine and pinned them to the foam rubber mattress.

"He told me all about you," he whispered.

"Yeah, me too," Paulie said, slipping under the covers, sliding up next to us.

"This is a hallucination," I said.

"Not exactly," Darren said.

"Move over," Paulie said, pushing Darren off of me and coming closer himself so that I had them on either side of me. I tried to move myself to give them more room.

"Ow," Darren said when I hit him on the head with my cast. Paulie's hand slipped into my shorts—at least I think it was Paulie's hand—Darren kissed me some more until he leaned back and said, "OK, who's going to suck who?"

"It's 'whom,' I think," Paulie said.

"I think he's right," I added. Paulie cupped my balls, his fingers edging the furry region around my butthole.

"Everybody could do everybody," Paulie said.

"I'm up for that," Darren said.

"How come you never let me suck *your* dick?" Paulie asked him.

"Wait a minute," I said, trying to sit up and shake this image out of my head.

There was no way this was really happening—I was having some intensely realistic dream, I was sure, and then Paulie stood up, hitting his head on the cupboards overhead—"Fuck!" he exclaimed—and tried to stick his dick in my mouth.

"Open up," he said.

"I want to turn on the lights," I heard Darren say, feeling him reach for the switch. Paulie whimpered as the pointed tip of his cock scraped against the stubble over my lips. I put out my tongue to taste him, the moistened slit of him. He could have used a shower, but the smell of him was almost like perfume, and I opened my mouth wide just as Darren ducked under the covers and nosed around the opening of my boxers. He pushed them down my thighs and licked my sudden boner, humping my calf with his sticky prick. Paulie hit the back of my throat, choking me, as Darren took me down to the pubes with all the ease of a sword-swallower. I made a noise that was supposed to sound appreciative.

"Did that hurt?" he asked.

I uncorked my mouth long enough to say, "Uh-huh."

Paulie started pumping himself into me, trying to talk like a porn star. "C'mon, baby," he whispered, "take it all, take it. That's a good boy. Suck my big dick, cocksucker. Suck that dick, faggot. Oh, fuck, yeah, fuck, that's awesome, fuck."

"Paulie," Darren said, "Shut the fuck up."

"Sorry," Paulie muttered, and then he began to moan.

"Paulie!" Darren barked, "Get down here." Paulie dropped to his knees to chow down on the bone Darren offered. I watched Darren's lips come off my dick, a string of drool connecting us. He gripped my shaft in his fist tightly. "I want to see you sit on this," he said to Paulie. Paulie looked up from his suck, appraising the fat head of my prick and the five inches that stuck up out of Darren's fist. Then he looked at me. I don't know why, but I winked at him. He looked cute down there with his mouth full of dick. He nodded, winking back.

The sight of his ass coming down on my pole was almost enough to make me lose it. He squatted over me and lowered himself slowly, and I saw his asshole glistening from the gob

Darren spat there. I quivered when my cock head touched Paulie's wrinkled puss. He slid on snug as a glove, and I heard Darren whistle.

Darren licked his palm and started jacking off, watching the two of us for a while, and then he got himself behind Paulie and lowered his ass until it was right in front of my face. I tongued his tiny hole, and fingered it, too. It was tighter than anything I'd ever touched, and I had to wonder how the guy took a shit. He gripped the tip of my finger and wouldn't allow any further access.

Paulie rode me, and I pulled Darren's thick pecker back through his legs and sucked on it, alternating between that and his little rosebud pinch. Paulie's ass lips made my hips buck, and I fucked into him, tonguing up Darren's shitter, making him grab my head and jam my face into his ass crack. "Fuck," he breathed, and I felt him shudder as he unloaded across Paulie's back.

My nuts tightened, and my knob caressed a tender button inside Paulie's cunt, and I let him pull the come out of me with his sliding ass lips. He stood up quickly, his hole gaping and dripping with gobs of semen. "Ouch," he said, bumping his head again. He jacked off over Darren and me, hosing us down with his hot spray of jizz.

"Hey," Paulie said, his shoulders heaving. "We need a shower now!"

We walked to the showers together in clothes we threw on. I think I was wearing something of Paulie's *and* Darren's. There was much hooting and towel snapping and soap dropping. I was still convinced that I was in some walking dream-state brought on by morning wood. I was ready to open my eyes for real and see the sun pouring in through the little camper's greasy windows. I looked over at Paulie under his showerhead and then at Darren under his and got hard all over again.

Darren said, "Looks like we've got a long night ahead of us, Paulie."

"Next time, you're getting fucked," Paulie said.

"What the fuck ever," Darren said.

"Chris?" Paulie asked, "Can't Darren get fucked next time?"

"Forget about it," Darren said, turning his back.

"Whose dream is this anyway?" I said, and Paulie laughed.

I woke up the next day to find myself snuggled up against Darren's back. He wriggled his behind. I turned, looking for Paulie, and found him up in the bunk, his foot hanging out of the covers. Had I dreamed the whole thing?

Darren rolled over and said, "Would you do me the kindest of favors and get your dick the fuck away from my ass's general vicinity?"

"Sure," I said.

"I told you no last night, man—you ain't gettin' in."

"What?"

"You heard me," he said.

We heard a loud bump. Then, "Shit!"

"Hey, guys," Paulie said, rubbing his head.

Noah stands by the water, bringing his arms up over his head to stretch them out. His shirt loses its tuck, and a swath of his belly flashes in the sunlight. The man with him—a man his father's age—takes it all in: the skin, the smooth brown hairs, the muscled midriff, and the fat contour of Noah's cock against the front of his jeans. Noah's not yet erect, but his prick is fattening and lengthening, making a drop to the left of his fly. The man swallows a suddenly flush of saliva that has collected on the center of his tongue.

Noah says, "This is no place to be at night," and the man agrees and says it's OK now because it's daytime. Noah agrees and turns toward the man, staring down at him, because the man is squatting and tugging blades of grass from the dirt.

"I'm not a gay," Noah tells him, and the man says he isn't either.

"But you are," Noah replies. "I can tell by looking at you. You've never even been with a woman."

True, but offensive, the man thinks, getting up out of his crouch, standing to his full height. He is a few inches taller than Noah is.

He is not a soft man—not in the way Noah's father is soft. His arms are thick with muscle, twice the size of Noah's, and his chest is full and wide. Noah has never touched a man with such a big chest. He's not sure he wants to now. Noah has a friend—Kevin—who is not gay either. Kevin's chest is nearly as big as this man's chest, but he does not come to this river with Noah. *Kevin doesn't even know about this,* Noah thinks. Kevin couldn't imagine what goes on here—the men that come here, the things they do.

Noah pictures Kevin shirtless and sunning himself. His cock stirs to life, becoming unmistakable in his jeans. Noah looks down and considers the meat hanging heavy and fat inside his pant leg. He looks up at the man, who tries hard to decipher Noah's expression. He hopes Noah is wondering, *What will you do about this?*

The man's name is Mike, and he was almost with a woman once, but it did not work out, and he ended up leaving her apartment and walking home at four in the morning through a cold mist. He did not live very far away, and the walk did not take him so very long, but the rain made him miserable. The whole evening had made him miserable. He did not like feeling like a failure and decided there, on his way home, rain running down the back of his neck, that he would try again and that it would be different. He never did try again.

They follow the river. Mike trails behind Noah, taking in his shoulders, his waist, his ass and legs. He likes the way this one looks, his short hair, the scruff on his chin, his shuffling feet. What Noah likes about Mike is the way he drove by Noah's pickup, catching sight of Noah, looking away and then looking back again, his admiration shaping his mouth into a wordless "Oh."

Noah holds a branch to keep it from swatting Mike, and Mike steps past Noah, his hand brushing against Noah's hand. Noah catches it up in his own because they are far enough from the dirt road not to be seen. He brings Mike's hand to his mouth and kisses the back of it, pressing it against his cheek for a moment, then taking one of the fingers into his mouth.

This is not what Mike had expected. He'd expected a boy like this one to go to his knees to accept the proffered erection, to suck at it like an animal; he'd expected to use the boy blatantly, without apology or thanks. That is what Mike has had before, what he wants again.

Noah puts his hands on Mike's chest, gripping his pecs. This is where he wants to put his cock, seeing the tight crease he makes when he pushes the two slabs of muscle together beneath Mike's unbuttoned shirt. Noah unfastens the last buttons and peels the shirt from Mike's shoulders. Then he runs his hands along Mike's smooth, trembling belly. He thumbs Mike's nipples, brownish pink, fat and hard. Mike's eyes close.

He fumbles with Mike's pants, tugging at the belt, the buttoned fly. Noah caresses the man's prick through thin cotton boxers, wet through already and outlining the bone-hardness underneath. He quickly drops to one knee, to put his face against the moist cotton, his lips against the stony cloth-covered shaft.

Mike plays with Noah's hair, with his ears. He slips a hand into the neck of Noah's T-shirt and traces the knobs at the top of his spine. Noah noses into Mike's fly and nuzzles his balls, licking them, biting at them, smelling them.

Everything is fine until Mike thumbs down the waistband of his boxers, baring his cock. Overwhelmed by the situation, Noah suddenly falls back on his haunches. He stands, almost losing his balance, and leans against a tree behind him. He pulls roughly at the buttons of his own fly and jerks out his throbbing prick, which has wedged itself into an excruciating angle in his jeans.

"You suck my dick," Noah says, the command sounding more like a question to both of them. Mike tugs at his own hard-on, contemplating the bulbous head and the sparkle of precome oozing from its slit. He is stalling, smiling slyly—he wasn't wrong about this one, after all. This one wants to think he's in charge, a textbook first-timer.

Mike says, "I don't know," hesitating, shaking his head, looking at Noah's beautiful uncut dick, its red head peeking out of a thick roll of skin. Noah sees him looking and pulls the skin back, revealing the whole of the head, the delicately flared flange. A few buttery drops dangle from the deep piss slit.

I hate them, Noah thinks, watching the bob of Mike's dark head, feeling the hot slide of Mike's mouth along his shaft, lips tightening at the base, taking all of him. "I hate them all," he whispers softly, the bark of the tree he's leaning against tearing between his shoulder blades. He touches the tree instead of Mike as he thrusts his prick down the man's throat, wanting to choke him, wanting to hear him gag and sputter.

Mike leans back, a thread of spit hanging between his lip and Noah's cock, a bright and sagging connection that droops and sways and breaks. "Fuck," Mike says, wiping his mouth with the back of his hand, taking hold of Noah's dick and squeezing it hard, the end flaring crimson.

He stares up at Noah's mouth. He licks his lips and then stands, putting his face into the crook of Noah's neck, kissing him there. Noah feels his breath catch in his throat. He lets Mike's caress linger only for moment, then he twists away, the bark scraping his back.

"I can't, I just can't," Noah says, gasping for air.

"I don't believe that" Mike says, a smile on his face. He thinks he can push this one. If he pushes hard enough, he suspects there's no boundary Noah won't cross. "You know you want to," he says easily, making his smile less knowing, more congenial.

He leans toward Noah, who looks away but draws himself closer, letting Mike kiss his chin and press his lips against the corners of his mouth.

Their hips meet and their cocks entangle. Noah moans, sliding up against Mike's thigh, finally accepting the man's tongue with a mouth wide open, acknowledging his hunger.

This is what he'd always wanted, since the first time he took his cock in his hand. How many times had he watched Kevin at the bar talking to some dumb fuck on a stool, chatting him up and drinking his shots, his mouth loose and easy, lips animated and seductive?

Noah opens his eyes and looks into the sun, still bright between green leaves overhead, sparkling and dappled. He brushes a few strands of dark hair from Mike's forehead. Their eyes meet, and Noah holds Mike's gaze.

Mike presses his lips against Noah's and pivots around, still tonguing Noah's mouth, until he feels Noah's cock against his ass. He presses himself back against Noah, making himself accessible, eager to feel Noah's cock in the split of his ass, the drippy head poking around, loose-skinned, hard as stone. He brings his arms up over his head, his biceps engorged and framing Noah's head, making him safe, held.

Noah licks each of Mike's biceps and strums his fingers over Mike's taut belly, fingertips catching on stubble, dipping into the divot of his navel, stroking a sudden puff of pubes and the stiff rise of Mike's hard-on.

Noah knows about fucking—just girls, though—so he does not catch on right away. He has never really thought about fucking a man before, but Mike's ass is dancing atop his slick cock, sending electric tingles coursing through his body. Noah's back is rasped and stinging, but he cares little about that now. He puts his hands on Mike's smoothly muscled hips.

"I'd like to draw you," Noah hears Mike say. He laughs because he thinks it's a joke. His cock bends painfully until Mike crouches a bit and his cock head hits tucks into a crevice that begins to give a bit.

"I'm serious," Mike breathes, feeling the bulbous end of Noah's prick against his asshole. He leans into it steadily and is filled with it, a painful plunge that feels like fire, and Noah puts his face against the back of Mike's neck, biting and licking, and croons, "OK, OK, OK."

"I like it," Mike says when Noah pinches his tits hard, twisting them, and pushes himself deeper into Mike's bottom. Noah smells sex all around them, and he wants not to be as close to the end as he is, but his cock is beginning to burst inside Mike's guts, sputtering creamy clots of come.

Noah pulls out. A stringy, stinking white rope hangs from the end of his dick. Mike turns, taking himself in a fist, teeth gritted and eyes hard on Noah's. He shoots a wet spray across Noah's shirt, spattering him, soaking him, making them both laugh uneasily. Mike dabs unhelpfully at Noah's shirt, and Noah stares down at deep crimson head of Mike's bubbling cock.

Noah watches Kevin tap beer, watches his hand, his wrist, his forearm, the crook of his elbow, the way the skin pales at his shirtsleeve, the big round bulge of biceps. He is nodding along to some rap song on the jukebox. Charlie is at the end of the bar, cheek bulging with chew, sipping beer over ice. Kevin places the beer in front of Noah, doesn't take any money from the pile Noah has in front of him. He has green eyes and dark hair, bright white teeth. He smiles now, doing his homey nod. A while ago he'd left Charlie in charge so he could blow a bone with Noah in the back. Noah scratches at his itchy chin, digging his fingers into the new scruff.

"Did I tell you how much that reminds me of my ex-girl-friend's bush?" Kevin teases.

"Fuck you," Noah replies, unable to stop himself from pinching the hairs and pulling them hard.

"You wish," Kevin says, and Noah thinks about it, about fucking Kevin the way he fucked that guy down by the river. He watches Kevin lean into the sink to wash glasses, but he can't imagine Kevin naked. He's tried.

Kevin closes the bar early because, after Charlie leaves, there's no one there but the two of them. He locks the door and stands in front of the surveillance camera, giving it the finger, saying, "Whitey's gonna love this." He grabs his crotch for good measure.

"Doesn't he get pissed," Noah asks, seeing Kevin shrug and dig into his pocket for another dollar for the jukebox.

"If he does, he doesn't say anything," Kevin says. He walks behind the row of taps, looking at himself in the mirror above the counter, brushing back the hair over his ears as though it were longer and unruly. Noah catches his eye in the mirror and looks away, and Kevin says he's hungry. He comes over to where Noah is sitting and leans on the bar, looking at Noah. "Are you hungry, Noah?"

"I am, kind of," Noah says.

"I had a teacher in fourth grade. His name was Keller," Kevin says. "He was a fag."

"Whatever," Noah says, and Kevin laughs, looks around for his beer, finds it by the register. He turns up the volume on the jukebox. The bass rattles the wineglasses that hang by their stems like dusty bats. Noah moves on his barstool, uncomfortable suddenly, and a little paranoid about his mouth, feeling his lips sticking to his teeth. He swigs down more beer and thinks about not going to work the next day, wondering what his uncle will say if he calls in sick again. He'll probably holler, "God damn it—do you want a job or not?" But he'll let Noah take the day off and pay him for it, too, and claim later not to remember Noah's not being there.

Kevin cashes out his drawer for the night and puts the money in an old shaving kit that he hides beneath one of the booths. Holding a finger against his lips, he says, "We're mighty up-to-date here at Whitey's."

He comes up beside Noah, shouldering against him. "What are you up for now?" he wants to know, and Noah shrugs.

"Anything, I guess," he says, and Kevin takes Noah's beer and drinks it down.

"You guess?" he says, as though he's only just heard what Noah said, and Noah nods because he doesn't know what else to do. Kevin starts to dance to the music. Noah watches him—the way he bounces, swings his arms, and pivots on one heel.

"I'll tell you, man," Kevin says, almost beaming, grooving to the music.

"What?" Noah asks, smiling in return, unable to help himself, feeling warm and foolish.

"I don't even fucking know," Kevin says, laughing.

Mike gave Noah his phone number, though he didn't say Noah could call him at 2:30 in the morning.

"It's Noah," he says, as though that's a good enough excuse for calling so late—and for Mike, it is. He tells Noah where he lives, and he greets Noah at the door, naked.

Noah falls onto him, his beery breath giving him away, and they grapple, kissing, wrestling for some purchase, some mutual dominance, only neither one wants to shoulder the responsibility tonight. It's too late for Mike, and Noah is suddenly too drunk, and they half waltz, half tumble into Mike's bedroom and fall onto the bed.

Noah stays on top and works his way between Mike's legs, his pants-bound cock throbbing, pressed hard against Mike's naked meat. "Take them off," he hears Mike tell him, and he struggles with the fastenings, only to find his clumsy fingers thwarted by the buttons. Mike rolls him over, straddling his stomach, inching up his chest, trying to get his cock into Noah's mouth. But Noah is fixated on his own fly and the effort of getting it undone. In a moment his cock has gone soft.

Finally, Noah gives up, gives in, and the beer sucks him up. He closes his eyes and is gone. Mike slaps his dick against Noah's lips, the fat head wet on its own, but Noah's lips are slack and a soft sigh slips out of them just before he begins to snore.

In dreams, Noah lies beside Kevin, on a beach, on a forest floor, on the cold, hard cement of the bathroom in Whitey's Saloon. Kevin puts his hand on Noah's chest, fingertips brushing his nipple, making him shy.

"I want to," Kevin says. "I want to. I want to." And Noah wants him to, but he can't speak—in this dream he's mute. He watches himself struggle with speech, but there's nothing coming out of his mouth except spit and frustration. Kevin shushes him with his finger and then his mouth and they're kissing. Noah is worried that his breath smells foul, and Kevin rolls onto him, putting himself between Noah's legs; his thighs bristle against Noah's. Kevin's cock rolls thickly between them, crushing Noah's doughy prick.

His mouth warm and moist against Noah's ear, Kevin asks, "Where's your cunt, bitch?"

In another dream, Noah is sitting naked on a barstool at Whitey's, and everyone is pretending they don't see him, but he knows that they do, and Kevin is on the phone, scratching himself and looking bored and saying things that sound German.

He wakes up in the dark, in Mike's bed, against Mike's shoulder. Mike's mouth is open and his breathing is quiet, but his hand twitches under the covers, near Noah's hip, which is bare. He realizes he is naked and unbelievably hard and unable to move for fear of waking Mike up. He can make out his profile, lighted by a pale glow from the clock on the nightstand beside him.

Mike curls into him then, saying something or maybe just making a noise. "What?" Noah asks, and Mike stirs. He puts his sleepy mouth on Noah's and they begin to kiss. They slide closer together, and Noah finds Mike's uncovered cock. He likes being in bed with a naked man.

Mike moves his hips and slips his cock beside Noah's cock. He slides his lips down Noah's neck, and Noah sucks in his breath. Noah presses his cock hard against Mike's cock, and they move together like that for a while, breathing into one another's mouths, tongues smearing spit, dicks smearing jizz that tangles in their short pubic hairs.

Noah's hands roam the muscled contours of Mike's body, the stony backs of his arms, the dips and divots of his back, a fur patch he discovers at the small of his back. He grabs hold of the meaty slabs of Mike's ass, his fingers dipping into the brushy crack, and Mike tightens his ass, making the slabs hard, and Noah laughs into Mike's mouth.

Mike twists around under Noah, giving him his back, his ass, and spreads his legs out across the mattress, feeling Noah's cock find the furred crack. Noah rides the hairy rut, his dick rasping and leaking. *It isn't right,* he catches himself thinking. *It isn't right at all.* But he is unable to keep himself from sliding into that warm channel, finding the soft button of Mike's asshole, the plush pout of it pursing before it gives in, letting Noah in, taking the shiny slicked head.

Noah gasps at the sudden heat that envelops his cock. He wraps his arms around Mike's huge shoulders and pushes himself deeper into the fire of the man's ass. His lips kiss the back of Mike's neck, the knobby vertebrae, his fragrant hair, the warm incense of his scalp. He shoves himself into the hole and drags himself back out. Mike tries to follow the trajectory of Noah's derrick, rising to meet Noah's hips with a loud smack. He receives Mike's long pole again with a gentle grunt. His hands reach back behind him and he holds on to Noah's bucking ass, bringing him deeper, faster, slapping the tightened cheeks.

"You're so good to me," he breathes, and Noah hears him. "You're so good to me." And Noah fucks him harder, faster, because he is not being good, not good at all, and he drives himself into Mike's ass with killing strokes, hips banging butt, gut sticking to the hairy patch. He pounds himself into Mike and it almost hurts and he closes his eyes, his forehead pressed between Mike's shoulder blades.

"Good, good," Noah hears again, and he grits his teeth at the tightening of his balls and the rush of his pulse, and he spits when he comes.

"Kevin! Kevin! Kevin!" Noah bellows with each furious thrust. Mike takes the abuse, relishes it, jerking himself off onto his own sheets, getting up on his knees and bringing Noah up with him, thinking nothing at all.

He kept his shorts up, dick out the fly, big and pink, making Billy Clark swallow his gum. His cock had a tiny pink head—the effect was like a wee thimble capping off a log. Kind of pretty, Billy was thinking. He squinted up at Bam Richards, who was looking down at himself, hands on his hips, his smile crooked and smug. "Well?" Bam said.

Billy shook his head. He didn't care much for Bam Richards, hadn't since high school, when Bam had said some unkind things about Billy. He'd said things that were unkind and untrue, about Billy and Jose Ortiz, which was just about fucking stupid. *Imagine me and Ortiz,* Billy was thinking now as he took the measure of the thick droop of Bam's cock. *Impossible.*

Bam made his dick sway. His boxers were blue, the same color as the vein that meandered the length of his swinging member.

"Patch'll be through soon," Billy said, and it was true. Patch was on his rounds, and he would hit the john like clockwork in just a couple of minutes. Bam understood. He bent over and hauled up his pants, tucking his prick away just as they heard Patch's footfalls down the hall. Bam stepped up to the sink and washed his hands, big raw-looking paws that wrestled one another in the suds.

Patch came into the bathroom, keys rattling like a tambourine against his hip. Billy pretended to piss, having stepped up fast to one of the urinals, leaning close to hide his erection.

"You still here?" Patch said, startled, his white hair wild over his head. He touched the front of his pants, and Billy pushed his engorged prick back into his pants, hitting the flush. The rush of water drowned out Bam's easy reply.

"I thought that'd be done by now," Billy heard Patch say. He was talking about the packing machine they'd been working on for the past two months.

Bam said, "Well, you know how fucked up it is around here."

"Cluster fuck," Billy said. "I'm thinking of going to Campbell's. Buddy of mine's there. Better benefits, and he gets a case of soup each month.

Bam gave him a look. He smiled the way he smiled when he was looking at himself—at his big joint.

"You boys leaving soon?" Patch asked.

"Soon," Billy said, and Bam nodded.

Patch looked at his watch. "Almost nine—where'd the time go?" He looked from Bam to Billy and answered his own question: "Damned if I know."

When Patch was gone, Bam reissued his initial proposition. "I'm not wrong about you," he said. "I never was."

Billy lifted his shoulders, running both his hands through his short blond hair, wiry as a terrier's. He groped the front of Bam Richards with his blue eyes. In high school, he'd sucked the bent uncut dick of Bam's best friend—not Ortiz, for Christ's sake—who was now singing country-western songs on the radio in a played-up hayseed twang. Billy was being offered Bam's prime piece of meat, the long drop of it apparent even through his green work pants. Bam hitched his pants up, further accentuating his impressive endowment.

"Fuck you," Billy said anyway. "You know I got a wife and a little girl at home. You don't know fuck about me."

Bam slipped his thumbs through his empty belt loops, puffing up his chest in his faded blue shirt. He grinned at Billy as though he just couldn't help himself and stuck the tip of his tongue into the space between his two front teeth.

"Well, OK, then," he said graciously, his eyes dropping to the fattened front of Billy's pants. "My bad, Billy-boy. No offense, no harm done. Our little secret, though, OK? Just between you and me? Nothing to talk about, right?" He stuck out his right hand, and Billy regarded it, wondering what was with the easy give. He took Bam's hand and shook it anyway.

"That's a mighty big hand you got there," Bam said, holding on longer than he needed. "And a nice firm grip, too." Billy broke the prolonged shake, his palm sweating, feeling the fuzzy buzz of desire redden his ears. He still had to put away his tools, get the Blakely machine cleaned up, and get home to eat the cold dinner that was waiting for him.

Billy wondered what Bam had to look forward to. He was married, too. His wife was a little hottie cunt he'd met—and knocked up—Senior Weekend at Ocean City. Billy had been there, at the same underage house party, and had gotten fucked up, too, but not so much that he hadn't taken note of the half-dressed Bam Richards. Even then, Bam's torso was rock-hard from his maniacal workouts and a brief stint with steroids. Billy remembered watching Bam escort the little freshman coed out of the house. Her hair was in blond cornrows with bent beer caps fastened on the ends; her T-shirt tied up to harness her enormous tits.

Must be as happy as me, Billy thought as he watched Bam turn and head out of the john, his ass twitching lazily.

Billy did not go home directly. Instead, he drove to the county park. He headlights spotlit the occasional deer, and the headlights of oncoming cars dazzled him. He parked in a pine-enclosed cul-de-sac between a newish BMW and an old wood-paneled Jeep. He'd been here before, sitting in his car, playing with the radio, ignoring the other men who'd come by to peer into his open window and ask him for the time while fingering the fronts of their pants.

Lights out: He went blind for a moment as his eyes adjusted to the darkness. He felt a small rush, a gut-flutter, a quickening hard

of his pulse that he blamed on Bam Richards. It was Bam's fault
he was here at all, detouring to this place because he didn't know
where else to go, where else to take the dull ache of his hard-on.
Where else was there? He turned on the radio, missing the noise
of it. He turned the volume low and waited, but not for long.

"What time do you have?" Billy heard, a rough whisper through
his open passenger-side window. He reported the hour without
looking at the man who'd asked for it.

The lights of the BMW went on, and Billy saw the driver
standing outside his car. He bent at the waist to study Billy, and
then reached back into his car and turned the lights off again.
Billy rushed to remember what he'd seen: a short man in a business suit, early 30s, thick-lipped, with straight brown hair parted
on the side.

"Do you hunt?" he heard the man ask.

"Hunt?" Billy said. He leaned toward the voice.

"Deer," the man said. "Have you ever seen so many?"

Billy tried to blink the man back into detail. The sky was black
and moonless, and his eyes wouldn't adjust to that kind of darkness. He tried to fill in details he'd missed. What color were the
man's eyes? What color was his suit? He saw the pale ghosts of
the man's hands on his door. Billy invited him in.

He learned too much about the man, who was compelled to
give Billy his name (Paul) and marital status, his approximate
address, his exact age, the names and grades of his daughters, and
his profession, although not his employer. "I'm very discreet,"
Paul said.

"Name's Bam," Billy said simply before he put his hand on
Paul's tie made of smooth silk, dark-colored and without pattern.
The song on the radio was Journey's "Open Arms." Billy loved
Journey. He felt Paul's chest—a thick slab of muscle that stiff-
ened under Billy's hand. He moved inside the suit and slid his
fingers over Paul's shirt-covered nipple. Paul put his hand on
Billy's neck and brought their faces slowly together. Billy tasted

the spearminty taste of Paul's mouth. His lips were fat and supple, his tongue lazy and soft. Billy's hand dropped down the front of Paul's crisp dress shirt and dug into the belted waistband of Paul's trousers, fingers poking groinward—but not making much headway until Paul tucked in his stomach, making it tight and hard. Then Billy felt more hardness.

There was a rustling in the woods that stopped them both. Billy thought about consequences and possibilities—police, arrest, shame. This was what usually stopped him from doing anything more than this—a quick feel-up, a flash of guilt, a stab of fear. And then a trampling that was undeniably the movements of a deer, but Billy quickly imagined a storm troop of authorities. He leaned against his door, wiping his mouth, cursing the weakness in himself.

"Hey, bud—where'd you go?" he heard as Paul leaned across the seat to put his face near Billy's. "Bam, you there?"

"My name's not—" Billy started, feeling Paul's hand on his thigh, traveling up to his soft mound of prick and balls, gathered tight in the crotch of his jeans.

"No," Paul said, leaning in for another kiss, running his fat tongue across Billy's lips before kissing them. Billy smiled at the rough chin, the aggressive thrust of Paul's face, and he let himself be kissed hard and for a long time, feeling himself stiffen in the crotch, his cock pulsing suddenly, happily inching up his belly hairs. He rolled himself over onto the man beside him, probably messing the press of Paul's suit, getting his fingers into the smooth straight hairs on the back of his head, trying his best to get his tongue to touch the back of Paul's throat.

They opened their pants, introduced their cocks. Billy felt his ass cheeks being pried apart. He wondered why his wife never put her hands on him this way. He bucked his hips and rolled his prick along the stubby length of Paul's cock, which matched Billy's in stature—short and squat, tight as hell, definitely a handful.

They rutted together on Billy's front seat, where his wife usually sat. The man in the suit, this Paul, had his trousers around his ankles, his rumpled suit coat opened wide. Paul's stomach, plaited and hard, was covered with a soft tickling fur, and Billy let himself bounce until he felt against his asshole the flat business end of Paul's cock, as hard and blunt as a transit worker.

Paul put his hands up under Billy's T-shirt, using his thumbs on his nipples. He breathed on the bared center of Billy's chest. Billy straddled him, head up against the ceiling of his Camry, fucked himself against Paul's gut, riding the trail of hair that rose from Paul's groin and spread thickly across his belly. Billy tilted his hips every now and then to kiss the tip of Paul's buttery cock with his stinking butthole. He grabbed the headrest and Paul wedged his head between Billy's elbows, squirming to find one of Billy's tits to suck. *The old lady would never do that!* Billy thought. His dick spilled a long trail of ooze, and he gut-fucked Paul until the man complained, "Chief, you're killing me!"

Outside the confines of the car, Billy dropped to his knees. He felt Paul's hands on his head, fingers toying with the struggling curls. Paul's cock, unseen but felt, was as fat as an ankle, almost as big around as a beer bottle. Billy's fingers barely closed around it, and his grip could not contain the length of the piece: its blunt cap rose thickly out of Billy's fist. He licked the cap first, the salty tip deeply split, a piss hole big enough to tease the pointed end of Billy's tongue.

"Bam," he heard above him. "What kind of name is that?"

Billy opened his mouth; the head just about filled it. He held on to it like that for a little while, twisting his tongue all around the head, getting under the rim of it. He felt like a suckling pig, mouth plugged with a ripe red apple. He slid his tongue forward, toward Paul's stones, and the shaft fluttered, and Billy swallowed. Paul's fingers curled around his ears, and there was a crackling sound of crushed leaves.

"Fucking deer," Billy heard Paul say. But the man's cock began to droop in Billy's mouth, and his thighs tensed. Billy looked blindly into the dark trees.

"Stand up," Paul said, his voice different, maybe deeper, Billy thought as he got to his feet. He faced Paul, who grabbed him by the back of the head and brought their mouths together hard, tongues wrestling crazily. He got both of their cocks into his hand and jerked them together, breathing hard into Billy's mouth. He held Billy's cock wrong, though—nothing was happening. Then Billy felt the warm splash of Paul's come in his pubes, and the introduction of some sudden lubrication made things right, and he held on to Paul's fist with both hands, fucking into it until he squirted his own load into Paul's hand.

Bam stripped in the locker room. "Fuck the overtime. I'm going home." He stood in front of his locker in the same blue boxers he'd worn last week. He looked over at Billy. "You want a beer?"

Billy shrugged. "Where at?" he asked.

"My place," Bam said, reaching into his locker for his jeans. The fly of his boxers winked, and Billy caught a glimpse of Bam's pale tool, its white heavy head.

"Darlene out of town?" Billy asked, thinking he'd gotten it, what Bam was up to. Bam hadn't mentioned the night he'd offered himself to Billy, nor had he offered again.

Bam stepped into his jeans, pulling them up his big golden-haired thighs. "No such luck," he said, zipping up his fly, looking over at Billy again with a shadow of a smile on his face. Billy, feeling embarrassed, wrong, got out of his work pants. He felt ridiculous in the green bikini briefs his wife had bought him for Father's Day this year. His crotch, tightly pouched, bulged obscenely, he was thinking, looking down at himself.

"Run out of shorts?" Bam said. "You gotta wear the old lady's?"

"Fuck you." Billy shrugged off his shirt and felt Bam's lingering stare. He pulled his wife beater up over his head.

"What do you bench?" Bam asked.

Billy shrugged. He knew, but he didn't want to say.

"You don't know?"

Billy shook his head.

The two were quiet as they finished dressing. Billy tied the laces of his new Adidas.

"We could go to the Canteen," Billy heard Bam say as he grabbed his lunch cooler and slammed his locker shut.

"Blue Marsh?" Billy asked, watching Bam comb his hair at the sinks. He had a big ass—not fat, just big—and his T-shirt covered his back like a second skin.

"You coming?" Bam asked, using the mirrors to look at him.

Billy said, "Yeah, I'm coming."

"I'm done," Bam said, pushing his glass away from him. It was crowded for a Tuesday, and Billy recognized a bunch of guys who worked at Carpenter. Bam was mostly quiet, and what little talking he did was about the packing machine they'd been working on and then about how fucked up management was. Other than that, though, he stared straight ahead, every now and then heaving little sighs that lifted and dropped his big shoulders. Billy swallowed the last of his beer.

"Me too," he said.

Out in the parking lot, Bam lingered, leaning against the fender of his pickup. "Saw Donny Krause last week at Sam's."

"How's he doing?" Billy asked, remembering the tall, skinny kid they'd gone to school with.

Bam shrugged his shoulders. "Who the fuck cares?" he said. He took a couple of steps toward the lake, passing Billy with a glance. He kept walking to the edge of the parking lot, out of the light, through the trees, disappearing. Billy watched him go, staying where he was for a moment, wanting to stay, to get into his car and drive away.

"Shit," Billy said to himself, feeling a pull of longing from the darkened edge of the lot where Bam emerged, lit by the moon, his arms crossed, waiting.

"You don't say shit, Clark. You just stand there looking." Bam turned away, the wind off the water coming between them.

"What are you looking at, Billy?"

Billy looked past Bam, past his profile, out at the dark water of Blue Marsh Lake. "I'm not," he said. "I'm not looking."

"You are, though," Bam said, turning to face Billy again. He let out a low belch that Billy eventually caught wind of—beery, sour. Bam hitched up his jeans.

"Why are you here?" he asked quietly.

Billy listened for the water to make a sound, but it was silent. The moon glowed through a haze of sheer clouds. Then there was a splash in the distance—fish jumping at insects, Billy guessed—and then there were more, and suddenly the lake seemed to be catching a downpour of water from the sky, its surface frothy and turbulent.

"Jesus," Bam said, his voice barely audible above the din.

They couldn't see the fish, but they could hear them, their collective noise, the air rushing through gills perhaps, or the mass fluttering of fins. It went on for a minute, a minute and a half maybe. The lake seemed to boil, and then it stopped and the air was quiet save for the settling hiss of the water.

"What the fuck was that?" Bam asked.

Billy shook his head. "Holy crap," he said finally. Bam stepped backward and Billy forward. They collided. Bam turned fast, his arms going around Billy's waist.

"There you go," he said, lips brushing Billy's ear, nosing in to the hair behind it, making him feel like a little boy. Billy kept his arms at his sides, letting Bam do it all. His hands were all over Billy's back, tugging the end of Billy's loosely tucked shirt, finally uncovering bare skin. Bam breathed again into Billy's ear, digging into Billy's tight jeans, grabbing up ass cheeks and squeezing them hard.

Bam got his mouth on Billy's, opening it wide, his tongue all over Billy's lips, dribbling spit down their chins. He pulled his hand free of Billy's jeans and held his head instead, pulling back and coming into focus, moonlit. Bam looked astonished, his eyes wide and staring.

"Stop it," Billy said, and Bam kissed him again despite his protest, holding him tightly. Billy felt the press of Bam's cock against his own, and then Bam's hand fumbling with the fastenings of Billy's jeans, pulling and tugging, struggling to get at what was inside. Once freed, Billy's cock stiffened thickly, throbbing in the night air. Bam gripped it, groaning into Billy's mouth. He fisted Billy tightly, squeezing up precome.

Bending at the waist, Bam lapped the ooze that smeared Billy's cock head and then he took the whole prick into his mouth. Billy gasped at the heat that engulfed him, the tender drag of teeth, snorts of breath into his pubes. Bam reached under Billy's shirt and touched his belly. He raked Billy's nipples with his thumbs and then reached around and uncovered his ass, grabbing his cheeks again, letting air get to the moist crack.

Billy leaned into the hot hole of Bam's mouth. He hit the back of the man's throat and stayed there, making him gulp and sputter. Bam gripped Billy's butt tighter. Billy pulled out and looked at Bam's lips, full and wet, wanting, and he smacked his dripping dick against them.

"Son of a bitch," Bam said, shaking his head, kissing the sticky cock head, standing up fast and undoing his own jeans, getting them down his thick thighs. His cock poked stiffly out of his bush of curly pubes. He licked his palm and took hold of himself, jacking the long shaft, pinching the little pink head with each cuff. He lifted each leg in a cocky strut, turning himself around, showing off his bright white ass. Billy played with himself, regarding the twin globes, the way they glowed. He touched them, the skin of them cool, and they tensed, turning to stone under his fingertips. Bam pushed it back at him, pressing his fanny against Billy's dick, getting it in between his cheeks, riding the length of him slowly.

"Put your hands on me, man," Billy heard him whisper, pulling off his shirt, putting his palms on his thighs and crouching in front of Billy. Billy stroked Bam's long back, kneading the tensed muscles across his shoulders. He reached around Bam's waist, looking for his prick, and pushing his own downward so that it rode over the tight ring of muscle around Bam's asshole. He dropped a gob of spit between them. It landed in Bam's split and drooled down onto Billy's cock.

He sucked on his thumb, wetting it before sticking it up into the hard bloom of Bam's anus, the inside of him hot and silky, his sphincter gnawing on Billy's digit. Now this is something, Billy was thinking. The closest he'd ever gotten to ass fucking was with his wife on their honeymoon when she'd passed out after too many Alabama slammers. They'd gotten no further than this, though, his thumb in her ass as he fucked her pussy. He fucked Bam this way, fingering him, making the man moan and look over his shoulder and wink at Billy, whose own cock dripped with need, stringy jizz hanging off the tip of it.

Bam dropped his ass, riding the thumb inside him, working it. He asked for the real thing. "Give it to me," he said, begging, making Billy smile.

"You're fucking cute," Billy told him. "Anyone ever tell you that?"

"I hear it all the time," Bam said back, bobbing his butt. "Just fuck me, Billy—you can tell me how pretty I am later."

Billy pushed his dick into the small aperture, and Bam yelped. "Christ," he said. "It looked easy in that movie."

"What movie?" Billy asked.

"Never the fuck mind," Bam said. "Just do it, will you?"

Billy got himself inside the burning hole and stayed there, feeling the race of Bam's heartbeat down there. He started to fuck the man slowly, holding on to his hips and pulling the ass on and off his aching throb. He fucked him gently, holding him tightly, putting his lips on Bam's back and kissing him there, licking his shoulder blades. His balls swung heavily between their thighs, bouncing against Bam's nuts.

"How you doing there?" Billy asked, and he saw Bam nod.

"Fine and dandy, pal, fine and dandy. Your dick feels like a fucking fist, though."

"Hurt?" Billy wanted to know. He couldn't imagine it, really, couldn't imagine taking Bam's huge slug, but the thought made his dick whimper in the hot sleeve of Bam's bunghole, and he felt himself sliding closer to the edge of a big bang. He pulled out and Bam's hole gaped.

"You can't stop now!" Bam said, pumping himself wildly. Billy used his thumb again, rubbing the hardening bulb of Bam's prostate. The man's ass cheeks shivered, clamping tight on Billy's hand. "

"What the fuck," Billy heard Bam say in the agitated tone he'd heard often enough at work. Bam stood up straight, banging his cock in his fist, bringing up veins in his neck, muscles rippling and colt-like under the skin of his back. He looked over his shoulder at Billy. "You," he said, and Billy smiled, using his free hand to tickle Bam's swaying bag of balls.

Bam uncorked himself and got up close to Billy, using his belly, knuckling against it, his dick in a stranglehold. He looked up, his eyes almost doe-like, moist and unguarded. He licked his lips, about to speak, but he stayed quiet and looked down again. Billy followed his eyes and saw thick ropes of come leap out of Bam's milky cock head, splattering across Billy's chest like wet ribbon.

"Now you," he said, getting on his knees, taking Billy's solid prick in his hands. He jerked it clumsily, licking the end of it, panting still from his own exertions. Billy played with his short-cut hair, thumbing the man's eyebrows, feeling each of Bam's tugs in his gut until he was once again toeing up to the precipice, about to leap. The feeling of falling rushed over him, wind in his ears, and he let Bam pull warm squirts of spunk out of him, He pushed himself into Bam's slick grip, splashing his come across Bam's fat lips.

It was quiet then, save for the pound of his own heartbeat in Billy's ears. Bam wiped his mouth with the back of his hand and stood up with a soft groan. He looked at Billy. "It wasn't so hard, though," Bam said, his hand on Billy's shoulder.

Billy said, "No, it wasn't so very hard. Just hard enough."

"We're bad, you know," Bam said, grinning wickedly, and Billy laughed, remembering the fish, the flying fish, and he looked out across the lake, waiting for something, anything, to present itself as a sign, anything at all, as Bam's come cooled on his chest.